HABITATION ONE

FREDERICK DUNSTAN, a recent graduate in English Language and Literature from Brasenose College, Oxford, wrote *Habitation One*, his first novel, after leaving King Edward's School, Birmingham, and before coming up to University. Several things prompted him to write it: a lifelong desire to be an author; a liking for the entertainingly bizarre in literature; a hope of making some money by writing; and the gradual growth of the germ of an idea (first conceived while walking home from school one day during his 'O' level year) about characters living on a fantastic man-made structure after the nuclear holocaust. This compulsively readable and thought-provoking book has brought to the fore a highly talented new writer. He is now at work on his second novel.

Besides literature, Frederick Dunstan's interests are mainly in the other arts; he plays the piano and the violin to 'modest standards' and is interested in painting.

Frederick Dunstan

Habitation One

FONTANA PAPERBACKS

First published by Fontana Paperbacks 1983

Made and printed in Great Britain by
William Collins Sons & Co. Ltd, Glasgow

FOR HARRIET

CONTENTS

PROLOGUE: THE DEAD PLANET

This is the earth.

In all directions, as far as can be seen, extends a brown plain. The sky is an evenly clouded grey. It is very cold. There is water: no streams or falls, but many clear, still ponds and puddles in the rifts and craters, between the broken stones and among the coarse grains of brown sand. A thin breeze is blowing; but there is no movement.

The plain is cracked and discoloured all over, as if by the action of fire. In some places the stones and jagged rocks are an ashy black and white; in others, a rusty red, with gleams of sooty, fiery orange. There are blanched, veined formations of rock like marble, where the whiteness has a sickly lustre against the reds and deep blacks, in which the pools of water twinkle like diamonds. The buff-coloured sand advances in smooth drifts to cover the base of every stone. There is no sound but the infinitely soft sibilance of the wind amongst the sand and the fractured boulders.

There are no round pebbles, no soft edges nor smoothness at all except the curves of the sand-drifts and the surfaces of the myriad pools. Although the wind and the sand have long ago begun their slow, eroding action, as yet this is unnoticeable. All edges are sharp and jagged. The rocks are twisted, fissured and smashed; similarly go the deep rifts into the ground, amid whose darkness is occasionally visible the shine of a metallic thread. There are a few peaked rock-masses dotted about the plain, more than fifty feet high; the depth of the ravines cannot be made out for certain. These little hills, with their tumbled, lined sides, recede into and punctuate the dreary distance.

The sand underfoot goes down only an inch or two – in places it has been swept away – and underneath are larger, dun-grey solids, like the corpses of clods of earth, which are hard and compactly fitted together. But in the lower depth of the sand are strange metal particles, the largest no bigger than raindrops, the smallest indiscernible: many of them perfect little spheres, some slightly rusty. They make a frosty sheen on the sand, not obvious at first sight, but unescapable when noticed. The wind rises. It is a harsh, sterile wind, with no smell but a trace of irritant dust. The pools ripple. The sand begins to move along the ground in flickering waves. Suddenly from nowhere appears a small whirlwind, six feet high, and at its slender base a sparkling cloud, formed by the grains of metal, which being heavier than the sand are not lifted so high. The whirlwind spins away over the stones, the sand, the rippling waters; another appears; the wind blows more strongly but less evenly, in varying gusts. The whirlwinds dance like ghosts, the one now pursuing the other, now independently, now disappearing together into the distance. A few drops of rain fall. The wind ceases and the ghosts are gone. A patch of sky lightens for a few moments, then darkens again.

Night comes: a night without stars or moon, after a twilight of grey sky and black desert. As darkness approaches a new luminosity is seen: some of the rocks are glowing dimly, others more brightly. Some flicker, and have a translucent appearance, as if lit from within by a cold, candescent fire. The pools of water reflect the drowsy radiance amid the blackness. Sky and ground are now equally invisible in the dead light. The luminous rocks are unevenly scattered. In one direction all is dark; in another the horizon is a pale line. The night is colder than the day. Nothing changes and the night continues for a long time.

Eventually there comes a lightening. Again the sky is a dark grey. No sun can be seen rising. The luminosity dies, the delicate slivers of ice which have formed on the pools during the night disappear, and the familiar sombre colours, brown, red, black, white, return slowly. This day is the same as the day before: the same endless vista; the same acrid wind; the same pools, the same twinkling sand, the same peaked hills. The same whirlwinds, the only inhabitants of this dead land, dance occasionally on their glittering feet. The sky remains uniformly overcast.

This plain continues northwards for a very long distance. But eventually come into view a distant range of mountains. They look grey, with white tops. The whiteness may be snow; but the mountains are not high. However the plain here abruptly ends

10

in water. This is the sea; the mountains are on the other side. In the east is open horizon; in the west the mountains appear to curve round and meet the plain. The sea has no distinct boundary. The pools in the ground become larger and more frequent, and join, until the land is an irregular disappearing network of ridges and islands in the clear water. Towards the west this coast rises, and distant cliffs are visible, with a splash of white foam beating against them. The sea is leaden.

At last the sky changes. Distinguishable cloud-masses form out of the uniform grey. A hint of blue appears. The sea, too, changes colour: there is a suggestion of sunlight on the horizon. On the other side of it, under the mountains, there are ice-bergs floating. The sun comes out, but it is still cold. The ice-bergs jostle as they float out into the arctic water. There is a sound of waves, and salt in the wind.

Onwards, upwards through the mountains, the cold becomes more intense, the sky is brighter and bluer; the dreadful ceiling of permanent cloud has been left behind. Now, miraculously, for the first time, there comes a faint sound of running water; a stream runs through a cold valley far below. Large mountains appear ahead: real ones, black-speckled, snow-covered. There are now only a few remaining wisps of cloud. The brilliant peaks cast blue shadows. Still higher mountains come into view. A sudden avalanche rushes down one of them with an echoing thunder. The still, rarefied air bites. It is midday.

Then, in the middle of the air, there is a flash. In front, between and behind the next two peaks, is a shining line, straight, vertical, ascending to be lost in the brightness. The place where it reaches the ground is as yet hidden. Slowly the mountains come forward and the lower parts of the line are disclosed. And there it stands, like a sculpture of wire and steel plate, higher than the mountains, delicate, gleaming, weightless, like a natural crystalline formation out of the rarefied air and sky.

A golden column rises from a wide plateau among the mountains. On the top of the column stands a tapering cone, which continues upwards to form the attenuated thread, apparently one-dimensional, which itself continues vertically until no longer visible. High above the highest peaks behind, the thread passes through a sphere, its diameter less than the thickness of the column; and from this sphere extends horizontally outwards a vast circular plane, as implausible as the vertical thread. At its circumference a shining wall rises and falls in two smooth curves on opposite sides of the sphere. The circle seems to be supported by a system of filamentary stanchions, which curve outwards and upwards from a swelling below the sphere, and meet the underside of the circle a little way in from its circumference. The circle is also supported by additional,more vertical struts which emerge from below the swelling. Yet more thready structures descend outwards from this swelling, widening into great shards that hang, unfixed, in the void. And the whole amazing, symmetrical, fantastically balanced structure, like a glittering metal flower, is held up by and poised on the single central thread which rises from the top of the cone; so thin, so straight, so effortless, that it is difficult not to believe that it is being kept taut by some celestial traction: a divine, invisible hand pulling at the top.

But the thing is enormous – incredible – incomprehensible. Measurements of distance become meaningless when applied to it. To say that the great circle must be more than four miles in diameter – does that mean anything? Or that from top – if there *is* a top – if the vertical thread does ever come to an end, far away from the earth, amid the cold and the steady shine of stars in the outermost reaches of the earth's atmosphere – to bottom, or at any rate which is visible of the vertical thread, must be beyond fifteen miles long – or rather high – is that comprehensible? It will probably be better not to try to realise. It is simpler, and perhaps even more accurate, to perceive it like a small model or toy: a magical creation, a fairy castle, or perhaps a mythical representation of the universe, with the flat world supported by a divine geometry. However, the circle is, in a more literal sense, a world. From a closer vantage-point a green skin can be seen on it. There, far away, minutely small, dwarfed by the fantastic proportions of the construction, trees are growing; there is a wood; and there are fields and rivers; and houses. There are people.

Approximately twelve hundred people inhabit this world – this hyperborean speck of warmth and greenness in the frozen, desolated wilderness. They are unaware of the stupendous structure over which they move; unaware, save for occasional glimpses, of any world outside it; and without inkling of any human civilisation or culture, past or present, but their own. They know of no other representatives of the human race thank themselves. Their world is a circular field four miles in diameter with a sphere at its centre; and they have lost the memory of its makers. Out of the small collection of facts they preserve – an unregarded assortment of momentoes giving evidence of a prehistoric, external culture – one of the most notable is the name itself, kept by tradition during unnumbered epochs, for the cosmic building which houses their existence. And this name, long ago conferred on it by its builders, is HABITATION ONE.

And now the events of Habitation One are moving, with gradually increasing speed, towards a climax. Though no one has yet realised it, the old system is breaking apart. A certain renaissance of interest and inquiry has begun, but it will soon be accompanied by a pessimistic awareness. Habitation One is now a wide stage, on which a strange and unique play is due to be enacted.

The date is the spring equinox of the year 32. Even living memory reaches back to times long earlier than the establishment of a fixed calendar. The fact that the years now have numbers is some evidence of a spirit of scientific observation, which itself is part of the slow general reawakening of the human intellect. It is a little after midday. To observe the action it is necessary to go closer.

PART ONE

I. i. THE SENIOR ASSEMBLY

The great Circle is divided by radial roads into eight equal areas.
A thick belt of woodland lines the circumference; from this the
roads, colonnaded with trees on both sides, emerge to run
straight towards the Sphere at the centre of the Circle. Fields lie
between the roads in an abstract, angular pattern of shades of
brown and green. Among the fields and hedges runs a rectilinear
system of streams. A small lake shines fitfully in the Circle's
south-west quadrant. There are many dwellings visible: most of
them low, wooden cottages, roofed with turf or ceramic tiles;
while here and there a grander edifice, a brick house of two, or
even three storeys and many windows, rises impressively. But
behind and above all runs the vast curving sweep of the
perimetral wall, a sheer, flawless band of white metal, eighty feet
high at the two lowest points of its curve, five hundred at the
highest.

Two men have just emerged from one of the larger houses and
are walking down a narrow lane towards the nearest radial road
– itself, like the others, no more than a stony track just wide
enough for two ox-drawn carts to meet and pass. The appearance
of the taller of these men is striking in many separate respects,
which in ensemble produce a startling, almost hallucinatory
effect. He is wearing on his brown, bald head what appears to
be a small mortar-board, dark in shade but unmistakeably blue
in colour. Otherwise he is dressed almost entirely in black:
boots, newly-pressed breeches, shirt, well-fitting jacket, relieved only by a loose gold chain of ceremonial appearance round
his neck, and a bright yellow handkerchief in his breast pocket.
But the really remarkable thing about him is an astonishing
moustache, more incredible than the unearthly lightness and
thinness of the composition of the Habitation itself. From each
side of his long, simian, muscular upper lip emerges a disciplined
jet of iron-grey hair, the individual hairs close-set, parallel, stiff
as wires, gently curving down and then up again to terminate in

sharp hooks a foot away from his cheek-bones, and on a level with his humorous brown eyes. A pointed chin, hooked nose, spiky black eyebrows and a black fringe around the occiput complete his gaunt physiognomy. His lean, black-clad frame adds another layer to the complex impression made by his appearance: a blend of philosopher, dilettante, clown, ascetic, school-boy, sage: comic, baffling, yet prerogative of respect. He is a man of between forty-five and fifty years old.

His companion is of an equally individual though much less arresting aspect. In contrast to the carefree movement and jaunty step of the other, everything about him adds to his air of heaviness and reposeful power. He treads the sun-dappled lane like an advancing tank. In spite of his wispy, greying hair and indeterminate grey-blue eyes, his face seems built like a fortress, with its massive chin and forehead, thrusting nose, heavy eyebrows and jowls, and greyish, puckered complexion. His clothes are a shapeless, nondescript assortment of khaki and brown; his trousers and boots are mud-stained; but his physique, though he is not much above five foot seven in height, is as imposing as his countenance. His shoulders are broad, his chest round, his hands big. His age is difficult to guess. There is dignity in his heavy stride, and intelligence behind his thoughtful expression and craggy forehead. Now a frown creases it and his lips are firmly closed as he listens attentively to his friend's high-pitched, but quiet and controlled, exposition.

'...No. I do not know what the cause is, but I have a faint awareness of hostility towards us.'

'And what form do you suppose this hostility to take?'

'Very well, Malcom ... You know that we – that I – founded the Scribaceous and Anagnostic Society some years ago because I thought that others – people in general – should have the opportunity of learning their letters. I thought then, and I continue to think, that literacy should be available to more than a handful of Doctors and Clerks. As you know, the Assembly saw no harm in it either, so I started the Society off. We had an attendance of ... seven in the first year, twelve in the second I think, twenty-five in the third, and twenty-one in the fourth, but now there are only the six of us. A year ago I was quite confident about everything, but now, suddenly, I'm not. Reading and writing and discussing and recataloguing and reclassifying – and simply sitting and chatting – these seemed worthy and satisfying activities. But now they don't.'

'I'm sorry to hear you speak like this, Settle. But why did you speak of hostility?'

'Because I'm sure we have enemies. Some people – I don't know who, but I'm sure the Priests at least – are concerned in what's happening, are putting pressure – probably through the heads of the professions – on the ordinary people of the Circle, who allow it to be known that they might wish to join the Society for a term.'

'It doesn't occur to you that the relatively large attendance we attracted in the first few years was perhaps no more than the natural attraction to a novelty?'

'No, it doesn't,' answered Settle firmly.

'And in any case, what evidence have you?'

Settle was silent for a minute or so. They came to the end of the little lane, opened a gate and passed onto the main road. In front of them suddenly appeared above the trees the visible upper half of the central Sphere, a superb, colossal, brilliant hemisphere many storeys high. The exterior walls of each storey (or level) consisted of no more than circular bands of arc-sectioned glass: not ordinary glass, for, though it was brighter and more transparent than the windows of the houses in the Circle, the midday sun could be comfortably regarded through it. The wall of each level was more than fourteen feet high, perfectly enclosed its own layer of the Sphere, and continued – except for the four wide doors at the ground level – the whole of the way round, a perfect, flawless ring innocent of frame or tracery. Between the storeys ran fasciae of black, polished metal, which contained the invisible vents supplying air to within the Sphere. The whole thing blazed in the windy afternoon like a vitrified sun, and as the two men walked towards it the black fasciae, subtly irregular with slight curving bulges and recessions, sent back dazzling reflections of the sun's rays that oozed and slid like white-hot mercury. Clouds and trees also, were darkly reflected; and between them could be made out the angular outlines of the solid apartments, doors, windows and furniture within, uncertain and faint.

But the member that, like a gothic spire, imparted to the architecture its feeling of miraculous, superhuman intention and achievement, was the great central column. From the summit of the dome it sprang up into the sky, like the flight-path of a rocket, vertical, infinite, and amazing. No one knew how high it was; the majority of the Habitationers believed that it reached heaven. Perhaps it did. Certainly, to look at the thing was an awe-inspiring, frightening, yet exalting experience: to follow the column, broad and shining amid the cloudy blue, higher and higher, up, up, and ever up till it became a silver thread, dwindling and receding into a blue limbo where strange perspectives soon confounded the observer's perceptions: the horizon seemed to rise into the sky, directly overhead, and the silver line bent backwards on top of the tired eyes and aching neck, so that the mind reeled and became uncertain whether the body was lying down or standing. It was very difficult to follow the column to the point of its disappearance unless a supine position was adopted, and even then a common sensation was that the flat ground was turning over through ninety degrees and tipping the observer out into space.

Reluctantly Settle brought his eyes back to the horizontal, keeping them closed for a few moments while he adjusted to the normal perspectives. His moustache fluttered stiffly in the breeze. The strain on his upper lip must have been considerable, but he gave no sign of minding it. He frowned and his hands clasped thoughtfully. Finally he said, in an undertone:

'There was a young fellow named Hugh Who wished he had something to do. So he looked for a stick Which he tied to his–'

'You were about,' Malcom interrupted heavily, 'to cite some evidence for me . . . I'm not at all interested in your poetry.'

'Ah yes.' Settle returned to the subject. 'Well, the trouble is that I do not think it advisable to name the people I talked to. They are naturally obedient to the authority of their own profession heads and I had great difficulty getting anything out of them.'

'All right. For the time being, then, I'll accept that these people are real and that you have some evidence. What?'

'It was about the same on every case. Each of them had been

persuaded to give up the Society. Most of them had had a friendly word from their fáthers or uncles. Some of them had resisted this and then they had been given a stern warning: their department manager, or a Clerk, might have met them and warned them plainly. I heard my confidants enumerate a variety of reasons for this: sanctity of labour, perpetual equilibrium, blasphemy in attaining to the Librarian's prerogatives, all the usual sort of mumbo-jumbo. A point to be noticed is that they all involved distinctly Priestly turns of language.'

'Indeed.'

The hemisphere and column ascended brightly in front of them. The wind stirred the budding lime-trees on the west side of the road. A group of farm-hands at work in a field close by shouted cheerfully; an old, wizened man dragging a hand-cart grinned and tugged respectfully as Settle passed him.

'Yes,' said Settle, smiling back. 'Well, the point I was coming to is that one chap did disregard the second warning and came to a Society meeting the next day. You may perhaps remember him – a nervous little man, fiftyish; we thought he had something on his mind at the time but he wouldn't mumble more than a few words about why he was worried. The next day he had a head's summons.'

'Oh dear.'

'The head – never mind which profession he was – no excuse or explanation, simply ordered him to cease to attend the meetings of the Society, to stop associating with them, especially me, and to surrender all the writing materials he had acquired. That was it. Of course he wanted to keep both his knee-caps –' Settle said this flippantly, but Malcom made a slight shudder – 'so he obeyed. I hope he's run no risk since in talking to me, but we were fairly careful to be secret.'

'Well. Why, then?'

'I don't know. The Assembly doesn't seem to object to us now. I don't see what we could have done wrong. The Priests are stupid, I know, but sometimes their actions have been rumoured to have sensible motives...'

'Have you asked them? There'd be no harm in a direct inquiry, would there? ... Oh!'

This ejaculation was provoked by an accidental collision

between the point of Settle's right moustache and Malcom's left eye. The moustache had been oscillating considerably and Malcom had carelessly allowed himself to come within range of it. He flushed angrily and moved to the other side of the road. There was a faint flicker in Settle's eyes; then his expression became blank. They went on in silence to where the road entered the Sphere, and said goodbye. Settle entered the Sphere through the high, arched doorway. After the brilliance of the outside, the interior was very dim. The door-keeper saluted him and a small gathering of people round the stores on the right moved hastily to avoid his moustache. At this hour of the day the Sphere was lit mostly by the sunlight outside; a few yellow-white neon-globes glowed palely. Settle walked down the passage, over the smooth flagstones, past the brick walls of the various apartments. As usual, at this time, the market was busy. Piles of goods, sacks of grain, of potatoes, strings of onions, vociferous crates of poultry, sides of beef, hides, furs, cotton bales, clay pots and jars, glass sheets and bottles, sawn timber, bundles of firewood, tin kettles and plates, stood and lay about, presenting a misleading appearance of confusion in the twilight as the representatives of various families from each profession went through the time-honoured rituals of barter. Further on the appearance of confusion was more striking, for the products were largely waste: buckets of broken glass, wooden boxes full of rusty knives and cups, an assortment of large, defunct pieces of machinery, pungent tubs full of decomposing refuse, even boxes of ash. This was where the more complex transactions of reclamation were carried out. On Settle's left was a wide, open area, called the Public Hall, apparently open to the outside – the glass walls of each level were invisible from the inside during most daytimes. It was occupied only by a number of indoor shrubs and trees, and a score or so of very small children playing in the dust under the supervision of a couple of old women. He came to the middle of the level, occupied by a complex architectural feature comprising a flight of stairs with a balustrade, several taut vertical ropes, some rising platforms, the upper third of a very large, spoked, slowly turning wheel, a gangway, and a small console of levers and handles. A large bundle of long steel pipes was being carefully unloaded from one of the platforms by three men. The lift-operator saluted Settle as he passed by and began lightly to mount the staircase to what was known as the Librarian's level. This was level 1, counting from the surface level (level 4): his own domain. The greater part of it was not in use. It contained his personal apartments and the large room where he had in happier times been accustomed to take the Scribaceous and Anagnostic Society's classes, and still held at regular periods the school for such children as the Habitation authorities might wish to receive a literate education. There were also several tall bookcases; these contained the books that Settle had retrieved and sorted out from the ruined library. But no one had read them, for they were cassettes containing spools of microfilm which needed a projector to be read, and there were no working projectors to be found in the Habitation. There was also one case, with one shelf in it, holding the other kind of books: these were massive, impressive, leather-bound volumes, two feet high and four inches thick. They had been written out in longhand by previous Librarians. There were eleven of them in the Library and they represented about two-thirds of the literature available in the Habitation. The rest of the area of the Library was in ruins, a roof-high chaos of smashed bookcases, fallen girders, gutted book-shelves, the tangled strings of unwound microtapes. It was clear that at some period a major disaster, probably not accidental, had overtaken the Library: for instance, many of the charred beams had round holes drilled in them, somewhat similar to those made by the laser-punch in the foundry on level 6.

This depressing sight did not affect Settle; he was used to it. He strode briskly into his room, took off his muddy boots and put on a clean pair of shoes with large brass buckles, washed his face and hands, combed his hair and brushed his moustache carefully, took from his wardrobe a long, trailing gown, in colour the same dark blue as his mortar-board, and put it on. Last of all, having carefully taken off his gold chain, he put another one, longer, thicker, with a heavy round medallion, over his head, drew his moustache through it, and settled it on his shoulders. He studied his reflection in the wardrobe mirror – cryptic, authoritative, dignified – ran a comb through his hair again, and turned as he heard a knock on the door. Outside two pages were waiting. The three proceeded to the lift, descended one level slowly, and stepped off to mingle with the decorous, richly-attired gathering in the foyer of level 2. There was a discreet hubbub of conversation. The heads of the twelve professional families of Habitation One were about to congregate in the half-yearly meeting of the Senior Assembly.

The Great Hall on level 2 was, in plan, an oval, with the pointed ends on a north-south axis, flattened. Of the long, curving walls, the west one was of glass, formed by a segment of the level's outer wall; the east was taken up with three tiers of carved wooden benches, where the heads of professions sat with their retinues. At the north end, on a dais, was an altar, a rectangular block of unfinished stone, filthy with congealed blood; at the south end stood by itself the seat of the President of the Assembly, who was the Senior Clerk – the head of the professional family of Clerks. Because of the one marvellously pellucid wall-window, the hall was usually well lit in spite of the drifting smoke from the charcoal fire under the altar. But the only access to it was by two narrow, unlighted passages which terminated near the north and south ends of the east wall. There was one other door in use, behind the altar, leading directly to the archive rooms, where the Clerks kept the few records whose value was thought to be greater than the worth, for reclamation, of the parchment or paper on which they had been written.

Outside, at that particular instant, the level 2 clock indicated that the time was 13.58.44. This unique timepiece hung opposite the lift, on the wall of the hot, airless foyer amongst the indoor greenery: climbing ivy, yellow and green; brown, waving ferns; two miniature, etiolated willows with their lank yellow strands; an ancient vine with a few hard, dusty grape-clusters on it; and the magnificent vermillion and light-green of the hypertrophied geranium bushes. The clock was fronted by glass covering a light yellow screen, upon which the six black digits came and went with silent, infallible regularity. No one knew how this clock worked: no means of adjusting it nor opening it were displayed on its casing: it did not need winding nor exposure to sunlight: it had never gone wrong. Except for the sun, it was the only trustworthy timepiece in the Habitation; there were also a few wind-up clocks and watches (Settle had one), one battered solar

24

chronometer which belonged to the Priests, and a quartz alarm-clock that was a treasured heirloom of the Doctors' profession. Settle looked at the clock, put his watch forwards five minutes, and wound it up deliberately. He conversed briefly with a few acquaintances, stolid and assured in their ceremonial dress among the dry fronds and foliage: the Master of the Glassworkers, splendid in leaf-green velvet slashed with silver; the Senior Clerk's secretary, a small man in grey and black; and in his surplice, Amiss Priest, a friend of Settle's, who occupied a subordinate position in the hierarchy of the Priesthood (hence his surname; the heads of the professions, however, were distinctively referred to with the definite article, so Settle's full name was 'Settle the Librarian'). Settle had enough time to tell Amiss that there was something that he would like to see him about later; then a bell rang, and it was necessary for Settle to take his place at the tail of the right-hand procession, where his two attendants were already positioned, awaiting entry to the Hall by the north door.

They plunged into the constricting, lightless passage and passed slowly along it. The entry into the Hall, as always, surprised Settle: suddenly, as it seemed when he turned the corner, he was walking out into the sky. The opposite wall presented a magnificent empyrean panorama. Huge grey-and-white clouds, stained and edged with silver, moved against the dark crystalline blue of the early afternoon sky like mobile towers drawn by elephants; swift in movement but with direction elusive, imperceptibly melting and changing like the fundamental, abstract tenets of an imperfectly comprehended philosophy. The topmost branches of trees, lightly veiled with the spring's new leaves, lurched and swayed, rippling like a submarine landscape. The floor of the Hall was wooden and polished, so that a diffused reflection of the bright wall added to the ambience of light within the room. The President's desk, far away from Settle's seat on the end of the highest bench, was a dark solid on the luminous sea; his head and shoulders, all of him that could be seen, were black against the light. Settle had mechanically reached his seat while looking at the sky. His gaze wandered over the smoky ceiling, with its faded gilt stars in the blue and grey coffering, towards the altar, where Amiss and another attendant were leading forward an old ewe. The ceremony was performed in a perfunctory, businesslike manner. The bleating victim was lashed to a special post, legs tied together, throat cut, blood efficiently caught. The High Priest, robed and stoled, took up some blood in a little cup and dabbled it over the altar and the invisible fire. He then turned and delivered, in a high-pitched voice interrupted by a frequent cough, the following prayer:

'O Lord God, who hast stablished Thy Habitation in the midst of the firmament, who hast raised it with angels and guarded it with seraphs, who settest Thy only Son on Thy right hand to be our master and our king, Thou who hast provided daily for our comfort and nurture, Thou by whom the winds are blown and the waters made, Thou who hast blessed the earth and made it fertile: be with us, O Lord, for this the next half of the year; safeguard the sense of Thy common people and keep them from waste and destruction; and be with us now, O Lord, Thy servants the heads of the twelve professions, in our counsels and administrations; increase in us piety and rectitude, that we may lead the people in thrift, in salvage, and in obedience in Thy godly laws. Through the merits of Thy Son our Saviour, Who led the cherubim out of Egypt, Yours faithfully, Amen.'

This invocation was not attended by any obvious display of religious feeling. Some of the heads stood to attention, but with their hands in their pockets; others leaned backwards against the benches or sat down. The members of their retinues, though, tended to be somewhat more deferential. However, no one talked or whispered and there was little disturbance. Settle himself watched and listened to the Priest with a frown on his face. A scattered 'Amen' sounded from the congregation, who then all sat down. A man came in with a wheelbarrow and removed the carcass of the sheep. The normal proceedings of a biannual meeting followed. The President read out the minutes of the last meeting and signed them, no one having any objection, as correct. He then ceremonially tore them up and dropped them in a bin to await repulping and recycling. The afternoon's real business followed: this was the formal delivery of observations, requests, protests, arbitrations and decisions concerning problems in the day-to-day running of the Habitation's communal life. The Master of the Glassworkers issued a warning that insufficient bottles were being returned, broken or otherwise, for the production of new bottles to be kept up, and required the heads of all professions to convey this message to their families. The High Doctor announced that mortality figures for the last winter were unusually high: 97 persons, nearly all of them aged over 50 or below 10, had deceased during the past four months, mainly through influenza and pneumonia. There had been complaints both from Circle and Sphere-dwellers about suffering from cold through being denied adequate fuel and heating energy. He appealed to the heads of the Electricians and the Foresters to account for this. Danyel the Electrician replied first: the lack of power had been owing to a fault which had appeared in one of the five main transformers. It had been necessary to shut down this transformer while the fault was traced, and eventually been found to lie in an inner circuit. This, as the Honourable Assembly might not be aware, meant that it was virtually irreparable. Therefore, reluctant as they always were to draw from the stores, an order for withdrawal had been made out, presented to the High Priests, granted, signed, countersigned by the Senior Clerk, and the components for a new transformer had duly been issued. This had now been assembled and installed, and power should soon be supplied to all homes as usual.

The heads not involved in the talking sat or lolled. Settle leaned back in his seat, bored, fingering a moustache-tip. The scribes scribbled hastily on their tablets and slates. At one end of the Hall the President sat motionless; at the other the High Priest dozed in his high, canopied seat. Outside the clouds sailed silently onwards; inside the patches of bright sunlight crept across the floor, motes gleamed and eddied in the sunbeams, blue curls of hazy smoke drifted from the altar. There was an occasional cough. Pens scratched, feet scuffled.

The head of the Foresters rose to give his report. He had been apprised of the winter energy-shortage, and had done his utmost to meet the increased demand for firewood. Unfortunately, as all those present knew well, the necessity for extreme economy of firewood imposed by the limited number of trees on the Habitation meant that the utmost quantity he had been able to supply had not been adequate. At the best of times a wood fire was a luxury; he had now exhausted large stocks. Unusual economy would have to be exercised for the next two quarters of the year. He therefore announced that until the autumn equinoctial Assembly, firewood would be available only to senior Habitationers, at the personal requests of heads of professions, and would even for them be strictly rationed.

Lazily Settle toyed with rhymes and rhythmic syllables like jigsaw pieces. Most of what had been said so far he already knew; his turn to speak had not yet come. An elegant limerick was slowly crystallising in his mind.

The Grand Watermaster, head of the profession of Waterworkers, gave his report. All was well. The condensers were functioning perfectly, rivers and channels were clean; the purifiers were in satisfactory condition for the time of the year.

The head of the Farmers spoke. All was well. The weather had been reasonably good and food-production was keeping up. His secretary read out some statistics.

The head of the Craftsmen had nothing to report.

The head Weaver expressed himself satisfied.

The head Metalworker was also satisfied.

Settle stood up. He said: 'I wish to remind all heads that, as in previous years, I will be happy to take classes in adult literacy. The Scribaceous and Anagnostic Society holds weekly meetings. I would be grateful if you would give notice of this opportunity to your own people, especially those of you such as the Farmer and the Forester, whose professions contain the largest numbers. Thank you.' He sat down again, uncertain what the faces beside and below him had registered. Most had seemed bored or indifferent. By the altar, Amiss was standing with a worried expression on his face. The other Priests seemed stupidly unconcerned.

The speeches of the remaining heads were soon over. The President rose.

'If there is no other business to be carried out and all heads have made a full statement, I declare this meeting closed. We will meet again after two quarters. You will be notified a week beforehand of the next Assembly.'

He turned from his seat and went out, followed by a small train of underlings. At the other end the Priests processed out solemnly. Settle smiled in private triumph as he selected the *mot juste* to bring his new poem to a successful conclusion, dismissed his two pages with a nod and stood waiting for Amiss. When he came back five minutes later, Amiss was revealed in the absence of his robes, to be a short, pleasant-faced, rumple-haired young man in his twenties. He now looked upset and vexed.

'If you want to see me about what I think it is – is it the Society?'

'Yes, it is.'

'Well, I think it would be most unwise to start talking about this now, in the open. I'll come and see you this evening. And I think you were foolish to make that announcement – to start spouting like that as if you had no idea what's going on!'

'But really, I haven't much idea. Why was it foolish?'

'I'll see you later.'

He moved away. Settle, slightly disconcerted, stared after him, then thrusting back his gown, stuck his hands in his pockets and walked out of the Hall, whistling softly. He sauntered up the one flight of stairs to the Library and made for his apartments.

I. ii. THE SCRIBACEOUS AND
ANAGNOSTIC SOCIETY

He opened the door and strode in setting his right whisker aquiver with the impact on the door-jamb. Two girls were holding hands on the sofa in his sitting-room. They remained in the same position, talking with an introverted, slightly forced disregard of Settle as he moved about, draping his blue gown and mortar-board negligently over the back of a chair, producing a bottle and some glasses from a cupboard, drawing up an armchair to the hearth, in which a wood fire was burning cheerfully, extracting a pipe and tobacco-pouch from his pocket, filling and lighting up with a brand while slumping comfortably into the chair. They surveyed each other. The look of disgust which had been on Settle's face as he had entered the room had been quickly replaced by a wry, dispassionate stare, emphasized by the set of his lips and jaw with the pipe. The less sullen-looking of the girls spoke, in a high-pitched, husky voice.

'Did you have a good Assembly, Dad?'

Settle was a widower. His daughter was a girl of twenty-three, medium height, and unprepossessing aspect. Her light brown hair was, in a Habitationer's eyes, unbecomingly short: that is to say that her ears were exposed and it reached, at the back, only as far as the collar of her shirt. Her complexion was very fair, unlike her father's, but in her his gauntness of face was even more pronounced. There was something skull-like in the sharp distinction of her cheekbones, the sunken uncertainty of her mild blue eyes, and in the pale tautness of her forehead and lips. Like his, her chin was delicate and strong. Her white throat disappeared into the front of a baggy, man's shirt, cream-coloured, which gave little clue as to whether or not she possessed a bust. She was otherwise clad – again, most improperly – in trousers (beige) and clumsy wooden clogs.

'Yes, thank you, Cathis,' answered Settle.

'I bet you didn't,' said Cathis's friend bluntly. 'I bet it was as boring and useless as ever.' She was a tall, strong-looking young woman, much more striking in appearance than Cathis; chiefly because, although dressed on similar lines, her costume drew attention to her figure, rather than away from it. Her trousers were nondescript in material and colour – an ordinary goose-turd green – but, her hips and thighs being big, they were tight, and the plump convexities of her belly and buttocks were shockingly exhibited. Her shirt, which had been dyed a bright scarlet, was tucked tightly under her belt, so as to emphasise equally her large breasts. This outfit tended to produce, as in Settle at the present moment, the impression of a somewhat self-consciously aggressive femininity. For the rest (a quantity much less prominent than the sexiness of her physique), she had small hands and feet, a head of long, dull, mouse-coloured hair, small greenish-brown eyes, plump cheeks and chin, a turned-up nose. Her mouth was full but pursed, set in a habitual pout.

'Boring, perhaps,' replied Settle between puffs of his pipe, 'but not useless, I don't think.'

'I do; and you know as well as I do that these fancy-dress meetings are quite unnecessary. At least, all the pompousness and mumbo-jumbo's unnecessary. It doesn't need all the Priests and prayers and Presidents to come to simple decisions about everyday matters.'

Settle, sunk in his chair, made no answer.

'Well, it doesn't, does it?'

'All right, Salla,' said Cathis, a trifle defensively, 'We've had this all out before.'

'I know we have! And what irritates me is that none of you take the slightest notice of it!'

'What do you expect us to do, then?' asked Cathis, slightly pink.

'What do I–? Oh, Habitation! there are hundreds of things–'

'No,' said Settle thoughtfully, interrupting Salla, 'I used to agree with what we all feel about the Priests, but I'm not so sure now.'

There was a pause.

'Do you mean that you can see a single good reason for them

continuing to exist, apart from the fact that we have no way of removing them?' asked Salla heavily.

But Settle made no further remark. A moment later the door opened and a man came in. 'Hello, everyone,' he said. 'Hello, Heron,' said Cathis; 'Good afternoon, glad you could come,' said Settle.

Heron Craftsman closed the door and seated himself in the other armchair. He was a tall, pale, handsome young man of about thirty, broad-shouldered, long-legged, with a powerful physical presence. His blue eyes sparkled with an immense vitality; his curly, dark blond hair seemed to fly about his head in irregular gusts. This was partly due, no doubt, to his habit of running his hands backwards through it; he gestured freely in conversation. His blond moustache, while hardly attempting to emulate the gravity-defying magnificence of Settle's, nevertheless bristled with an energy of its own. His hands were fine, strong and capable. He was wearing ordinary working clothes, but with a fresh white shirt. There were traces of sawdust on his trousers and boots.

'Have you seen the two others?' Settle inquired.

'No, I didn't. Is Christofer coming, Salla?'

'Yes.'

'Well, I've got a little something to show you all – a rather amusing little toy I've invented. In the meantime, Settle the opulent Librarian, what about a plug of tobacco? It's only the first day of the quarter and I've used the quarter's allowance half up already. Thanks.'

Settle tossed the pouch over and Heron helped himself lavishly. His pipe, which he had made himself, had a large, black, square bowl, with a mouthpiece fabricated from a piece of copper piping. He too took a brand, lit up, and replaced the brand. 'I must say I love your fire,' he said, smoking with relish, 'I do wish firewood wasn't rationed so severely. A good blaze looks so cheerful. . .'

'We heads of professions are entitled to our modest luxuries,' replied Settle.

'You know, Dad,' said Cathis nervously, after a pause, 'this is really another example of what Salla was saying just now. It's not only the Priests who take advantage of all the mumbo-jumbo.'

'Indeed?'

'Yes,' she said, suddenly fluent. 'All the heads of professions do, and – and you, you yourself are among the worst of them. You have many things, in abundance, which are allowed much less to poorer people. Tobacco, firewood, running water, lavish electricity – but what work, what serious work, do you do in return for this? Nothing. It's all just empty ceremony.'

'Come now, Cathis darling,' said Heron jovially, 'let's not get worked up. Anyway, you know that's not true. Settle's the Librarian, and that means – it means that – well, we accept that the head Librarian always has what's proper. At least –'

'Look, Heron. My father takes one class of children, three times a week, at odd times. And he goes to the Assemblies – twice a year. And occasionally he is called in to arbitrate on some abstruse point of Habitation law or grammar usage for the Clerks or Priests. That's all, but he is one of the richest men in the Habitation. Do *you* think that is fair?'

Settle drew on his pipe calmly a few more times before answering. 'What would you, then, especially considering that you're in my family and habitually accept a considerable portion of the benefits, do with these riches you say I ought not to have?'

'Share them out among the poor, of course,' said Salla firmly.

'And all the family possessions of the Priests and the Clerks, as well, I suppose?'

'Yes; why not?' Cathis was defiant.

The door opened again and the last two of the six regular members of the Society arrived. These were Malcom, who had changed his clothes and was wearing a tie, and another young man, whose name was Christofer Clerk; he was Salla's husband. He was of medium height and of amiable, unstriking appearance. His dark hair was short and combed, his mouth set in an uncertain smile; his nose and spotted chin were moderately firm; but his narrow, sloping shoulders, thin chest and rather limp hands gave no promise of much physical strength. His feet, though elegantly clad in fresh-polished boots, were large and clumsy. He moved awkwardly. He and his wife had no children.

'This discussion sounds very interesting,' said Malcom as he lowered himself into the last vacant armchair. Christofer stood looking around him, somewhat at a loss. The two girls remained motionless. He sat down uneasily between them. Both withdrew from him on either side. With affected nonchalance he said, 'Yes, why not what? What were you talking about?'

'Oh, come off it, Settle, that's enough of this gloomy talk,' interrupted Salla loudly. 'I can't stand all these boring old arguments any more. Heron! Wake up! What about that invention of yours you were going to show us?'

Heron, who had indeed been lying back in his chair with his eyes shut, apparently also bored by the conversation, now sat up suddenly. 'Eh? Oh, yes, certainly.' He took from his pocket a small round wooden object and held it up. The others saw that it consisted of two thin discs of wood, a small distance apart, with a string protruding from the narrow space between them. There was a loop in the end of the string. 'Now, who can guess what this thing does?'

'Go on, show us,' said Settle, interested.

Heron fitted the loop over the middle finger of his right hand, bent his fingers round the device and flicked it sharply downwards. To everyone's surprise the wheel descended quite slowly, revolving as it unwound itself from more string hidden between the discs. It reached the full length of the string and hung six inches from the ground, spinning rapidly.

'Now what?' said Cathis.

Heron's wrist made a dextrous jerk, and the wheel rose miraculously, like the platform of a lift, and darted vertically back into his hand. There was a general cry of surprise and amusement. He grinned broadly and performed the trick again. Settle and Christofer, having deduced how the wheel was able to levitate so magically, looked on smiling, as Cathis examined the wheel curiously. Malcom and Salla however, seemed less impressed. Cathis inserted a finger into the loop and dropped the wheel. It descended inertly to the floor. 'No,' said Heron, 'you have to flick it and jerk it back.' He wound the string round the central axis, demonstrated, and returned the object to Cathis, who was now able to work it herself. Settle and Christofer had a few goes, while Malcom regarded them impassively.

'What do you call this thing, then?' Settle asked. His spirits had recovered. 'It's certainly very clever.'

'I call it a Bouncer.'

'Bouncer, eh? Well, it's very good.'

'Thanks.'

'Talking of inventions,' said Settle, 'I composed a very nice limerick today.'

'Oh, no,' said Cathis.

'Not *another* one – I hope it isn't as disgusting as the last one you gave us,' said Malcom grimly.

'Yes, it is,' said Settle cheerfully, 'worse.'

'Let's have it,' said Heron and Christofer together.

Settle recited the limerick he had made up during the assembly:

> 'When Grandma's awakened from sleep,
> By what feels like a cold woolly heap,
>   She understands why,
>   For Grandpa close by
> Has a weakness for screwing dead sheep.'

Christofer and Heron guffawed loudly at this, and Cathis giggled, embarrassed; but Salla and Malcom were not at all amused. After a few minutes more chat, the latter turned the conversation to the things Settle had told him earlier that afternoon. 'The Priests', he said, 'are not so much hostile to us, as towards the idea of illiterate, lower-rank men and women joining us. They are preventing them from doing so. They are trying – and succeeding – in crushing the life out of the Society; they're destroying its function, trivialising, castrating it. They have succeeded, in two or three years, in reducing us from a constructive, progressive force, to an inbred group of sterile, dillettantish intellectuals.' He spoke with a grave finality.

'Malcom has put it a great deal more strongly than I did, but he's quite right.' said Settle.

There was a reflective silence for a minute.

'Well,' said Heron, 'Why d'you think they're doing this?'

Malcom spoke slowly in reply. 'Knowledge is a kind of power. Every member of the Habitation has a certain quantity of specialised knowledge, and this gives him the power of his trade: over materials, or plants, or animals, or fluids like water or electricity. But access to this kind of power is very limited: it takes skill to acquire it, and it can only come through listening to others, and through practice and experience. However, when a man learns to read and write well, a gate is opened to all kinds of other knowledge and ways of thinking. I know there aren't many books, but well, we've all experienced it, except Settle and Cathis because they learned in infancy ... the wonderful feeling of enlightenment, the astonishing widening and broadening, the ability to form concepts and abstractions. I know myself that the year in which I joined the Society made more difference to me than any other year of my life ...

'Now, for example, Cathis and Salla are in the habit of making attacks on the way the Habitation is run. Whether or not these attacks have any substance I leave aside, for the moment. But if they had never learned to read and write, their powers of reasoning would have probably never developed to their present level. The Priests and Clerks are afraid of what might happen if *everyone* learned to use their minds more. I know a lot of people are not at all intelligent, but still, there are many people with deliberately uncultivated minds. The stability of the Priestly power depends on its acceptance by an illiterate populace. It is not really at all surprising that the Priests should wish the populace to remain illiterate.'

Settle broke in with excitement. 'But none of you seem to be taking any account of what the Priests are actually like! These ideas sound all very well – but you are building up a picture in our minds, a presentation of the Priests as a cynical, self-consciously tyrannical bunch – as if they had no other motives but the desire for power, and as if they had a lot of power. But they haven't. More than half the control of people's lives rests with the heads of their Profession. The heads are the real despots – they are quite straightforward about it. The priesthood really is nothing at all to do with power and domination – it is to do with people's religion and worship.'

'Oh! that!' said Salla in disgust. Promptly Cathis and Malcom proceeded to demolish religion as a possible concern to rational people. Christofer sat silent, thinking about Malcom's verdict on the Society's usefulness. Although Cathis was in the habit of snubbing him every time he opened his mouth, he eventually gathered enough determination to ask Malcom, boldly, whether he had any constructive suggestions to make on the subject of what the Society should be doing with it's time.

Malcom's reaction startled them. At first he seemed at a loss for words. He ran a hand through his wispy hair, and patted it down; his grey face suddenly took on a weak, lost expression.

'I don't know,' he said. 'I don't know. There doesn't seem to be anything. . .'

'You give up hope for us, then? Oh dear.'

'Don't laugh! It's not funny! There's nothing . . . *nothing.* And if there's nothing, it's the *end.*'

'Old Malcom seemed very quiet there,' observed Christofer to Settle some hours later as they sat by the fire again. Supper was over and everyone else had gone.

'Yes. There were some rather worrying things said. Cathis and Malcom seemed to have a lot on their minds.'

'Cathis's points weren't all that far out, you know.'

'I feel she's got the right motives, but the conclusions she's reached are all cock-eyed . . . It's very difficult to say exactly how, though.'

'What about Malcom's grumbling?'

Settle got up and went across to the window. Outside, darkness was gathering and the brilliant northern stars had begun to appear. The wall on the rim of the great Circle was distantly visible, faintly luminous, behind the dark haze of woodland. Scattered lights, yellow and red-lit windows, revealed the locations of homes in the Circle.

'I had no idea that he'd take what I said this morning so seriously.'

'Settle – does the thought of futility, of aimlessness, strike you in that way? Do you really worry about the Society's value?'

'No, not really. I was just – well, a little depressed when I thought of it. I think our friend has a mild thing, a neurosis (that's

it) about things having to have value, purpose, meaning. I mean
–'

'He's so unnervingly serious.'

Settle took a plateful of crockery into the kitchen. Christofer picked up a few glasses and followed him. On the way he peeped into Cathis's bedroom, briefly inspecting the small white bed, the painted chest of drawers, the walls covered with childish drawings. She had begun these many years ago and still added to them occasionally. There were birds and strange flowers and the curiously stylised figures of girls; executed in charcoal or crayon or ink-brush, they combined a delicacy of tone with a sureness of line, but the subjects were touchingly immature. The little girls had exaggerated heads and diminutive breasts, great, liquid eyes and vestigial noses. The birds had long, curly tails and humorous beaks.

'Is Cathis going to be in tonight?'

'I don't suppose so. Hasn't Salla invited her back to your house again?'

'Probably.'

'I don't know why you put up with it. She behaves disgustingly to you, though I haven't an idea why.'

'Oh, I don't mind Cathis. I like her, really. It's Salla I can't stand ... Habitation! Why my parents married me to that bitch I don't know and I'll never get rid of her now.'

Having cleared all traces of the supper away, Settle returned to his sitting-room and sat down, muttering to himself.

'Salla, shallow, sallow, fellow – There was a young lady named Salla, Whose conduct was lickerish and shallow. She said, "If you're stuck When a lesbian you–"'

'What's "lesbian"?'

'It's what those two are. It's in the dictionary, but I've never seen it written down anywhere else. I believe moral law reserves some very unpleasant penalty, theoretically, for it, though I don't know of any case ever having turned up in reality. I don't remember the details. I'll look it up – some painful form of mastectomy or clitoridectomy or some other ectomy, I suppose.'

'Please – *stop* being so flippant!'

Settle looked up; Christofer's expression dismayed him.

I. iii.   EXPLORATION AND DISCOVERY

Two days after the Society meeting Settle came down the stairs to level 5, whistling as usual. He went into the Electricians' workshop, found Malcom and after another slight contretemps with his moustache, offered him supper that evening.

'Thank you,' said Malcom, mollified, 'there's something I'd like to talk to you about, too,' and went back to the task of supervising the rewinding of a large coil.

Promptly at seven, he came in through the Librarian's front door, ruminatively, like a strayed ox. He stopped in surprise, seeing Settle at work on the construction of a tall, solid-looking edifice of playing-cards, on the dining-room table. These playing-cards, shiny cardboard rectangles, marked with their numbers and mysterious emblems in red and black, were ancient heirlooms of the Librarian family. The Clerks also possessed two incomplete packs. They were believed to have magical, divinatory powers of some kind, and were hence regarded reverently; Malcom, though one of the least superstitious of Habitationers, was slightly shocked to see Settle treating them so indecorously. He gave a disapproving cough, and Settle, turning his head without sufficient caution, brought one whisker into sharp contact with the middle storey of the card-castle, with ruinous effect. The structure promptly disintegrated.

'Hallo, Malcom,' he said cheerfully. 'Glad you could come. Sit down.'

Malcom sat down. Settle ladled out some soup for him. It was compounded of onion, potato, cabbage, leek, celery and hot-house asparagus in a fine beef stock, and smelled very appetising; Settle's eyes glistened as he poured out a lavish bowlful for himself. Malcom, however, gave no more indication of interest in it than the requirements of politeness.

'Very nice soup,' said he. 'Did you make it yourself?'

'Yes.'

Settle was, most unusually for a man, devoted to cookery. Having an excellent digestion and taking a keen interest in food, he did all his own cooking himself. This arrangement suited Cathis; in return, she did the housework, what little was done. Settle kept no servants, preferring to spend his comfortable income on expensive luxuries. He poured out a glass of wine now, and a half of one for Malcom, who filled it up with water. The scene, lit by four candles, the last light of the emerald evening sky outside, and the dim rosiness of the electric fire, was rich and tranquil. Four huge, vague shadows of Settle's head and moustache flickered and faded behind him on the wall. The lustrous gleams from the golden bottle and the glowing red wine in the glasses fell along the tablecloth. The soup-pot sat in the middle, massive and brown.

After a time, Settle began to speak of the matters he had been deliberating for the last two days. 'On the evening of the last Society meeting,' he said as a piece of bread disappeared under his moustache, 'Amiss came to see me. You remember, on the same day you said I might make some direct inquiries. Well, all I did at the Assembly was to make a routine announcement about enrolment in the Society. Nothing further. But Amiss was pretty upset about it.' He blew gently on a spoonful of broth before conveying it to his mouth.

'Well?'

'He told me several things, but they don't all seem to hang together very well, now I've thought things over a little ... In the first place, the routine auguries have been consistently worsening for some time. When the insides of the ewe – the sacrificial victim that is, were examined after the meeting, she was found to have three livers or no lungs or something. I don't really know how to react to this kind of information, but there it is. And this is only the latest incident in a series of upsetting omens.' He reached for the salt (a great luxury).

'The Priests may take omens seriously, but I don't see how that need affect anything.'

'Of course not. Like yourself, I am anagnostic, I mean agnostic, about divination, as about all other religious matters. But the second thing is that the Priests are actively hostile to the Society; a lot of what you said at the Society meeting is true, I'm afraid. They aren't hostile towards me, or you, or any one individual, but towards the idea of a literate, thinking populace. They don't want *people* to know how to read. Amiss was not specific, in fact it's probably that this feeling is vague and diffused, rather than originating from the thinking of one or two individuals. The Priests are a thick lot anyway. All the same, you were right to a certain extent.'

'So,' said Malcom thoughtfully, 'They wish no harm to us, only providing we remain as we are. . .'

'That's right,' the words came from the kitchen, where Settle had taken the empty bowls and spoons. He came back with a cold roast joint and a jar of pickled onions, and busied himself with carving. 'But there's something else. And this really must be confidential. Amiss has found what he thinks may be a reading apparatus.'

'What do you mean?'

'It's a little gadget – like a box with a glass window, he tells me. He thinks it's made for the purpose of reading those cassettes of ours. There's a slot of some kind in one side of it, which would be just the right shape for a cassette, he said. He was rooting around in the archives, looking for some old document or other, and he just stumbled across it, buried in dust. He doesn't know if it would work, even if it did turn out actually to be a reader.'

'And if it did?'

'The annoying thing is that the other Priests have got their hands on it. He's too conscientious, Amiss is. As soon as he'd puzzled over it for a bit, he realised that he thought his duty was to hand it over to his superiors; so now of course they're sitting on it and slowly wondering what to do next. I only hope . . . however, scrupulous as old Amiss may be, he's still favourably disposed towards our ideas – he regrets the decline of the Society – and he'll do his best to help us.'

'How can he be sure that it is what he thinks it is?'

'Oh, I forgot. He says that he pressed a switch or a button of some kind, and it threw out a bright light, a big square, on to the wall. He thought he could see markings of some kind in this square, but they were very blurred. Now you don't know, but Amiss does, because I mentioned the subject to him a long time ago, that in one of the earliest volumes of the Library records – wait a moment, I'll get it.'

He put a pickled onion into his mouth and disappeared. Malcom remained, chewing regularly, for a minute or two until Settle came back through the door, staggering under the weight of an enormous dusty volume. He moved some crockery and placed it carefully on the table. He turned over the large, sepia pages, muttering to himself.

'Rattle – Pickle – Nettle – Parottle – Ottle – Ottle! Here we are. It's in Ottle's records. As you know, they aren't dated, and they don't come at the beginning, but from references to him made by other Librarians we gather that he was probably the first Librarian who kept a regular, private diary. Ottle's the man who identifies those cassettes and strips as books in miniature – microtapes, he calls them. He describes how a projector, as he calls it, was found, and almost immediately destroyed as an "abhomination". He doesn't say how he recognised it as a projector, or why it was thought "abhominable", but he drew a little picture...'

The drawing, executed like the large, crabbed, difficult handwriting, with a wide-cut quill, showed two stylised human figures, their hands held up, their faces contorted with horror and disgust. Before them on a table lay an innocuous-looking little box. The dark slot was clearly recognisable at its side, and lines representing rays of light led from it to a square, drawn without regard for perspective, on the receding wall. The box stood on four short legs.

'Did Amiss's machine have legs?' asked Malcom, bending over the drawing to inspect it closely.

'No, but it has four holes, one at each bottom corner, where they might have gone.'

Settle closed the book and returned to his meal.

'Well then,' said Malcom. 'You've been thinking about this for two days. You must have realised many of the implications.'

'The situation is somewhat tense – that's why Amiss didn't want me to go talking rashly. As I see it now, it's the Priests and not me who are going to make the first move. They don't know I know about the projector, and they think they have as much time as they like to decide on a proper course. They would like to obey their natural, or at least habitual, inclination to give the thing to me. It's clearly in the Librarian's province, and by normal thinking I ought to take charge of it immediately. But they have realised that with the aid of that projector I'll be able to read a great deal; to find out all sorts of things that they might not be able to do anything about.'

'Nobody knows *what's* on those strips,' said Malcom after a pause. 'They might have – they might – there's no way, no way at all of telling what information one might pick up. There might be an answer to – to everything. . .'

'That sounds rather optimistic.' Settle gestured with his fork. 'Anyway, what I'm coming to is this. In Ottle's time a projector was found, and destroyed. Amiss has just found another, which has been confiscated. I rather doubt we'll get our hands on that one. The Priests will probably withhold it from us for the same reason that they suppressed literacy, their blind, rigid stupidity. They wish to preserve the status quo. I don't know whether it's through a merciless desire for power, as you revolutionaries keep suggesting, or for some other reason . . . anyway, the point is that there have been two projectors, so there may be more. And the most likely place to find another is in the Library itself.'

'That's probably so. The thing to do, then, is to search the Library.'

'That, my dear Malcom, is what I have also been attempting to do for the last two days. However I have encountered some unexpected obstacles. If you come with me, if you've finished eating, I'll show you.'

The sky outside was now a glowing sapphire at the horizon, darkening to a deep prussian blue. The stars were numerous and brilliant. Settle blew out the candles and switched on the electric light in the other room. He led the way out. At the same moment Cathis came in, ignoring her father, and went to her own room. With a grimace, Settle took hold of a small dynamo-torch and went out into the Library foyer. He switched on the lights there too. The two men stood at the top of the stairs, unnerved as usual by the chaos confronting them. Signs of efforts made, now that Malcom's attention had been drawn to them, could be seen. In one place stood a small cardboard box full of carefully rolled

43

tapes. In another was a heap of broken cassettes, tapes spilling out of them in glittering streams, awaiting assortment. One of the leaning book-cases had been straightened. But the spectacle was, by and large, as appalling as ever. In addition, the unpleasant, dry, burnt smell that hung about the roof-high wreckage was a great deal more noticeable than previously.

'As soon as I got seriously started,' Settle was saying, 'it became clear that a lot of this junk has been put here deliberately by someone. I cleared out a lot of old chairs and tables, and a smashed-up cart, as well as a lot of terrible, old, dead brambles and spikes which couldn't have found their way up here naturally. There was also a fair amount of barbed wire.' He went up a narrow alleyway, just wide enough to allow for his moustache, between two tall blackened book-cases. 'But I struggled through, minding my moustache carefully, until I came to this.'

It was dark in the alley and the disgusting smell was much stronger. Settle gave the dynamo-handle a few turns and switched on the powerful beam. Most of the plastic cassettes on the shelves on either side had melted and run, forming unpleasantly and inextricably congealed shapes, black, white, livid orange, and repulsive greys and browns. In front of them the alley was blocked by a massive girder, a blackened metal beam eighteen inches broad. Its foot was embedded in the charred wooden floor, its top seemed to be about an inch away from the ceiling. It was inclined backwards, away from them, at an angle of about sixty degrees with the horizontal against another huge, dense, impenetrable pile of rubbish.

'If we can move the girder, the stuff behind it doesn't look too difficult.'

'I see.'

'I'll just give this another wind – I'll need both hands.'

While Settle was winding the torch, Malcom looked round, examined the book-cases again, put his hand on the congealed plastic and drew it away with distaste. 'Settle', he said, 'in an odd sort of way this has a bearing on what I was going to say to you. Who do you think built this Library? And who destroyed it?'

'Well, it could have been an accident, I suppose. A fire. Or some madman set fire to it deliberately.'

'Perhaps. But who do you suppose *built* it? Who created it?'

'But that's – that's stupid. It's like asking who created the Habitation itself. The Library's part of the Habitation really, you know, even though it's all ruined. It's always been there.'

'I think it was built by men.'

'*Men?*'

'Yes.'

'Oh, come on, stop talking nonsense. You lay hands on that end, and I'll –'

Together they lifted the girder and slowly eased it forward. It was far too heavy for Settle to have moved it on his own, but Malcom was a very strong man. They laid it down on the floor without mishap, and then began to clear away the debris behind, both getting covered with dust from head to foot in the process.

Malcom made one or two other attempts to reveal his thoughts to Settle, but the latter was in an excited, flippant mood and paid little attention to him. It was very late – nearly eleven o'clock – before the passage was clear. Malcom accepted a drink of water from Settle's tap, submitted to being vigorously brushed by him, and left, feeling rather annoyed. It was not uncommon for him to leave Settle with a feeling of annoyance; but this time it was, for some reason, stronger than usual.

'Surely you object to the Bin and the Ejector because they're so awful and cruel?'

'Yes,' said Salia impatiently, breaking an egg into the frying pan.

'But isn't it equally cruel to use it on the heads and Priests? They'd suffer as much as their victims did.'

'Habitation! Cathy, you are so like your father sometimes! Niggle-niggle-niggle! Nag-nag-nag! You know as well as I do that it would be only fair, only ordinary justice. Have you ever seen anyone binned? Well, I have. It's horrible. Those Priests deserve all we can give them.'

'But, Sal,' said Cathis, and then lapsed, defeated.

The institutions they were discussing were properly known as the Ejector-Seat and the Loony-Bin. These were the instruments for the most frightening forms of capital punishment in the

Habitation's imaginative penal code. The Ejector-Seat was, in essence, a large immobile catapult; it was situated in the north-west quadrant of the Circle. The procedure for ejecting a convict was as follows: his arms and legs were thoroughly broken, so as to prevent struggling and wriggling. His hands and feet were then all tied together behind his back and he was placed in the Seat. Pressure for the ejection was generated electrically, by a large filament in a cylinder full of water. This water, heated to boiling-point, was not allowed to expand or to turn to steam except through the safety-valve which emitted a piercing whistle, until the cylinder's close-fitting piston was released. Enough pressure had been produced by this time to cause it to leap obliquely upwards at an incredible speed. The chair would swing round in an enormous semicircle, with an audible cracking sound as the man's pelvis and spine disintegrated, and he would be flung many thousands of feet into the air. At the same time would come a loud explosion and a scalding, shuddering burst of steam. Most eyes, however, would be fixed on the sky, where the convict, a rapidly diminishing speck, would remain visible for a few seconds, always rising. The popular belief was that a man's sins were expiated by his ejection; thus he did not return to earth at all, but was received directly into heaven. Certainly, this was what it looked like. Pragmatists like Malcom, however, maintained that he would eventually sink, and fall to whatever kind of ground existed outside the Habitation. But as few people could conceive of there being any kind of ground outside the Habitation at all, death by Ejector-Seat was regarded by most with a peculiar blend of horror and admiring awe.

Death by Loony-Bin – 'being binned' – was a very different and much simpler affair. There were seven inhabited and known levels in the Sphere. The seventh, the lowest, contained, as well as vast quantities of stores of various kinds, a bare, whitewashed corridor about twenty-five yards long. The ubiquitous neon-globes seemed dismaller there than anywhere else. The corridor decreased in height and width towards its end, so that at its entrance there was room for a large crowd of spectators. At the end of the bleak corridor, grim and isolated, stood a large black metal bin, like a dustbin except for the facts that its lid was heavy and could be bolted down, and that it had no bottom. This fact was literally and terrifyingly real; the Bin had no bottom. The Bin-corridor was left open and unattended, so this unpleasant truth had fresh confirmation from time to time, by such daring spirits as might wish to descend into the nightmare alley, examine the Bin, and confirm the fact for themselves. What happened was that the convict was simply pushed into the Bin, the lid was bolted down on him, and no one at all knew what became of him after that. Those executed by the Bin were never unconscious or drugged; they were always, as part of the deterrent effectiveness of the punishment, manhandled and physically forced into it by the several strong, masked attendants, chosen by lot from among the younger Priests and carefully instructed in their task. Resistance was always unavailing. Thus the gagged victim would be dragged away down the corridor, usually squirming and struggling wildly, by the five ghastly, anonymous, silent executioners, to the place where the Bin waited with its lid open like a black toilet bowl. The scuffling noises would reverberate in the narrow confines of the corridor. Ages later the combatants would arrive at the Bin. An interval would ensue while the thrashing arms and legs were seized and secured; and then the convulsed body would be slowly forced in, head first, like a rat swallowed whole by a python. The protruding legs and feet would flutter briefly, hopelessly; finally would come the echoing clang of the dropped lid, and the snick of bolts. As may be imagined, this method of execution exerted a powerful grasp over the minds of the people of the Habitation.

These two deaths, however, were used only rarely. Of the two dozen or so executions Settle had witnessed during his lifetime, most had been conventional hangings. (A portable gibbet was kept in the Foresters' centre on level 5.) He had seen only two ejections and one binning; these punishments were reserved for the 'abhominations' – crimes so vile that they were not mentioned in the penal catalogue, nor in open conversation.

Salla began on her fried egg. She and her husband occupied a small cottage in the North-West quadrant of the Circle. It was eight o'clock in the morning and the rising sun poured in through the open window. At other times this room often appeared squalid and shabby, but now the brisk spring sunlight, the curls of prismatic steam which rose from the crockery on the table, and the flowers Cathis was in the habit of arranging about the room, snowdrops and daffodils, lent it an air of freshness and brightness, distracting attention from the sink full of burnt pans, the unclean wooden tub standing in a corner, the filthy stove, the cobwebs, the mouldering refuse on the tiled floor. Christofer's cat, Arnold, entered mewing. Cathis tickled its ears and filled a small wooden bowl with milk, which she set on the floor.

Salla drew two slices of toast from under the grill, buttered one, and munched it absently. 'Well, whether we bin them or eject them,' she said presently, 'they've got to be rooted out completely.'

'Well –'

'Cathy dear, you know what those Priests are like. You know the terrible laws they've made up.'

'What laws do you mean? I'm sorry, but I don't quite –'

'Oh you know! About women having to have babies or else be flogged in church, and no woman to have more than three babies, and no women being allowed to make their own way in life, or to do what they want to do – always looking after the household, cooking the husband's dinners, scrubbing floors, changing nappies . . . no woman is allowed to belong to a profession in her own right. Men have everything. Oh, Habitation, when I think of the future I could–' Her voice broke off. 'I don't mind Christofer with me really, but it's the thought of having babies . . . giving birth . . . ugh!'

'But you know that the population has to be kept level very carefully. It's terribly important to have the right number of babies.'

'One woman is not going to make enough difference to justify the punishment for sterility! Fifty lashes! You know what that means! And even the poor women who want to have babies and can't, they're still punished for it! It's frightful!'

'Oh dear,' said Cathis in great distress. 'Oh dear, Sally – I–'

'We must stamp it all out *completely*.'

'Yes, I'm with you there; but binning them –'

'Who are you binning now?' asked Christofer, who had just entered, carrying two large pails full of water.

'You,' said Salla coldly. 'I think we might include the ban to cover Clerks as well, don't you Cathy?'

'Yes, definitely.'

'Good morning, my dear, good morning, Cathis,' he said mildly. He advanced towards the table and kissed his wife on the cheek, seemingly unaware that she was still chewing. 'Any breakfast for me?'

'Go and see for yourself,' she answered dully.

He found some bacon and put it in the frying-pan. Cathis was staring at him in contempt; then her eyes met those of her friend and they both giggled.

Christofer was filling a copper with water. He said, 'Are you doing some washing today, dear?'

'I suppose I've got to.'

'Then we'll need some more water. I don't want to go to fetch it twice in one morning.'

'Well, you'll have to, darling, if you want your shirts washed.'

Christopher sighed. 'Very well,' he said. Again Cathis and Salla both giggled and he affected not to notice. 'Now, are there any eggs left?'

'Catch!' said Cathis suddenly, throwing an egg at him. He managed to catch it, but missed the next one, which was thrown by Salla, repeating Cathis's action with a brutal, senseless joy. The egg hit Christofer squarely on the mouth; his face was bespattered with albumen and bits of shell. He stared ridiculously at them for a moment and they both burst out laughing.

'Sorry, Chris, but there aren't any more eggs,' giggled Salla. 'You should be better at catching.'

'Don't throw the other egg at us, will you, Christofer?'

'Don't worry, I won't,' Christofer replied in an emotionless tone. He stepped back, wiping his face with his handkerchief. This was a mistake. Temporarily blinded, he failed to notice the buckets of water, tripped over the one which still remained full, fell, and next moment was sprawling, soaked, on the mucky floor, while a large part of the water he had just fetched ran swiftly out of the back door. Arnold, who had jumped out of the way, began to lap it up. Although incidents involving a greater or lesser degree of humiliation for Christofer happened quite often in his home, the two women felt that he had surpassed himself this time. As he stood up again with water running off him, his discomforture was complete. He had bruised his knee and cut his hand on the metal rim of the bucket.

The two spectators were evidently enjoying the scene. Cathis smiled and drank some milk; Salla, more extrovert, buried her head in her arms and laughed with extreme abandon. 'You'll definitely have to fetch some more water now, Chris,' she said at last, between hiccups, 'but never mind, the floor could have done with a good cleaning. Come on, Cathy,' she continued as Christofer made two steps towards her, his eyes glittering, 'you can finish your milk outside. Let's get out of here before he rapes us.'

Christofer sat down in a chair. He put his elbows on the table and rested his forehead in his hands. He remained in that position for about ten minutes, while the water continued to drip out of his clothes. He was aroused by the smell of burning, and returned to the stove to find the bacon crisp and black in a heavily smoking pan. He looked vaguely round for the egg, then discovered it, intact, in his clenched fist.

Outside the sun was still shining but grey clouds were advancing from the north. Salla and Cathis sat on a gate together and continued with their discussion.

'It's all very well thinking about what we do when we have gained control,' Cathis was saying, 'but we ought to consider some practicalities, things we must set about doing now. We must start getting support. We can't sweep away the established order on our own, much as we'd like to.'

'Don't be sarcastic, Cathy. Who is there?'

'I've thought of some names. I think Angela Forester's nervous about having another baby after two miscarriages; Gyllan Craftsman hates the idea of getting married; Alis Glazier, Susan and Rosan Clerk –'

'I don't know them.'

'They're likely to be sympathetic. Oh, and Ellis Farmer.'

'I know her.'

'Those would do for a start. We'll have to go cautiously, of course, and we aren't in a hurry. Now, go and give poor old

Christofer a hand tidying up, and we'll go round and make a start on seeing them this afternoon. I've got to go up and see Daddy this morning.'

They kissed goodbye. Cathis slipped off the gate and began to make her way up to the Sphere which loomed ahead of her, now that the sun had gone in as a great, steely, grey-and-black dome. The tall column had disappeared into a lowering ceiling of cloud. It was getting colder. She walked briskly. Drops of rain were falling by the time she reached the Sphere.

At the top of the stairs, gloomy and grey now that rain was falling outside, Cathis came upon her father. He was smoking his pipe, having evidently just breakfasted, and thoughtfully regarding the results of his labours over the past few days. He had not yet found a projector, but more of the thickets had been cleared away.

'Hello, my dear,' he said. 'Have you come to give me a hand?'

'Yes, if you like,' said she. 'Have you found the thing you're looking for?'

'No, but there's a lot of ground to cover yet.'

'What's this horrible smell?'

'I wasn't sure till yesterday, and I'm not sure now, but yesterday I came across some things which enabled me to make a shrewd guess.' He put down his pipe and picked up a torch. 'Time for another stint. Are you coming?' He went into the lane which had been opened, and Cathis followed.

It was the first time she had penetrated the Library. She was conscious of a horrible stink, an increasing claustrophobia, and an unpleasant, illusory suggestion of spiders' webs constantly brushing over her face and hands. Her mouth and nose seemed to be full of dust. Loathsome deformities of twisted, congealed plastic met her eyes. Under her feet the surface was loose and slippery. The obscurity increased as they advanced. Settle shone the torch around.

'Careful, now' he said. 'Don't trip over the girder.'

They stepped over it and plunged further into the thick, cindery, stifling, dark-grey gloom.

Soon Cathis had her first shock. 'A face!' she cried. 'There, on the ground. Stop!'

'What?'

'A face with huge black eyes! It looked at me! Let me go!'

'Hold on a moment, Cathis. Don't run away,' said Settle, releasing her wrist and bringing the torch round. 'Yes ... I thought so.'

On the floor lay a skull, partially calcined but still gruesomely recognisable. It was a mottled greyish-brown in colour, with black, shadowy eye-sockets, an empty nose, and splintered, whitish teeth, two of which shone with silvery gleams. Several other, unidentifiable bones were scattered nearby.

'Only a skull, Cathis. You've seen animals' skulls, haven't you? This is a human skull.' He picked it up and handed it to her. 'You'll have to get used to them, I'm afraid, if you want to be of any use to me.'

She turned it over in her hands, fascinated. 'A human skull...'

'Come along now, and prepare yourself for something much uglier.' He took her by the hand again. She came without protest, bemused. The darkness opened in front of them and closed behind as they walked along, with the occasional stumble, and eventually came out into a wider place. Settle put the torch on the ground and took his tinder-box out of a pocket. 'Brace yourself.'

He struck the flint; a spark appeared briefly; the tinder caught. He lit several candles rapidly. Their soft, bright radiance waxed slowly to reveal a small chamber with several dark alleyways leading out of it.

Many skeletons sat or lay in this chamber, dim, tall, inhuman, ghastly, chill-looking even in the warm light.

'You've seen a skull,' said Settle cheerfully. 'These are skeletons. They look rather offputting, I know, but they're quite harmless really.' He chattered on, unheeded by Cathis as she gazed dumbly about her. Actually there were fewer of them than appeared at first sight. She counted them; five in all. Two were sitting, their arms by their sides; the others lay on the ground. One of these seemed to have been crushed or pulled apart. One of the sitting ones had a neat round hole in its forehead. They were all very clean-looking. Ribs gleamed, teeth twinkled. There were more skulls, hands, arms, rib-cages and miscellaneous osseous fragments scattered in profusion around the small room. She felt faint and cold, and suddenly heard her heart beating very loudly. The skeletons watched the living beings like sentinels, attenuated, motionless, silent and terribly ancient.

'. . .Must admit they gave me quite a shock yesterday evening. I didn't like the thought of visiting them, alone. I'm glad you turned up. But – I think it would be a pity to disturb them or take them away, don't you? I think they look rather grand as they are, and they needn't interfere with our searching.'

The skeletons' looks seemed to serve as a reply to these statements; they made an oral response, supposing that the skeletons could be endowed with the power of speech, seem superfluous. They were unassailably, irreducibly self-sufficient.

'Daddy, I know I haven't helped you at all yet, but I'd like to get out of this as quickly as possible. I can't stand it any more.'

'All right, my dear.' He was winding the torch and blowing out the candles. For an almost blissful second they were in complete darkness. Then the torch went on again. He handed it to her. 'Be careful not to trip over on the way back. It's not very far. . .'

Cathis hurried back as fast as she dared. Outside the passage the air was fresh and cool and delightfully scented; the rainy light was delicious; and the Library foyer seemed an architectural miracle of broad, relaxed spaciousness. Her spirits soon recovered, and a short time later she was able to return to the skeleton chamber without overwhelming fear.

Soon she began to ask questions. Settle told her that he had found no clue to the reason for the skeletons' presence, except that it seemed likely that they had been involved in the same disaster that had ruined the Library. He had no idea about the round hole in the skeleton's forehead. But he had noticed odd holes drilled in the floor, or in the book-cases, in many other places.

'If you don't mind, Cathy, we'll go back there and do a bit more exploring. It's only about a quarter to ten.'

Cathis was not averse and they returned along the dark passage to the skeletons.

'Hello again, chaps,' said Settle; then, to Cathis, 'Any of these four exits looks as good as the others. We'll try the right-hand one.'

The right-hand passage was equally pitch-black, but it seemed to have suffered less from the burning than the areas previously surveyed. The air was a little fresher. Settle stopped and began trying to prise a cassette free from a shelf. It was very dusty, but only slightly warped, and it withdrew quite easily. Like the others, it was constructed of some material unlike wood or metal: hard, but slightly flexible, and giving the impression of warmth to the touch. Unlike them, however, it was neither black nor orange nor grey, but dark green.

'There's a label on the other side,' said Cathis as he fingered it in the torchlight. But the label was disappointing. It said only: 'ORD QX1/7/aaptn. cuTR 5/49799'.

'Oh, well,' said Settle as he replaced the cassette and rewound the torch, 'at least they aren't all melted. On we go.'

Quite soon they came to another room; this had three other exits. An incomplete skeleton sat in one corner. They halted in the middle of the room. The same thought had occurred to them both simultaneously.

'Daddy,' said Cathis, 'I'm beginning to think there's not much point in going further.'

Settle played the torch round the room. Black walls, grey floor, dark openings, skeleton, in fact nearly everything seemed to be the same as in the other chamber. A chance swing of the torch-beam momentarily lit up his daughter's face and figure: dishevelled, slim, white, appealing, her eyes brilliantly blue in her thin face. 'I agree with you,' he said. 'We'll almost certainly get lost if these passages go on much longer. We need to do something to distinguish these chambers and passages from each other. I'll try and make a map.'

He turned, but she continued to stare up the middle passage. She said: 'Just a moment. I saw something twinkle out there.'

'Oh?'

'Shine the torch up this passage.'

This time they both made out, ahead of them in the obscure distance, a tiny but distinct twinkle.

'Let's have a look,' said Cathis.

They walked towards it. The mysterious spark rapidly grew brighter and it turned out to be not very far away.

'Here's your sparkler,' said Settle, picking it up and handing it to his daughter.

It was a beautiful little key, undamaged and clean, apparently made of gold: about three inches long. It shone in her hand like a piece of jewellery. To those accustomed to the rude, clumsy effectiveness of Habitation locksmithing, it was marvellous, a miracle. Cathis thought that it was the loveliest object she had ever seen. 'How beautiful,' she said.

'Would you like to keep it? You found it.'

'No,' she said after a reluctant pause. 'I'd better not. I'd probably lose it, or have it pinched. You keep it. And besides – you're the Librarian. It might be important for something or other.'

'Yes. It certainly looks like a very important little key.' With an unusual solicitude Settle wrapped the key in a clean handkerchief and put it in his pocket.

They went, past the headless skeleton, down the second passage, into the room of the five skeletons. Cathis plucked at her father's arm.

'Hang on a moment, Dad.'

'Found something else?'

'I don't know. Look, isn't that skeleton on the ground, in that corner there, holding something?'

The skeleton in question was sprawled, prone. One fleshless hand was resting in a heap of ashes and cinders.

'However did I miss that?' muttered Settle as he bent down, raised the bony arm, not without some repugnance, and tried to disengage it from the buried object. He pulled at it. The hand came off the arm, disintegrating. 'Tch'k,' said Settle. He carefully exhumed the object with his fingers. When it came to light it was unidentifiable. Part of it seemed to be a hollow tube; there were some levers and moving parts. It was heavy and made of some dull, black metal. Settle rubbed it carefully on his sleeve and said with a shrug: 'I don't suppose you have any idea what this thing is?'

'No.'

'Neither have I.'

'Can I have it?'

'I suppose so, seeing as you found it again. It doesn't look very – well, I don't know. You could ask Heron to have a look at it. He's very clever at that sort of thing.'

Holding the object at the tube end, which was just as well since it was a fully loaded pistol, Cathis followed her father back through the dark, airless passage into the lighter regions of the first level. They spent the rest of the morning clearing away more of the debris in an attempt to open up another passage into the Library, but at half past twelve they came upon a final check: an enormous, vicious-looking tangle of barbed wire that entirely blocked the way, giving additional confirmation to Settle's theory that the Library had at some time been deliberately sealed off. However, they sat down to lunch together in a relaxed mood. There was an unusual and rare sympathy between them, greater than Settle could remember there having been for a very long time.

It did not last. Soon Cathis's talk, in spite of all Settle could do to direct it elsewhere, was returning to the opinions she had been expressing at the Society meeting. Settle could not prevent himself from opposing her pronouncements. The argument descended to personalities. Finally he said, coldly: 'I will not disguise from you, Cathis, that I think your friend Salla a foolish, vacuous, worthless young woman, her political opinions the merest cant, and your friendship with her a relationship that is laying both of you increasingly open to the vilest conjecture.'

At this declaration Cathis went white with anger; then she blushed redly. Then, with her mouth hardened and her eyes narrowed, she rose from the table, said, 'Thank you, father, for this meal,' and left the room, closing the door firmly behind her. Not till she reached the second level stairs did she begin to tremble.

Christofer was away, at work in the Sphere. His job was that of Liaison Officer to the Foresters, or at least so it had been termed one day by Settle in a mock-solemn mood. Since the Priests and the Clerks were, with the exception of ex-Scribaceous and Anagnostic Society pupils, and a few Doctors, the only Professions commanding the power of reading and writing, a number of Clerks were employed in secretarial positions with senior officials of the other Professions. Christofer was one of these. He was thus in charge of and conversant with all records to do with the Forestry profession: the number of trees in the Habitation, their yields, ages and states of health; the production, storage and dispensation of timber; the culling of the small avian and ferine populations; the cottage industry of papermaking. Although his official requirements were merely to provide ready information and advice to the Forester, it would undoubtedly be true to say that in the long run he exerted a considerable degree of control over the conducting of Forestry business; hence, that this important section of the Habitation's economy was largely within his power. The other liaison officers were also, to greater or lesser degrees, in control of the professions to which they were attached. This arrangement benefited the illiterate heads of professions, while enabling the Clerks and Priests to keep closely in contact with affairs that might seem, on a superficial level, to be out of their own provinces: another instance, as Settle or Malcom might have observed had they thought with sufficient penetration on this subject, of the powers secured by the monopolisation of literacy. Few persons realised this, however. It had never occurred to Christofer to think of himself as the man who dictated Forestry business, nor did the heads ever realise how dependent they were on their Clerks' supplies of systematically collected information. It is likely that only the Senior Clerk, that lonely, aloof, celibate figure, fully grasped these realities of the distribution of power; hence, that in spite of the unnecessary, superficial, largely ceremonial appearance of his role, he was not inappropriately titled the President of the Senior Assembly.

Salla filled the copper, switched it on, and fetched the week's washing as Cathis told her about her morning's experiences. Listening without much interest, she dumped some shirts and vests in the bathtub and added a handful of brown, semi-liquid soap from a sticky jar on a shelf. Cathis came to the finding of the metal object. 'Anyway, the other thing was in one of the skeleton's hands, lying on the floor. I glimpsed it as we came back. I'll show it to you.'

She took it from a leather bag she was carrying. It glinted

darkly in her hand with a blue-black lustre. Salla stared at it curiously, her arms in the soapy tub.

'What is it?' she said. 'What does it do?'

'No idea.'

Cathis put her eye to the muzzle and looked down it, inadvertently pulling the trigger as she did so.

'Let's have a look,' said Salla, drying her hands. Cathis handed the weapon to her. She turned it over in her hands, found a lever and pressed it. It clicked into a different position, and the gun was now cocked and ready to go off. She puzzled over it like a child or a monkey playing with plugs and switches, on the point of being electrocuted. 'How was the skeleton holding it?'

'I didn't see. It was nearly covered with dust, and I'm afraid I couldn't stand the thought of going over and – touching it. Ugh.'

'Well, it looks as if it might be meant to be held in a certain way. It's heavy, but I can fit my hand round this curved thing, and then I can – *Habitation!*'

A shatteringly loud explosion rang out as Salla pulled the trigger. The gun had been pointed downwards: a tile exploded and a plate crashed from the dresser as the bullet ricocheted. Neither of the two women was injured.

There was a long silence as they faced each other, astonished. A faint trail of blue smoke, lit up by a rare sunbeam straying through the window, drifted slowly upwards from the muzzle.

'What did you do?' whispered Cathis at last.

'I don't know! Are you hurt?'

'I don't think so. Are you?'

'No.'

There was another pause.

'It must have been when I pulled this little bit. But I hardly touched it at all.'

'There's a tile broken and a plate smashed. And look ... yes, look at this.'

Behind where the plate had been the plaster was cracked and a small round hole had been drilled into the wall. Salla came to look at it. 'It looks,' she said, 'as if, when it happened, something shot out of the tube, hit the floor, then bounced off and hit the plate, went through it and made this hole. Cathy, you were very lucky not to have been hit. You were nearly in the way.'

'Yes ... but why didn't it just go into the floor?'

'I expect ... yes, you see there's a thick iron pipe running under the tiles just here. And there's a dent here, underneath the broken pieces. That's why the thing bounced off.'

'Try again – no! Don't point it at me!'

'Sorry, Cathy.'

'What can you use? I know, a tree. Point it out of the door at the apple-tree.'

Salla grasped the butt with both hands, put her finger on the trigger, and fired a second time. Out of doors the report was much less loud than they were expecting. Cathis saw some splinters fly off the tree. Salla had hit it not far from its circumference, so that the bullet had not remained embedded but had forced a way right through. They went up to it, examined the entrance and exit holes and fingered the protruding splinters.

The sun had gone in for good. The sky was a heavy grey, with faint yellow gleams revealing the outlines of cloud-masses. It was very cold. Suddenly Salla said, in an expectedly hard tone. 'There's one more test to make.'

'What?'

'Finding out if it works against living things.'

'I should think it would.'

'Do you think I could kill something with this thing?'

'*Kill* something? Why?'

'I could try pointing it at a pigeon, but I'd probably miss.'

'Why do you want to kill something?'

'Aha, the very thing.'

She returned to the doorway where she had left the pistol, picked it up, and before Cathis could say anything had raised it, sighted, and fired. There was a short scream from the thick, dark green undergrowth behind the house, not very loud, but appalling: thin, coughing, retching in agony. Cathis had not noticed the cat, Arnold, returning through the hedgerow for his afternoon saucer. Now he was twisting and jerking in the grass, legs stiff, claws flexed, feet scratching and scuffling. Blood dripped from a hole in his head. She watched him dumbly.

'He's dead,' she said as Arnold ceased to move.

'That's all right then.'

'You shouldn't have killed him!' cried Cathis in distress. You *shouldn't!*'

At these words Salla, on her way back to the house, turned, still holding the gun. Cathis was kneeling on the grass, stroking the warm fur. She looked up at Salla in horror and bewilderment. Salla was nonchalant, slightly uneasy, surprised at the force of Cathis's reaction. They regarded each other. A few flakes of snow began to fall past them.

Then, suddenly, Salla made a small, involuntary movement with the hand that held the pistol. The same dreadful thought entered both their minds simultaneously, as if the fear was borne on a drifting gas. Cathis stood up: terror was in her eyes. She stared at the pistol. Salla glanced down towards it too. Her eyes seemed to have become veiled, inscrutable, lost in a private world. Cathis found herself speaking timidly.

'Sally, I'm sorry if. . .'

The fear passed; the spell was broken. In the Habitation no memories or reminders then remained of the times when firearms could serve as an instrument by which one man was able to impose his will on another. Those times had now returned. Salla smiled. 'Did you think I was going to shoot you?'

Cathis tried to smile back. 'Of course not. Let's go in. I'm freezing.'

In the evening of the next day Christofer was out in the field adjoining his cottage, despondently shooting arrows into a target leaning against a sodden bank. Behind him the red sun was setting; before him the Sphere flashed like polished copper. In the amber light he presently beheld a silhouetted figure picking its way towards him from the far side of the field. He recognised it by the two horizontal lines that streamed out of its head on either side. A faint cry floated towards him: 'Don't shoot!'

Christofer grinned and sent an arrow skimming over Settle's head. He was a skilled practitioner with the bow and arrow, though it was for him no more than a hobby. Archery was practised mostly by the Foresters, and the shooting of animals carefully monitored by the authorities, who were, as it happened, mostly Christofer himself. Thus he was in a position to relax his own rules from time to time, and take a potshot at a rabbit or pigeon; though he confined himself more often to the target. Settle also was a keen, though no more than competent, archer.

Settle retrieved his friend's arrow from the tree-trunk in which it had embedded itself, and came up to him. 'Good evening, Christofer,' he said, proffering it. He too was carrying a bow, and wearing a quiver and a leather sleeve.

'Good evening, Settle. How's the exploration going?'

'Progress made, progress has been made, though of course there's still an infinity of work to be done. I came out to get some fresh air.'

'Yes. Nice evening.'

Christofer turned, drew an arrow, set it on the bowstring, bent, and shot. 'Blue,' he said, referring to the blue spot that always formed the centre of the concentric target.

Settle bent his right whisker and took the end of it in his teeth, so that it should not impede the drawn bowstring. He aimed slowly and shot high. 'Habitation,' he said in a tone of annoyance, the whisker springing back as he opened his mouth.

As Christofer shot again he grounded his bow and savoured the beauty of the evening. The sky was clear and pale, presenting a lovely blended continuity of yellow, green and blue. Small clouds, pink and mauve-grey, drifted wispily in the light evening breeze. The sun was a ball of brilliant amber, poised above the outer wall of the Circle. In the field the shadows stretched and twilight deepened; the turf was a dark, vague green, deepened by the bright slits of puddles. From trees, far and near, came a quiet, diffused rustling, and the subdued twittering of birds. He had spent nearly the whole day in the black, choking depths of the Library's inner recesses.

'How's married life going?' he asked a little later as they splashed forward to retrieve their arrows from the target.

Christofer sighed. 'Really,' he said, 'I've no idea what's going to happen, but there's bound to be some terrible row before long. No, that's not even true. There could be a row, but I don't know if ... Oh, I don't know at all. I am at a loss.'

PART TWO

II. i. THE HIDDEN WORLD

A reunion of spirits had succeeded the temporary estrangement between Cathis and Salla, and the latter had been persuaded to hand the gun over to Heron, as the best-known and most sympathetic of the Craftsmen, for investigation. As yet Christofer knew nothing of its dangerous properties, although Settle had told him of its discovery.

It was eleven days after the Society meeting, a pleasant spring morning. Cathis and Salla were sitting on the wooden bench by the lake in the south-west quadrant of the Circle. Christofer was on the other side, among the osiers, examining the young shoots, which were used for making baskets. The lake sparkled, the reeds whispered, and small white tufts of cloud mounted into the blue from above the broad white wall of the Perimeter; a couple of small pink dragonflies were hovering, swerving and darting above the sunlit surface of the water.

A shout came from behind; Heron and Malcom were approaching. Heron had a new yo-yo, larger, heavier, and painted bright red. They squelched over the wet grass and sat down on the bench, Malcom at one end, Heron solidly between the two girls. Salla shrank away from him but Cathis did not seem to resent his proximity.

'Have you looked at the thing?' she asked him, rearranging her knees under her skirt.

'Yes. Here it is.'

'How does it work?' 'What does it do?' the girls asked simultaneously.

Malcom looked down at the pistol with interest.

'I unscrewed it carefully, and tinkered about with it for a little, and I've grasped what it does. How it works, though, I'm not sure at all.' He showed them a small, shining, cylindrical object with a pointed end. 'There were three of these inside it. I think, but I'm not sure, that there's some kind of stuff inside this thing that, when you hit it very sharply, burns up very quickly and the gas pushes the pointed bit out of the tube. Very quickly. Look, if you look closely you can see that it's made of two different kinds of metal.'

Cathis weighed it in her hand, impressed. He took it from her and loaded it into the pistol.

'When you pulled the trigger you released a mechanism on a spring, which makes a sharp point hit the blunt end of one of these things. The top flies off and hits something...'

'But what's it for?' asked Salla. 'Is it meant just to kill things with?'

'For all I know, yes. But you've only got two of the missiles left. I used one.'

'Well, don't worry: I'll use them carefully,' said she, taking the pistol.

'There may well be some more in the Library,' said Malcom thoughtfully.'

'Hey, yes, there may be,' said Salla.

Heron stretched and leaned back expansively on the back of the bench, putting his arms round Cathis's and Malcom's shoulders. 'Well,' he said to Malcom, 'why not go on with what you were just saying. I'm sure Sally and Cathy would be interested.'

'Oh,' said Malcom, slightly surprised. 'Yes, right. I've been meaning to tell this to the Society for some time now,' he told them. 'Now: start by considering the following ideas. One: The Sphere is constantly being repaired and looked after by human beings. I've just had to repair a coil. The water, the electricity, the lifts, all the essential services are maintained by men. The equipment they use is repaired and replaced continually by human artifacts.'

'So?' asked Salla.

'So, who do you think produced it all originally? Who installed the very first coil? Who was the first to condition a water-purifying system?'

'I don't know. God, I suppose,' conjectured Heron.

'I do not believe in God. Neither do you. These things were first done by men.'

'You think the Habitation was built, was created by *men?*'

'Yes.'

66

Cathis gasped. 'But how could – how possibly – how ever – those huge round glass walls in the Sphere? That column? The circumference wall?'

'Obviously an extremely advanced technology is implied.'

'Oh, well,' said Heron. 'Go on.'

'Two: all the processes of everyday life involve some wearing out. Most of the things we use, like clothes, food, wood, and so on, we can grow replacements for. But we usually replace worn-out things with new ones when they cannot be saved and recycled. The Glassblowers can melt down bits of broken glass to make new glassware, but all the same they are continually dependent on a very small supply of fresh silica from the stores. Similarly with all the others – the Metallers, the Waterworkers, the Doctors for their drugs. Now, as we all know, the stores are extensive but finite. We never add to them. Therefore, somebody, sometime, must have put them in, though we can't tell when that was. But it seems reasonable to assume that the stores date from the establishment of the Habitation, don't you think?'

'That means . . . that someday they are going to wear out. I'd never thought of that before.'

'Yes: depressing, isn't it? But it won't be till long after the ends of our lifetimes.'

'Good,' he said.

'That's all, really. But it's quite possible that there may be more to be found out in the Library. Things like, why was this place created, why we have completely forgotten the creators, what happened to them afterwards, where they are, and what they are doing now?'

'Blimey!' Heron was flabbergasted; Cathis was almost equally startled.

'I imagine Settle will find it eventually if it's there. But there's one more thing. I've got a job for you.'

'Oh?' A trout jumped out of the water and fell back with a splash. Heron removed his arm from Cathis's shoulder, to her secret disappointment, leaned forward on the bench and began to throw his red yo-yo. He had acquired the knack of flicking it over his hand, so that it returned to its downward journey at an

67

increased speed and without having returned to the grasp of his fingers.

Cautiously Malcom stood up and looked around. They were in one of the more secluded spots in the Circle; there was no one within earshot.

'Cathis and Salla, you must promise to keep this strictly secret,' he said, sitting down.

'All right,' said Cathis.

'Now, Heron, it may or may not be useful, but I want you to climb the outer wall and find out what's outside it.'

Heron looked blankly up at the great white wall. His yo-yo descended and lay inertly on the ground. 'What?' he said. 'Me?'

'Yes, you, my dear fellow. There's not much to it; nothing simpler. I've thought out all the details. Don't worry.'

'Habitation! why *me*?'

'Because you're in the Society. I'd do it myself if I was a little younger and nimbler. *He* couldn't possibly manage it.' He gestured towards the distant figure of Christofer, still pottering about among the small willow-trees. Cathis giggled; Salla, in a daydream, did not notice this reference to her husband.

'And I'm not sure why,' added Malcom, 'but I don't think we've any time to waste.'

'But, Malcom, *why*?' asked Cathis, bemused. 'I mean, what's the point?'

'I've told you: to see what's outside.'

'What do you think it will be?' asked Heron, frowning.

'I've no idea. You could take a pencil with you. You're good at drawing and it would useful for others to have an idea.'

'That's all very well, but you seem to have forgotten that climbing the wall is illegal. There are some strict penalties.'

'Priestly nonsense. Do you give a damn for any of that? There's no reason why you shouldn't get away with it.'

Heron continued to resist, but this was his weak spot: the notion of a dare had a great attraction for him. Within another couple of minutes he heard himself saying,

'All right' – with an expulsion of breath – 'What the hell, I'll do it.'

'Excellent,' said Malcom. He began to speak about ways and

means of making the attempt, but Heron, feeling perfectly capable of dealing with such technical matters himself, cut him short. He knew that the outer wall acted both as a wind-deflector and a water-condenser; moreover parts of it were electrified to deter climbers.

'Malcom,' Cathis asked again, 'what do you think there should be outside?'

'There must be something . . . some kind of ground, at least. We must be resting on something. Something to hold the Circle and Sphere up and stop them falling.'

'Whatever –? Oh, I see what you mean,' said Heron. 'I must say, Malcom, all these ideas of yours are amazingly clever, but I shouldn't worry. . .' His voice tailed off as the impassivity of Malcom's face deepened.

'It *does* matter what we find. It matters a great deal.'

'Supposing there's nothing there?' asked Cathis.

'There'll be something. There's got to be *something*. But what will it be?'

'What, indeed?'

'Do you realise, Heron, what will happen if there's no one out there? We will be left on our own.'

A silence fell, as often happened when Malcom made one of his vaguely ominous pronouncements. Heron put away his yo-yo and took out his pipe. Salla started out of her dream as if struck by an idea. She picked up the pistol and pointed it across the lake.

'Going to murder your husband, Salla?' laughed Heron.

'No,' she said, 'just give him a fright.'

She held the pistol at arm's length, in both hands, looked down it, and shot, apparently straight at Christofer. The bang rolled loudly over the lake. The other three were startled by the speed with which she had aimed and fired, but amused by the reaction of the small figure, which leapt violently backwards and fell over, though not into the lake itself. Christofer picked himself up and began to run stumblingly round the lake towards them, through the reeds and the unsteady, soaking tussocks.

In a little while he arrived, red-faced, dishevelled and puffing. His right side was muddy and wet, his boots were plastered with mud, and his shirt had become detached from his trousers at the back. He briefly surveyed their expressions. His wife's face bore a contemptuous smile; she still held the pistol. Heron's jovial expression looked rather more brutal than usual. Cathis stared at him scornfully; Malcom was preoccupied and indifferent.

Heron made the attempt, and was successful, two days later. He arrived at the foot of the wall as day was breaking, climbed it with the aid of a rope and grapnel, and found a place at the top where he could sit and sketch the mountainous scene before him. The climb, however, was extremely taxing and dangerous, although he never attempted seriously to describe it afterwards. Towards evening, chilled to the bone and wet through, he made his way safely down to the ground again. It was about seven o'clock and he was very hungry. He set off for the Sphere, walking briskly. He took his yo-yo from his pocket and manipulated it absently as he walked. His mind was busy with memories, appreciative delight, a flush of elation at the success of his lawless daring, pride at his achievements and physical prowess, pleasure in the beauty he had had some success in recording. His mind was elsewhere, but an observer would have marvelled at the unconscious dexterity with which he now flicked, repelled, caught and released the yo-yo: backwards, forwards, sideways, sometimes almost vertically upwards from his hand. It seemed to hover around him like a midge as he tramped through the dusk.

In front of him the Sphere now rose brightly like a great warm opal, horizontally striated in layers of thin black, and broad bands of shining, varying colour, reds, greens, yellows, ambers, areas of dim gold or dull, frosty silver, depending on the kind of illumination and curtaining in use in the different regions inside. The sky was now cloudy and starless; but above him, through a rift in the clouds, the fixed star burned watchfully in the blue darkness. Unlike the other stars, this bright star never changed its position at all, and it twinkled far less noticeably than the others. It always appeared vertically above the gazer, like the column in the daytime.

It was half past ten; or, at least, so the level 2 clock indicated

(22.29.17.) when Settle went down to check. His watch indicated only three minutes past. It seemed to have recently developed an alarming and increasing tendency towards losing time. He put it forward half an hour and returned to the Library to make the final run for the day's round of cartographic exploration. Level 1, as he arrived at the stairhead, now presented an unusually tidy and well-kept appearance. He entered the Library, traversed several passages and side-alleys, made a turn of ninety degrees, and found himself in an unfamiliar, unmarked passage which he labelled 'Dq' with a piece of chalk. It was in good condition. He was half-way down it, shining his torch along the floor, when he received a shock of a nature totally different from any the Library had so far administered to him.

He saw a line of footprints clearly marked in the dust.

They were pointed towards him: about the same size as his own footprints, ordinary footprints typical of the leather boots, the alternative to clogs, worn by men in the Habitation. He stopped and stared at them incredulously. He knew that he had on no occasion entered passage Dq before that day.

At about the same time Christofer, having spent the evening in solitary communion with a bottle of mead after a hard day at the office, drained his last glass, remembered to switch off the fire and the light, and stumbled upstairs. He lurched into the bedroom. His wife was lying in bed, only her head and one hand visible on the grubby pillow in the light of a naked, low-power light-bulb. Like their other rooms, the small, cramped bedroom was shabby, untidy and frowsty. A dusty chest-of-drawers stood with its drawers open as if newly ransacked, and a drift of crumpled blankets and linen lay in one corner. Christofer went to his wife. At his approach she closed her eyes. He said:

'Salla, is it –'

In answer she shook her head, briefly, without speaking or opening her eyes. Christofer was drunk enough not to be greatly offended. This response was about what he had expected. He went out of the room, decided to go down for another drink, remembered that the bottle was empty, and sat down heavily on a couch in the darkness of the landing. He heard the click of the switching-off of the bedroom light. He lay down on the couch,

71

postponed his undressing for a few moments, and removed his boots. He felt uncomfortable, but too unhappy to want to do anything but sleep, and too tired not to fall asleep in a few minutes.

Later that night the clouds parted further, allowing the round crescent moon to shine intermittently through walls and windows. Malcom, awake in bed at half past one, saw it. With one hand behind his head, the other unconsciously occupied at his groin, he stared at it sleeplessly; its celestial purity awoke no response, save perhaps a faint, emphasized pang of self-pity and regret, as the turbid currents of his thought flowed coldly and swiftly through cavernous recesses of deepening, darkening anxiety. Some way ahead, he was coming to be aware, there must be an end; but whether a relieved emergence into the light of day, or a sudden violent plunge into unfathomable depths, he could not tell.

The next day there was a meeting of the Scribaceous and Anagnostic Society, at which all its members were present. All the events of the last few days were discussed: the exploration of the Library, the key, the pistol, the pistol's powers, and, after a general swearing to secrecy, Heron's adventures and his drawings of the mountains he had seen. Settle said nothing about the footprints. The talk continued into the evening. Malcom was white and overwrought; there were dark hollows under his eyes. Settle was superficially calm, but his frequent outbursts of flippancy did not cover the strained vigilance with which he continually regarded the other five. Christofer, unshaven and untidily dressed, was attentive and taciturn; the few contributions he made were immediately, and unfailingly ridiculed by Cathis and Salla. Cathis argued wildly and passionately. Salla spoke little and made even less attempt than usual to disguise her sovereign contempt for the Society, for the Library, for the drawings, for the four men and men in general, for the discussion, and by implication for all forms of original intellectual activity. Heron was the most relaxed, in spite of the tensions surrounding him. He played incessantly with his red yo-yo.

II. ii.   CONTACT AND CRISIS

'You'd kill all the Priests? You'd shoot the Clerks? Is that it? Would you kill Settle?'

'Why are you so bothered about him? You told me you hate him.'

'But, Sally, that's frightful!'

'Why are you so astonished? Habitation, we've talked about this enough.'

'But – but it seems so wicked.'

'Don't you think the Ejector-Seat and the Loony-Bin wicked?'

'Oh dear, oh dear.' Cathis sat silently and tried to marshal her bewildered thoughts. 'Fancy killing them all,' she murmured presently. 'But don't you think it – that it – that there'd be something wrong?' She took Salla's hand. They were sitting on the bed, in the room in Christofer's house where Cathis sometimes spent the night.

'No. Why should there be?'

'Just killing – shooting – I hated it when you killed poor Arnold.'

'I don't believe in Heaven or Hell, Cathy, and I don't believe in souls.'

'Nor do I, really. So what?'

'It makes no difference really, whatever happens, whatever we do. All this talk, all this argument of Settle's and deep philosophical thought, it has no – it doesn't mean anything. I don't really care much whether we take over the government or not, except that I don't want to be whipped. It would be something to do. It makes no difference whether or not Malcom's stupid theories are true or not. I don't care if men did build the Habitation. It doesn't make any difference to us now ... nothing does. And if you think that killing a few is going to alter anything important, you're wrong.'

Cathis had begun to feel somewhat dizzy. 'Sally,' she said at last, 'in that case, what's the good of being alive at all?'

'Not much,' answered Salla dully. 'Sometimes I wish I was dead. But I don't really want to be dead; I just want a release. I hate all these stupid petty fears and worries, all these little thoughts and emotions. Has it ever occurred to you how unnecessary, how meaningless, nearly all, everything we say and think is?'

'No. It hasn't.'

Salla began gently to caress Cathis's hand.

'But – what about people?'

'What about them?'

'Don't you believe in love?'

'Whose love? Can you think of anyone you know who gives a damn for anybody but his own self?'

Cathis thought. She thought of Salla and her husband; of her parents (Salla had become an orphan only recently); of her own father; of Heron; and of some of their other friends and acquaintances. Finally she said: 'There's me.'

The grip on her hand tightened.

'I like you, Sally ... don't you like me?'

Salla's spirits appeared to return. 'Yes, Cathy,' she said, 'That does make something worthwhile.'

'Oh, good, good.'

'You're right.'

'I'm very glad.'

'Thank you ever so much.'

'You do think that our friendship can mean something?'

'Oh yes, oh yes.'

'And the way we feel has meaning?'

'Yes.'

'And love can be demonstrated in action? It can take physical form?'

'Yes.'

'Then we don't live in a meaningless world, and some of our actions have value!'

'Oh, thank you, Cathy!'

'That's all right.'

'Shall we?'

There was a pause.

'Sorry?'

'Shall we?'

'What do you mean?'

'Come on, let's.'

'Whatever –'

'You said so yourself, Cathy – you said it!'

'I'm sorry, I –'

'Our friendship can be demonstrated! "Physical form"! You said it!'

'Yes, but –'

'Come on, then.'

Cathis was still sitting on the bed. Salla came up behind her and put her hands on her shoulders.

'I'm sorry, Sally, but I still don't know what you mean.'

'I mean this, you foolish girl.' She put her hand on Cathis's left breast.

'What *is* this?'

'I've been longing to for such a long time, Cathy, you know.'

'What for?'

'But you do know, don't you. I was waiting for you to say.'

'I *still* don't understand you. Why are you undoing my shirt?'

'Don't be frightened, Cathy darling. Just relax.' She stroked Cathis's hair while sliding her hand underneath her jumper and shirt. Cathis turned her head to look up at her.

'What –?'

Smiling, Salla placed her hand firmly over Cathis's mouth. Her groping fingers found their goal. For one moment the two girls were both immobile: Cathis craning backwards, gagged and uneasy, her eyes fixed on Salla's face; Salla leaning a little forward, eyes blissfully closed, one hand on Cathis's mouth, the other embracing her bare breast inside her clothes. Almost immediately, with a gasp of horror, Cathis bounded from her chair, wrenching herself away from Salla's caresses. Salla, too, started, but remained where she was, between Cathis and the door. They stared at each other, Cathis disgusted and terrified; the happiness of Salla's expression faded. Her mouth worked without producing any sound. A look of anguished entreaty came into her eyes.

She said, uncertainly: 'Won't you –?'

Cathis made no answer; she stayed leaning against the wall, breathing hard, her clothes in disarray, her shoulder bared.

Salla's beseeching expression vanished, and her former, unfamiliar aspect returned, withdrawn, introverted, temporarily blinded, the appearance Cathis still remembered vividly from the occasion of the killing of the cat. She wondered what she was thinking. Abruptly Salla returned to the present and ran out of the room. Cathis felt warm relief flood through her. She began to adjust her clothing. She heard a sound of rummaging in the next room, but attached no importance to this. But before she could think of leaving the room, the house, of removing herself to as great as possible a distance from the scene and the author of the loathsome overture she had just received, Salla was back. She held an object which Cathis easily recognised, feeling a ghastly pang of fear as she remembered that one cartridge still remained in it and that Salla had so far shown herself to be a surprisingly good shot.

In thick darkness Settle groped his way along tunnel D/Qa6. He had dropped his faithful torch a few paces back, and it no longer functioned, but he was confident about finding his way back and he had decided to advance to the end of this tunnel in order to bring the foray to a planned conclusion. He had called this passage a tunnel because it was much lower and narrower than the other passages. It was so narrow that there was no room for his moustache, and he was forced to advance sideways, moving his legs with a stiff, latitudinal motion while his hands felt along the bookshelf behind and before. He could see nothing at all. As always, the air was dusty and dry. His footsteps scraped and shuffled loudly. He had two candles and a tinder-box in his pocket, but was anxious to save them for the return journey. His fingers ran delicately over the endless ranks of even, uniform spines.

He came out into a wider place, lit a candle and looked round. The chamber had a skeleton and two exits. He held out the candle and looked down the righthand one.

He said later that it was, after all, providential that he had broken his torch. Had he not done so, he would have played the powerful beam down the passageway and failed to notice anything unusual. As things were, however, he looked down the tunnel in candle-light, found that the candle served to hide rather than lighten the darkness, and put it behind his back.

The first tunnel was completely black.

In the second, he thought he could see a faint greyness.

He blew the candle out, closed his eyes to accustom them to darkness, suppressing the rising hope and excitement within him, and looked a second time. This time there was no doubt. Some way ahead of him, an aperture on one side of the tunnel was admitting a dim luminosity, like the dying effort of an adventurous daylight.

Later on in the same morning Heron was working in his studio in the Craftsmen's workshop on level 3. Outside it was raining heavily. His section of wall-window stood before him, visible as a bright, blurred screen, composed of millions of thin, flickering drops and rivulets. Small, ghostly patches of condensation travelled evasively on the inner side. At rare intervals there was a faint rushing sound as the great wall-wiper passed by, a confusing array of dark, rotating brushes, big and small, churning vigorously up and down in a welter of fine spray. This mechanism, maintained by the Electricians and the Craftsmen and operated by the Glaziers several times a year on rainy days, was responsible for keeping the exterior walls of the levels in their accustomed state of cleanliness and complete transparency. Today, however, nothing could be seen of the trees and houses outside but diffused, broken forms of grey and black.

The studio was warm and comfortably lighted. On a bespattered table in the centre of the room, Heron was engaged in grinding up some charcoal on a slab of thick glass, before adding enough of a dubious concoction of egg-yolks, linseed oil and distilled alcohol to make a tolerable lamp black. As usual, the room was untidy, with a number of objets d'art, carved chairs, painted canvases, wooden brackets and panels, standing about in various stages of completion. They were all by him. The soft puffs of his pipe blended soothingly with the crunch of the steel

77

roller and the faint sounds of rain outside. To Cathis, who entered suddenly without warning, the room appeared like the embodiment of an unhoped-for ideal, a miraculous haven of tranquillity.

Heron looked at her in astonishment. She was in a most disordered condition. Her soaking hair clung to her shoulders and skull in bedraggled rats'-tails. Her face was flushed and wet and her eyes were swollen. Her mouth was open; she was panting heavily. Her hands were pressed to her stomach. She was wearing no cloak or waterproof. Water trickled out of her clothes. Her trousers were thickly splashed with mud. Heron also noticed that her jersey and shirt had both been put on back to front.

Two apprentice Craftsmen came into the room. 'Do you wish to see this woman, sir?' one asked. 'She ran past before we could stop her.'

'Yes, that's all right.'

They retired quietly.

'Come on in, Cathis. Always glad to see you. Sit down, no, not on that one, you're rather wet. Here. Draw it up to the fire.' He rummaged in a drawer and brought out a moderately clean towel. 'Dry yourself with this.'

She accepted the towel.

'Would you like anything to drink?'

She shook her head, rubbing her hair with vague, mechanical movements. She had come into the room with a limp, as if her ankle pained her. It was obvious that her physical distress was owing to something more than violent exercise in the rain. There was an air of langour and exhaustion in her movements; a shocked, astounded expression seemed to have set and stiffened on her features. She looked down at her trousers, and around the room. Heron had picked up his roller again. He continued grinding until the charcoal was a smooth paste. Then he turned, his face expressing nothing but friendly concern.

'Would you mind telling me what's happened to you?'

His eyes met hers. For a brief moment her set expression wobbled and crumpled like a subsidence of earth. She opened her mouth, shuddered, and gasped as if about to be sick. He saw that there were traces of what looked like vomit down her front.

She shut her mouth and the hardness returned to her expression: a different kind of hardness, detached, cold, clinical, reminding him of her father as he had occasionally seen him. She said in a controlled, even tone:

'I have just been subjected to a lesbian attack by Salla Clerk.'

'Habitation!' said Heron, somewhat taken aback. He knew what 'lesbian' meant, having heard the word used by Settle. That such a thing should have happened did not surprise him much; like the other members of the Society (who were, out of all the Habitationers the people best acquainted with these two girls) he had unthinkingly assumed that their friendship had already passed the boundaries of physical reticence. Such perversions, proscribed and punished with great severity, were by no means unknown or inconceivable in the Habitation. His surprise now stemmed from learning that an overture had only just been made, and that this had evidently been entirely repulsive to Cathis.

'Good Heavens,' he said at last, 'how awful. Did she –?'

'Please, Heron, *please* don't ask me anything about it.'

There were fresh tears on Cathis's cheeks. She took a comb out of her pocket and began making abstracted attempts to untangle her hair. 'I ran all the way here.'

'I'm sorry.' He turned back to the table and began scooping up the black mess with a knife and a spoon, scraping them against each other to transfer it to a small, clean glass jar.

'It was so – frightful, so vile, oh, you can't imagine how disgusting, how repulsive. . .'

He gave her a handkerchief.

'I liked her so much – I would have done anything . . . But not, oh, Habitation, but not. . .'

She began again. 'I didn't realise that such things really happened. She doesn't care for other women at all. All those things she used to say, all those ideas, they were just lies. She doesn't care about anything at all but herself.'

'I didn't know.'

'I didn't know either until today. I never suspected–' she sniffed. 'But they *are* important, whatever she's said. Oh, Heron, I didn't know what to do! I was just helpless!' There was

a note of desperation in her voice. 'And it's all my fault, too . . .
I found the wretched thing and *gave* it to her.'

'I'm sorry.'

'I gave it to her. Didn't you know?'

'No. . .'

'Oh, I see. Of course I haven't explained what I'm talking
about yet.'

'What did happen? – If you don't mind my asking.'

'Salla threatened me with that shooter. She has still got one
shot left.'

'Oh . . . I see. I didn't understand why you felt so powerless.'
He picked up a small yo-yo and began playing with it. 'She didn't
shoot you, did she? Are you sure you're all right?'

'Yes, there's nothing wrong with me.' But she burst into tears
again. 'The memory was so awful that I just wanted to escape
as quickly as possible. Oh, that feeling. . .' She was choked with
sobs. Heron went quietly to his stove. He heated some milk in
a saucepan and handed her a cupful. He poured out some wine
for himself.

'It's nearly lunch-time. I was going to have it here anyway.
Will you stay?'

'Yes, thank you, Heron.'

He scraped off the last of the black paint, closed the jar tightly,
and cleared away the implements. He put a pot of cold bean-soup
on the stove to warm up. Cathis collected herself and wiped and
tidied her clothes. Presently she made him promise not to repeat
what she had just confided to anyone else.

During the meal, desiring to turn her mind to less distressful
thoughts, he asked her about Settle's exploring. 'No,' she said,
'I don't think he's discovered anything else. He's getting a bit
fed up with it all, poor man, and no wonder. I really think the
whole thing's a waste of time.'

'Oh?'

'Yes. Silly fool. He's trying to bury himself in the Library
because he doesn't want to come out and face the real
problems.'

'Indeed.'

'And now Sally – and now Salla's turned into – and now, well
I have no more faith in her – and I don't think there's anyone else

who really cares about things – the injustice, the cruelty – I'm all alone.'

Heron took a swig of wine.

'...*Alone*. There is no one else. You don't care much, Heron, do you?'

'I don't know,' said he. 'I haven't thought much about these sort of things. I know you've talked about it, but there are other things which seem to me much more interesting to think about.'

A minute passed in despondent silence, which was broken by Heron.

'Cathy.'

'Yes?'

'Why did you come to me? Today, I mean.'

Cathis closed her eyes. Her air of forced, cold bluntness returned. 'You, Heron,' she said 'much as I hate having to make this sort of admission, are the only person from whom I could count on a measure of kindness and sympathy.'

'Oh,' he said, blankly.

'Yes. That's the truth.'

'But – but – what about your friends? What about your father? What about –'

'I realised, as soon as I escaped from – *her,* that I have no real friends. Hardly anyone who wouldn't be shocked if I told them. I haven't led a very respectable life so far. But I know what they think. You thought it too, didn't you? About Sally and me? That we were – that we were – lovers?'

'Of course not.'

'Thank you. I hope that's true. But Sally was the only real friend I had. Sally...' Her face contorted but she managed to avoid breaking down again.

'But what about your father?'

'*Him?*' she cried angrily. 'Heron, do you know what he would have done if I'd gone back to the Library and told him what had happened to me? Do you know? I can tell you. He'd simply have *laughed.* He laughs at nearly everything except his stupid books. He's all dried up inside, he doesn't care for me at all.'

'I see. Well, well.'

'So there it is.' She laid her knife down and looked vaguely at her clothes again. 'Goodness me – I'm still in an awful mess.'

'You will at least go home sometime? Or do you want me to put you up here?'

'That won't be necessary, thank you, Heron dear,' she said, regaining some of her usual astringency. 'I'll go home now and get cleaned up.'

'How are you feeling now?'

'I'll be better when the memories are a little less vivid and horrible . . . but that won't be in a hurry. Luckily I'm not injured, she let me go after . . . it.' She stood up straight, went to the door and opened it. A hum of voices and machinery came in from the workshop.

'Come and see me again, then,' he said, 'if you want to talk about it, or about anything. Drop in, any time.'

'Thanks. I will,' she said quietly. 'Thank you for the lunch. Thank you very very much – and –' Very quickly she stood on tiptoe, putting her arms round him, and kissed his cheek; and was quickly gone, shutting the door behind her, before he could respond.

Settle moved cautiously forward. But he could see his way clearly, without the aid of a candle or torch. Light was coming from around the corner in front of him, and he was sure that when he turned this corner he would have arrived at its source.

He had not plunged into tunnel D/Qa6B immediately, on seeing the faint light ahead of him. Instead he had retired to his study and brought the master map, by now a diagram of considerable complexity, fully up to date with his latest findings. He had then eaten, spent a pensive quarter of an hour erecting constantly-collapsing card-castles, and finally, having made up his mind, returned to the maze. On the way in, to his alarm, he had noticed more alien footprints. He arrived at the end of the tunnel, dusted himself, turned the corner, halted, and slowly took in the scene in front of him.

He was standing in a large retangular hall – large, that is, by Habitation standards, about twenty feet by thirty by twelve. In front of him hung a cold, bright, flickering curtain; as he had expected, he had reached the circumference of level 1 and was now looking through a wall-window. To his right the wall had been opened to let out a ramp which sloped upwards with a low declivity into darkness. On his left a sheer wall rose from the floor to the ceiling, apparently made of black glass. There were many objects in the room. Settle recognised some of these as corpses, repulsive in the hard afternoon light. Unlike the skeletons in the passages, these had no dignity: fully clothed, but grey and shrouded with cobwebs; ragged with tattered yellow skin, stiff with protruding bone; sprawled and grotesque in the abandonment of death. They looked as if they might have died in pain and not suddenly. Settle averted his eyes to the ceiling. There were several vents in it. Then some more facts presented themselves to his consideration: the air in the room was clean and odourless; there was actually a light draught; and the draught was, if not strikingly warm, certainly much warmer than it ought to be in an unheated room at the circumference of a level. There also seemed to be faint, low, almost undetectable humming or vibration, as much feeling as sound, coming from somewhere. Settle gingerly examined the other objects, some of which fell to dust at his touch. There were metal chairs; a table; a long black cylinder mounted on a tripod which Settle took for some kind of gun; three more pistols; crumbling cardboard boxes spilling ammunition of different kinds; some books, volumes of printed paper, which he examined eagerly, only to find them all more or less pulverised; tangles of cassette-tape; glass bottles, some of which Settle greatly admired, never having seen green glass before; implements of various kinds, power-drills, a blowlamp, a miniature laser-punch in working order, as Settle soon found out (but, like Cathis and Salla examining the first pistol, he was lucky enough to avoid punching a hole in himself); a jumble of incomprehensible and smashed-looking electronic tools and components; a dead torch and several broken light-globes; some simple, identifiable items, mostly tools, which included three spare hacksaw blades without a hacksaw, an unpowered screwdriver, some spools of copper wire, and an assortment of rusty nails and screws; a few complex mechanical items, mostly broken, probably parts of larger machines; more human remains; and dust, dust, dust. In the course of half an hour's careful, often nauseating investigation, however, he discovered no projector.

He turned his attention to the ramp. It was an extremely rickety structure, and gave every sign of having been contrived in haste. Before Settle had unsuspectingly advanced more than six paces up it, there was a loud crack and it collapsed without warning. Settle found himself sitting on the tiled floor in a cloud of dust. Only a small area, however, had fallen. Settle stood up, brushed off the splinters, and continued more circumspectly. He reached the top of the ramp without falling again, and found that it led to another black glass wall. It was not entirely featureless, however; at its centre was a small square excrescence. Settle fumbled for and lit a candle. It shone almost as brightly from behind the door, in reflection, as it did in his hand. He had a moment's unnerving glimpse of himself, eyes gleaming and deeply sunken in the faint yellow light, mouth set, the great grey bows of moustache quivering against the ghostly light of the lower level. Then it occurred to him, with a horrible shock, that this door must lead to a level higher than level 1.

This apparently trivial thought brought home to him as none of the other various weird manifestations had yet done, the loneliness and strangeness of the task on which he had become engaged. That there should be levels above level 1 must have occurred to any sensible person who had set eyes on the Sphere's exterior, and Settle himself was naturally aware of this possibility; but so far it had never occurred to him that the search for a projector might entail exploration to these hypothetical regions. The majority of the Habitationers, the peasants and artisans, lived on the Circle and regarded the Sphere itself, as well as the bewildering and disorientating column, with a certain amount of awe; and this feeling increased with regard to the higher and lower levels. Many had never gone beyond level 4, either upwards or downwards. The lowest level, 7, was naturally dreaded on account of its association with the Loony-Bin; and the uppermost was inhabited by an obscure figure of occult, esoteric wisdom, the Librarian. Settle did not share this view of himself, but even so, especially after having partially explored it, he felt some sympathy with the popular view of the Library as a kind of unimaginable, demon-tenanted limbo. There were of course innumerable stories and legends about rash spirits who had ventured up to the Library and had never been seen again. The posited levels above level 1 were never talked about at all: they were too ominous. This general background was enough to give Settle a tingle of superstitious fear as he examined the small rectangular boss in the mirror-black wall or door. It was apparently made of gold and there was a small neat keyhole in it. (He had unfortunately forgotten about the key Cathis had found.) He pressed it tentatively but nothing happened. Having ascertained that there was no way off the top of the ramp except through the door, he blew out his candle and slowly descended.

He spent the next ten minutes wandering around the room, stepping over the corpses and debris, peering through the wall at the amorphous curtains of rain drifting across the Circle fields. He could just distinguish the pale curve of the outer wall amid the watery confusion of the atmosphere. He felt frustrated and sad. Below and in front of him tree-tops shook and dripped. It had seemed, briefly, as if he had at last reached a goal – but the goal had turned out to consist largely of more of the same elements that had already become so wearisome to him: obscure violence, sterile decay, dust, darkness, and a perpetual, at first exciting but by now oppressive and enervating, sense of unfathomable, infinitely distant mystery. He wondered how long these people had lain there, how they had died, and who they were. Their fates were as entirely inscrutable as his own future. There was another exit from the room, similar to the one through which he had entered. He had looked down it, not expecting to see anything new, and had not been surprised. In front of him the bright, white drops of water skipped, trembled and ran. Settle turned, fingering his moustache listlessly. His eyes travelled once again over the tall black wall, and stopped suddenly.

On the other side of this wall a dim red glow had appeared. He gazed at it. Certainly it had not been there when he had entered the room. Then he realised that the faint vibration had also ceased. There was now no sound at all but his own breathing.

He approached the glow; from the other side his own grey image approached him. He stood in front of the wall, straining to descry the source of the redness. He thought he could see the dark silhouette of some piece of furniture, perhaps a desk. Then the light went out, but almost before he had had time to feel disappointed several other things happened.

He realised that his reflection had also disappeared; in front of him was simply an immense blackness; but now this seemed not in front of him, but below him. He was suspended – he was falling through space. He plunged downward and felt a violent impact. He opened his eyes. Light had returned; he was lying on the floor, extremely scared, his heart pounding, in the same room although the light now seemed curiously weak. He could see clearly the disordered heaps outlined against the window, with the partially fallen ramp rising behind them. It occurred to him that he must have fainted and the red light had been an hallucination.

His next shock did not affect him so much like a blow, as a numbing, paralysing faintness. He was lying, not on grimy tiles or metal planks, but on *carpet*. It had a rough, curiously hard and abrasive pile. He stood up, advanced half a pace and struck an invisible barrier. He felt it with his hands. It was smooth, cold and unyielding and stretched as far as he could reach in all directions. He knew that he must somehow have passed through the black wall and was now on the other side of it. He turned back and saw the piece of furniture. It was a desk, with a padded chair behind it. A small red circle was glowing on its top like a wintry sun. The area behind the glass was no more than a small carpeted annexe; there was no furniture in it, nothing at all except the metal desk, the chair, and a large off-white screen attached to one wall. There was no way out. Settle walked round it, tapping and feeling the walls with his hands. Then he tried hurling himself against the glass barrier and bruised his shoulder badly. Trying not to despair, he went up to the desk and looked at it. It was covered in an array of identical rectangular buttons, arranged in lines and squares. He put his hand on the desk and a blue spark of static electricity pricked into his finger. He was more upset by this than by any of the other events of the last hour. He sat down in the chair, which was very comfortable, and tried to think. A minute later, absently, fingering the top of the desk, he pressed the red button.

Instantly the surface of the desk lit up in a multicoloured display, yellow, green, amber, violet, blue and white. After a time he looked up and saw that the screen on the wall in front of him now bore a luminous superscription:

If you can read this, press a yellow square on the desk in front of you, then a blue square, then a green square, then a blue square, then a yellow square. If you do so you will receive a chance of escaping.

Settle's spirit, already much cowed, shrank before this manifestation, like a savage transported to a European city. Huge, impersonal authorities seemed to tower before him; effortless, anonymous wizardry held him trapped like a baby. It occurred to him to pray to the Habitationers' God, which he was not accustomed to doing. He did so, briefly, then obeyed the instructions. Each little square went out as he pressed it.

II. iii. THE LAST MEETING

Plying his yo-yo, Heron came up the stairs to level 2 and found Malcom, Christofer and Salla standing below the clock, arguing.

'It must be wrong. It *must* be,' said Christofer.

'It never goes wrong,' said Malcom firmly.

'It has now. Habitation, Malcom, we've only just had lunch! Look at the sky – there, yes, the sun has come out. Look at the shadows. One of the two must be wrong. Personally, I'd prefer it to be the clock.'

The clock said 17.20. Malcom regarded it doubtfully. 'I don't know...' he murmured.

'Hello, everyone,' said Heron breezily. 'How are you all? Fine? Good. What's up?'

'It's the clock,' answered Christofer excitedly. 'Now look, Heron, do you believe that that's the right time?'

'Habitation! No, I certainly don't. What's wrong with it?'

'How are we to know?' asked Christofer. 'You're the mechanical expert.'

Heron flicked his yo-yo a few times. It was a new one, painted white, and the string was very long, about seven or eight feet. 'I know nothing about clocks, I'm afraid. You could try taking it to bits to try and find out the trouble. What do you think, Malcom?'

'I don't think you'd be able to get it off the wall without damaging it. And the black case is all of a piece. I don't know what it's made of, but it doesn't look as if it would come off.'

'And there'd be a row if we started messing around with the Priests' precious clock. Yes – best leave it alone, Chris. Perhaps it'll mend itself.'

Malcom's tone was grave. 'Do you think it will?'

'How am I to know?' answered Heron.

Here Salla, who had been standing listlessly apart from this conversation, opening her mouth occasionally as if to interject but closing it without speech, burst in with her characteristic abruptness: 'Oh, what does it matter about a silly old clock? Why should you be so upset about it? It's easy to tell the time by the sun, or by a candle or something.'

Heron regarded her curiously. She appeared to him rather less attractive than usual. Her hair was an unkempt, greasy mass; her face was sunken; there were dark shadows under her eyes. She looked as if she had been wearing the same shirt and trousers for several consecutive days and nights. Christofer, by contrast, was remarkably spruce.

Heron said: 'Bravo, Salla. Come on, Malcom, tell us. What's the problem?'

Malcom made a gesture of despair. 'I can't tell you in a few words. You really ought to have picked up some idea by now, especially you, Heron. . .'

They turned and went up the last flight of stairs together. Settle had summoned at short notice an important Society meeting. None of them had seen him for several days and Cathis had not been able to supply much information. A fire was burning in Settle's sitting-room; it was a cold, showery day. Cathis was there, wearing a woolly white jumper over a plain grey dress. Settle sat at a table, writing busily. 'Come in, come in,' he said. Heron promptly sat down on the sofa next to Cathis. Christofer sat on his other side. Salla squatted on the floor next to her husband. Malcom lowered himself solemnly into an armchair.

After a short pause Settle got up. 'Welcome, everybody,' he said. 'I apologise for dragging you along like this at such short notice, but I've found out a lot of things and had some very interesting experiences which I'm sure you'll be anxious to hear about.' He picked up some papers and sat down in his own armchair.

'Well then, Settle, let's have it,' said Heron. 'But let's have a drink first.'

Settle passed the bottle and glasses around. The two smokers lit their pipes. Heron's left hand became unobtrusively engaged with Cathis's right.

'Now, as you know, for the last two and a half weeks I've been engaged in the task of exploring and charting the Library. My

89

original aim was to find a device that would enable us to read the cassettes with which we are so liberally supplied.'

'"Liberally"—?' asked Christofer conscientiously.

'Never mind that now. This intention, however, soon became subordinate to the task of finding out the dimensions of the Library; of getting to the end of it, or even of feeling that I was getting somewhere, or anywhere at all. Some of you have been in it and know what a depressing place it is. Well, two days ago I at last arrived at a definite end. I came out on the other side of the Library; I entered a room, with a window-wall that looks towards the south-west. I've called this room the ramp-room on the map, because there's a ramp in it.' He described the contents of the room and the actions he had taken there. The Society listened attentively. 'Now, from this point it becomes very difficult to tell you what happened, because it's all so strange and incredible. I have difficulty believing it myself. I will do the best I can, and I must ask you not to interrupt or ask questions. You can do that later. All right?'

'Yes.' 'Yes.' 'Go ahead.'

Choosing his words slowly and carefully, Settle described his falling through the glass barrier and putting the computer into action. 'The most important thing to get clear, which I admit I have not yet really myself succeeded in doing, is that these events were all controlled by a machine, called, so I understand, a computer; not something alive. The Habitation – Malcom is right – was created and built by men. They must have possessed fantastic, unimaginable kinds of knowledge to have done it; and one of the things they could do was to build computers. I don't begin to have the faintest understanding of how a computer works, but you can tell it things, which it will remember; you can order it to do things and it will do them. When you press a switch, you are, I suppose, giving an order to the light-bulb; when you wind a watch, you are, in a way, ordering the hands to go round. The actions you perform are only indirectly related to the effects you require; the results are much greater, and have little resemblance to the effort you supply. In the same way, when I pressed certain buttons on that desk – don't ask me how it works – I was giving the machine an order which resulted in words appearing on the screen. I have no idea of the processes involved and I fancy that probably everyone else on the Habitation but us – at least, I hope I can rely on all of you – would dismiss the whole thing as witchcraft, an abomination, and have tried to destroy it.'

'What happened?' Christofer presently asked.

'The next thing that happened was that I was made to go through a series of tests. I can't remember all of them; it seems blurred and confused now; but it was made clear to me that I would be kept imprisoned, till I starved, unless I passed them. There were a lot of tests to do with words – defining meanings, that is, choosing the best definition out of a series of three or four alternatives, pressing the right button. The buttons kept on changing colours. It was lucky I can read. Then there were some sums I had to do – calculations – a mathematical problem appeared on the screen which I had to solve, but that was easier than I expected because a lot of numerical signs and symbols suddenly appeared on the desk-buttons and I was told to use these. The computer did most of the calculations for me, but I had to tell it what to do. The answers appeared in red on a little screen on the desk. I know I talked just now of giving the computer orders, and this sounds as if the computer was giving me orders, but you must remember that it was only carrying out instructions someone else had already given it.

'There were a lot of other tests and they went on for a long time. There were a lot to do with logical deductions – those kind of arguments which are called syllogisms. There was one that went, "all carrots are vegetables, all carrots are red, therefore all vegetables are red," and I had to say, I mean to press, one of two buttons which said true and false. It all went on for ages, but eventually all the lights on the desk went out and another announcement appeared on the screen. It said: 'You have passed. In a few minutes you will be allowed to depart if you wish. First, however, you must listen to a recorded message. Try not to be alarmed at hearing the sound of a voice, if you have not heard tape-recordings before. There is no one else here apart from yourself. Tape-recordings are a means of storing and reproducing sounds.' Then it went out and I was left in the dark again. But soon the red button – the original one – lit up again. I felt rather nervous, but I touched it, and the voice began·

speaking to me. It was a shock, but I closed my eyes and tried to imagine someone sitting a few feet away from me, and then it wasn't so bad. It was a gravelly kind of voice; he sounded rather old and tired; I'm sure I heard a yawn at least twice. The first thing he said was, "Congratulations on passing our little examination. We must first of all apologise for inflicting this uncalled-for ordeal on you, and in addition subjecting you to a good deal of anxiety and strain. But the tests have indicated that in all probability you are a man or woman of intelligence and rational persuasions. There is, we realise, a small possibility of error, but we are sufficiently confident in our contrivances to feel sure that the kind of person you almost certainly are, will entertain no resentment against us when you know our reasons." I remember that much very clearly – obviously he meant to be flattering – but I can give you only the gist of what he said after that. He explained a lot, but I've spent some more time at the desk since then, yesterday and this morning, and so I am more fully aware of the whole story. He told me how to work the computer so I could find things out for myself. I took notes . . . yes, here we are.'

He filled his glass and looked round at the Society. Cathis, sitting upright, met his gaze curiously. Heron ran his hand through his hair, stretched out and crossed his legs. 'Fascinating.' He grinned. 'I didn't know you Librarians led such interesting lives.'

Settle placed a couple of logs on the fire. 'I think it will be clearest if I go straight through the history in a chronological – excellent word, that – order. To begin at the beginning: Habitation One was built about three hundred and forty years ago. What we have not realised is that it is only very small, absolutely tiny, compared to what's outside. Heron has only seen the minutest fraction of it. In reality it is a huge round thing called a planet, moving in the sky as the stars and sun move, and men used to live on it and move about all over it. And there were enormous numbers of them. Do you know what a billion is? It is a thousand millions, a thousand thousand thousands. One can't conceive of this kind of number at all. But there were four and a quarter billion people living then, mostly on the earth but also in other places in the sky. The Habitation took eight years to build and by their system the dates were 2188 and 2196. The reason for building it – well, I'll have to digress here.

'They were always fighting and quarrelling among themselves. At times half the population would be involved. People were killed in their thousands – even millions. They had developed tremendously powerful weapons: guns of different kinds, missiles that could fly through the air and kill huge numbers of people a long way away, and ways of causing dreadful diseases and poisoning the air and turning people mad. I admit it all sounds most unlikely, crazy, almost ludicrous; I can't really believe it myself; but if you simply accept these facts with your minds without trying to feel what they mean, then that'll do. Apparently, from the latter half of the twentieth century – the Habitation was built in the twenty-second, remember – mankind had the technical power to destroy itself entirely, to kill practically every living thing in the world. I know it's crazy – please believe me. I promise you I haven't made all this up for a joke. It's true. I don't know how people managed to live with this or why they didn't do anything about it. Don't ask me. Anyway, what the computer said was that during this time the world was divided into two opposing halves; both halves had the means to destroy the other, but neither did because it would immediately be destroyed in retaliation. And neither half could surrender its own weapons, as many people wished, indeed as most people wished, because that would leave it vulnerable to the other side. It sounds rather a thin explanation ... they managed to survive without a major war happening for a surprising length of time – until the year 2042. Then it happened, and about half the population died at once, and about four-fifths of the rest died within the next two years, of starvation and various diseases. But the remainder carried on and they multiplied, and the hostilities came back, and this time the world was divided into three armed groups. But they were again able to avoid war for a long time. At this time, about 2150, they began to leave their own planet and establish colonies in space. Now new resources were available to them, from the moon and other planets, and one group – I forget its name – determined on constructing a series of buildings, Habitations, which would be proof against all kinds of attack. There were flying machines which had to be deflected, or destroyed in the air, and there were things called radiation and fall-out which had to be guarded against and gases and missiles of various kinds. But they were able to do all this and they built the Habitation. The purpose was to ensure that a small number of people – comparatively small, that is – would survive. And so twelve hundred people were chosen, when the building was finished, and they came to live here.

'What went wrong was that the next – and the last – world war happened much sooner than expected; in fact almost immediately. They were barely in time. And this time it really was the end. War broke out, and literally the entire population of the planet was killed, and the people in space were included in the war, so they were all killed as well: everybody except the first Habitationers. So there they were, by themselves on a dead planet. They couldn't get away, and there was nowhere to get to anyway. Instead of a round planet 7,900 miles in diameter they were confined to a round plain with a diameter of four miles. And they stayed like that for another five years or so. Then – and this is where it begins to concern us – there was a dreadful time.

'The old man whose voice I heard – I think he said his name was Levinsky – described this trouble, briefly on the recording, and then in a great deal of detail, in computerised notes. But he admitted that he felt he could explain and analyse it only partly. He had certain views about the reasons for what happened, and other people had other views. He said that the causes and reasons were obscure and complex, though the results were plain. In short, I know what happened but I don't really know why it happened, and it's not very likely that we ever shall, for sure. To put it as briefly as possible, there was a short period of rapidly mounting trouble followed by a popular revolt – "insurrection" was the word he used. The Habitation was governed by a body called the Habitation council, which should have regulated all the business our own Assembly and heads of professions look after, but because the war happened so much sooner then they expected, they were unprepared and unable to deal competently with the task of governing. There was an increasing hysteria and panic. Levinsky gave some figures: in the five years and seven months between the terminal holocaust

(I liked that) and the insurrection, 283 people – that is, nearly a quarter of them – commited suicide in various ways. At the beginning of this period about a tenth of them professed religious faith; at the end, the Habitation was sharply divided into two groups, those who did and those who didn't, and the former outnumbered the latter by about seven to one. There seems to have been a kind of orgy of expiation and atonement – but more about that in a minute. The average age of the Habitationers fell, because most of the older people, people over fifty, died very quickly, nearly all of sickness and shock and despair. The birthrate fell very sharply as well. And a lot of people suffered agonies and died, from a disease called cancer which had been caused by the radiation, which affected them in spite of the defences. Anyway, what with one thing and another, and an extremely miserable time it must have been, the population of the Habitation fell to nearly half – six hundred and fifty – its former level.

'But all this wasn't what caused the insurrection. Levinsky, as far as I can make out, says it was caused, fundamentally, by a superstitious desire for atonement and the expiation of guilt. He says he was aware of a huge collective sense of sin in people's minds. People felt that the world they had lived in had been unendurably wicked, and had been punished for its sins, and they felt guilty for having escaped divine punishment as well; and they had a desire to punish themselves. There was a general movement into the Church and the Priests became very powerful. All sorts of new services and rites were devised, sacrifices of animals, taboos and penances, flagellations and self-torture. It makes our own Church seem very restrained . . . However, I do not see exactly where the connection between this and the next thing comes. The next thing was a passionate and intensely irrational hatred of technology. There was, from the second year onwards, a growing, deepening conviction among the mob that since the holocaust had been brought about by man's enormous technical knowledge, which had enabled him to create the terribly powerful weapons, sophisticated technology must be associated with the devil. This belief gained strength from the fact that nearly all the more trained, intellectually cultivated people, the teachers, Doctors, council members, scientists, held themselves determinedly aloof from the growing mania. The troubles got worse and worse. At first it showed itself only in small things – rejection of automatic, labour-saving manual appliances such as power-tools, and so on: but of course technical sophistication is a product of culture, and by and by it inevitably came about that culture, rationality and thought were also hated and stigmatised. Soon books, especially ones in cassette form, were regarded as suspect. Children ceased to receive education. (All children were taught to read before those days.) They stopped using their ploughing machines and cultivators and went back to ox-drawn carts. Levinsky gives a great long list of separate aspects of the general regression. But, as I say, I don't see how the first cause – guilt – ties in with the second – hatred of culture. The second seems to me more important than the first.

'To resume: by five years the Habitation was deeply divided against itself, with intense fear and hatred on both sides: on the one hand a massive, voluntary withdrawal into barbarism, on the other, an elite determined to stand fast to secular ideals. The government was carried on in theory, by the second side, but by now it had very little power left. There was a small executive police force at the beginning, similar to the one the Clerks run, but the Council was unable to retain control over it. Its remaining power lay in its retention of the few sophisticated weapons in the Habitation: guns, exploding things called bombs, gases. But as you can imagine these were dangerous assets, they were regarded with especial horror by the majority, and of course the fact that the Council had these weapons, and was determined on keeping them, made the other side much angrier. By the end of the fifth year the leaders of the two sides had emerged: Levinsky and two friends of his called Clarry and Miller; and on the other side the Chief Priest Harkness, backed by the Church. The Priests were also very anxious that the computer should be done away with. Eventually things came to a head. There was a proposal to introduce human sacrifices into Church services. The Priests were in favour of this, and so were most of the common people. One can guess whom they'd have chosen for the job of being slaughtered. The Council, still nominally in control, vetoed this emphatically. At the same time came two demands: that the Council should surrender its small arsenal, and consent to the shutting down of the computer. These were both denied, the same day. That night Levinsky and Miller were both murdered. Harkness renewed his demands the next day. Clarry refused them. In the afternoon a mob, of whom twelve were women, gathered outside the Sphere whose doors were locked, broke in, and was repulsed by the defenders, who were now fewer than fifty. By evening they were running low on ammunition. They retreated to the upper levels – there were only about twenty-five people left by now – still led by Clarry. But level 1, the Library level, had been carefully prepared. Levinsky, who was undoubtedly an extremely intelligent and resolute man, had foreseen several months ago what was likely to happen. And they realised in advance that their own cause was hopeless – they were bound to be defeated by greater numbers; their own ideals had no hope of surviving. But, rather admirably, they would not give in. So they decided that the best thing they could do would be to fortify the Library and computer; to store up the knowledge they possessed and make it inaccessible to anyone for a long period of time; three hundred years was the figure. By the end of that period, they thought, the chaos would have sorted itself out and a new, calmer order established itself – as has actually happened. Or else the Habitation would have fizzled out completely into a band of savages and morons. As an additional safeguard they devised the series of tests which I had to pass, so as to be sure that the computer could only be reopened, once the three hundred years had passed, by a reasonable, cultivated person, therefore, necessarily, the product of an ordered Society.

'The thing they used was called a neutron-blanketer. Neutrons are invisible particles, that can kill men but have no damaging effect on inanimate things like furniture and equipment. Under Levinsky's supervision they built a blanketer and installed it in the computer. The computer was also protected by a power-damper, which meant that no electrical tools could work against it. A few days before he was killed, he made the recording and put it in. Again, they were just in time – the history of the Habitation seems to have involved a number of hair-breadth escapes. Fighting broke out. Clarry's little band retreated into the Library and set off the blanketer, which meant that they were safe as long as their supplies lasted, and the Library was safe for three centuries. Clarry made another recording and brought the story up to date. They had a fortnight's food-supplies. I suppose they were just sitting down and wondering what to do next when someone told Clarry that two cylinders of poison-gas were missing and must have been left downstairs. It sounds rather implausible as a story, but that's the way things often are. At any rate the last addition to the records is a bald, uncommented-on observation to the effect that the two cylinders were missing. And there it ends. One can only recreate the rest. I suppose that Harkness gave orders for the gas to be used against them, and that they were probably all dead by the end of the same day . . .

'But the blanketer continued to do its job. No one could enter the Library without being killed, either failing to return or dying shortly afterwards. So, not surprisingly, it must have developed a bad name. The only thing to do was to block it up. Meanwhile life went on. There must have been great hardship and misery at first, but in time things evened out. All references to the past history of mankind must have been suppressed as far as possible – and even so, I find it a little surprising that it should have been forgotten so completely . . . Children must have grown up in ignorance, and their children in greater ignorance. Memories *must* have been kept, for some time, secretly. Perhaps there was a deliberate campaign carried out by the Priests, to make sure all reminders and memories of the outside world were eradicated. The stores continued to supply what was essential and slowly order and prosperity returned . . .

'Well, that's it. Now, for the first time in centuries, we know where we are and why we're here . . . Does anybody want to ask anything?'

There was a silence in the room which lasted about five minutes. The fire had burned low. Rain pattered soundlessly against the window. Each member of the Society was busy with his or her own thoughts.

Salla yawned.

'I'd like to see those computer-records,' said Christofer slowly.

There was another pause.

'Poor wretches,' murmured Cathis.

Malcom spoke: 'Thank you, Settle. That was very illuminating.' His voice was lowered almost to inaudibility. 'But – but – this is very bad. This is worse than I expected, much worse...

'Oh, Habitation, do none of you realise? Can't you see? What's wrong with you?'

But no one heard these words. Settle stood up and everyone except Malcom relaxed. There was a general stir as he began the preparations for tea. Under cover of the bustle Heron whispered to Cathis, 'Well, what about it? Will you?' and she nodded.

PART THREE

III. i. FIRST CONSEQUENCES

It was half past four, by the level 2 clock, on the next day. Settle had got up late, being rather worn out through the exertions of the past fortnight, and was having breakfast. Cathis had gone out somewhere. A little pale, mid-morning sun shone fitfully through his kitchen window. He spread a slice of toast with butter and munched it thoughtfully. Mentally, he seemed to have become adrift in a nebulous, uncertain environment. Possibilities and implications drifted past him like mists. Fears and hopes percolated through the fog like familiar but muted sounds, strange echoes and resonances, dim knockings and hootings. He took up the cards again and began to stand them end to end. Suddenly a totally new idea occurred to him.

It was a unique and delightful perception. He contemplated it, entranced, for a few moments, and then, abandoning his ruminations with relief, prepared to put it into execution. He took an untouched, stale loaf from the bread-bin, sliced it skilfully, and proceeded to toast the slices under the grill. This took twenty minutes. When they were all done he sat down on the floor and began building with them. He had realised that slices of toast would do very well instead of playing-cards for card castles. It was realisations like this that contributed in a large measure to his enjoyment of life. For ten minutes he was extremely, childishly happy. The sun continued to shine; the toast was crisp and dry under his fingers; its pleasant smell filled the air. The darkness and horrors of the Library receded. He whistled to himself as he built two houses and dismantled them as architecturally unsatisfying. His third attempt, a symmetrical, buttressed, overhanging edifice eighteen inches high, pleased him greatly. But no sooner had he finished it than he recognised, with a slight feeling of dismay, a heavy approaching footstep outside. As if in sympathy, the sun went out. He stood up hastily, dusted the crumbs off himself, and went to the door.

Malcom came in, looking even more preoccupied than usual,

and asked for half an hour's talk. Settle went back to the kitchen and continued with his meal. Malcom refused his invitation to sit down. After a time Settle looked up, smiling. 'Well, go ahead,' he said.

Malcom's answer burst out as if from a bottle. 'No one else seems to have realised how *bad* the truth is ... If I understood you correctly your findings indicate that we are, in truth, completely isolated. We are the last remnants, the dregs of a corrupt, wicked, self-destroyed race. What have we to look forward to?'

Settle made no answer.

'Please don't laugh at me. Think. We grow our own food and we make our own clothes. We get water from the atmosphere. I don't know where the electricity we use comes from, but the cables that supply it lead up into the central column and most of the Electricians think that there must be a large solar cell up there. But we can assume that the Electricity won't run out. So we are assured of most of the necessities of life – and the rest we get from the stores in the lower levels.'

'And?'

'Settle, those stores are finite. They won't last for ever. We depend on them for many things, most of which are vitally important, which we can't make for ourselves. Wire is the most important of them. Wire, and sand for glass, and clay for ceramics, and large numbers of chemicals for the soil and for purifying the water, and for the foundry; and all kinds of small components, little screws which we can't cast accurately enough, lenses and filaments for light-globes and ... other things. The Electricians and the Metallers are the professions who rely most heavily on the stores. We're all as careful and economical as possible, and they won't run out in your life-time or mine, and there are still a lot left, but someday they *will*.'

Settle got up and began clearing away the breakfast things. Malcom, too deeply immersed in his own perplexities to notice the curious object on the floor, came further into the room. 'And another thing is that we are totally dependent on the machines the founders left. We depend on their continuing to function perfectly. One of them has just gone wrong: the level 2 clock. It's worked perfectly for three and a half centuries; now it's failed and there is nothing we can do. We won't be able to mend it. Now we can't measure time with the same accuracy any more. You may say that this isn't a necessity. We can get by without it. I agree. But whatever would we do if the water-condensors ceased working? Or that great solar cell I mentioned just now? Or the purifying system? These things were all made by humans and humans are fallible. What do you say to this?'

'I'm afraid I can't think of anything to say at present,' said Settle shortly.

'And ... there's something else which I find even worse. To think of the stupidity and folly of the world; to think of the things men did to each other ... it's easy to understand why so many people committed suicide after the destruction.'

'Do you wish to commit suicide, Malcom?'

'Sometimes; but it's not just me. It's all of us – the race in general – the futility ... If only we had something to do, some purpose to achieve, if there was only something to believe in, then that would be all right. The stores wouldn't matter. But there is nothing. All we can do is wait for the end.' The bitterness and tension had gone out of his voice, which now sounded only sad.

Settle busied himself with drying a few plates. Some time later Malcom said:

'In addition to that, there's something I should apologise for. You see, it was me who –'

There was a loud crunching sound and Malcom fell heavily to the floor. Perhaps wearied of remaining on his feet for so long, he had attempted to sit down; but the seat he had selected was Settle's toast castle. He had evidently been under the impression, without ever having noticed or looked at it directly, that it was a kind of stool or wooden box. He may be forgiven for his lack of perspicuity: it was about the right height and shape for a stool, and in the right position relative to the kitchen table. It collapsed immediately in a shower of crumbs. His coccyx struck the floor painfully. Malcom sat on the floor; Settle stood at the sink. They stared at each other incredulously. Malcom picked up a piece of toast and examined it. An unconscionably long time seemed to pass before he realised what it was. He broke it between his fingers and dropped it.

Malcom looked at Settle's face again. The old inscrutable mask had come over it; but he could discern, deep in Settle's eyes, a very faint gleam, a tiny spark of amusement.

'This is *toast*?' said Malcom.

Settle nodded.

'Why?'

Settle's moustache was quivering very slightly. He said nothing, but the gleam grew and his lips parted in a soundless chuckle.

'Habitation, why – oh, *why*? I don't understand you at all!'

Settle had turned away to hide his face, forgetting that there was a mirror on the wall and his profile was visible to Malcom in it. He stayed silent, but was obviously laughing.

'You devil! Why do you keep on doing these things to me? Why do you –'

Settle was now laughing helplessly. His moustache jerked, his shoulders sagged. Gasps came from him.

Malcom's face was a dark, furious red. His great hands were clenched. 'Curse you, Settle! Say something! Come on, I want to know. I wish to know what amuses you. *Say something*,' he shouted, '*Habitation, or I'll* –' He stood up swiftly. Settle made no response. Malcom advanced three steps and drew back his fist as if to hit him on the back of the neck. Settle, shuddering with mirth, his face in his hands, was not aware of this gesture.

Malcom dropped his fist. 'I see,' he said. 'Very well. Goodbye.' He went out, closing the door surprisingly quietly.

In the early morning of the next day Cathis entered Heron's studio. The Craftsmen's workshop was quiet now. A faint, bleak light fell into the deserted workshop, across the dusty tools and scraps. She had come, extremely nervous and afraid, in response to his recent solicitation; renewed, and assented to by her, at the end of the last Society meeting. She had not been able to let him know when she would come, and hoped he would react kindly to being surprised. She knew he kept a couch in his studio and was accustomed to sleep there. Her light foot-steps made little sound. She opened his door quietly and stole into the darkness. The wall-window was curtained with black-painted canvas. She heard the sound of breathing but could not locate the couch. She felt her way to the curtain and moved it so as to admit a little light. What she saw transfixed her with horror.

It was a large couch, wide enough for two, and there were two people on it. Heron she saw, his pale bare arm lying on the grey blanket, in the attitude of a relaxed embrace, over his partner's shoulder. Little was visible of her face; all that could be seen was a mass of long black hair. They were both fast asleep. Cathis wondered distractedly who, out of all the girls and women she knew, had such long black hair. Heron's hair shone dimly, a dull gold. Cathis saw that Heron's other hand was linked with the woman's on the pillow. The room was cold. Cathis shivered. Her heart seemed to be striking violently against the front of her chest. Carefully she drew the curtain back and left the room, in a greater agony of mind than on the occasion of her last encounter with Salla.

'How are things with you and Salla nowadays?'

'She goes around with her mouth open and a glazed expression, like a zombie. I ask her what's the matter and she says nothing. She does the housework in a dream and spends the rest of her time sitting staring at nothing.'

'Last corridor – we'll be out in a minute.'

'She hasn't given me much cause to be fond of her – I hated her, until just recently; but after all, I loved her once and I don't like seeing anyone in, well, such obvious pain.'

'What do you think you can do?'

'I have no idea. But after all, Habitation! Settle, she is my wife, isn't she?'

'Certainly.'

'Something has evidently gone wrong between her and Cathis. Perhaps . . . I don't know.'

'Well, here we are,' said Settle, entering the ramp-room. It was much as he had left it. 'Hello,' he said, looking down, 'that's odd. I'm sure I left a pile of things down here. I wonder where it's gone.'

'Is that the terminal?'

'Yes. One moment please.' He found a small panel on the wall by the entrance, opened it, and pressed a six-figure code on the digital buttons inside. The darkened glass slid effortlessly up into the ceiling. Christofer looked into the annexe, impressed.

'I told you I got there at first by falling – I felt as if I was falling and the glass seemed to melt away. I got out simply by pressing some coloured buttons on the desk. A handle appeared on the wall – it seemed to lift itself out – and I turned it and this door opened.' He opened the door. A short, narrow, steely, ramifying corridor led away from them. 'There's a trapdoor and ladder at the end. They take you down to level 3. That's the way I eventually got out. The computer told me the way to open up next time I came.'

'Good. Now what about this, then?'

'The thing practically teaches itself. The red button comes on when you open the glass wall. When you press it . . . you see what happens . . . There's one particular programme . . . red, blue, green, red . . . which gives information, an index, about the computer itself, and how to get what you want out of it. You see . . . blue, now the figures nought three nought three. And there you are, I've been through some of it.'

'Goodness. How amazing. Thanks . . . Could I come back tomorrow morning?'

'Certainly.' Settle cancelled the display. 'Hey! Listen!'

From some source outside, in the Library, was coming a series of bumps and scraping noises. Settle moved forward; but it was not possible to tell from which area of the darkness the noise was coming. They stared into the black exits. The bumping sound grew quieter and quieter and faded away.

Settle fingered his moustache. 'We agreed, didn't we,' he said, 'in the Society, not to mention the computer to anyone?'

In the evening of the same day Cathis returned to Heron's room, where he was in the process of cleaning up after the day's work. He greeted her with his usual pleasant raillery. She sat in a chair, painfully upright, replying in monosyllables. After a while her taciturnity obtruded on his notice. 'What's wrong, Cathy?' he asked.

'Heron,' she said, looking past him through the window.

'Yes, love?'

'You told me you wanted to –' her expression became rigid.

108

After a few moments she forced herself to go on: 'You told me you wanted to – to make love to me.'

'Yes, I did. You agreed, remember?'

'Have you done this before? Am I the only one?'

Heron frowned. 'Yes, of course,' he said.

'Oh? Are you sure?'

'Of course I'm sure, darling.'

Cathis's face crumpled. To her intense vexation, tears began to flow from her eyes.

'What's the matter?'

She struggled to control her voice. 'I'll tell you what's the matter, Heron.'

'Good.'

'*You're a liar.* I thought you cared for me. . .'

'What's this you're saying?'

She noted his alarm. 'I was ready to trust you. I thought you loved me. I resolved to – give – I resolved to give myself to you. I would have done – anything –.' Her voice became choked. She took a handkerchief from her sleeve and wiped her face. But she was not so upset as to fail to notice Heron's rising fear and anger.

'Why are you saying this to me now? What have you come for?'

'I admired you very much, Heron. I was willing to love you. I came this evening to give you a chance. I hoped you would have something to say. I thought you might have some excuse, or that you would have owned up and asked my forgiveness. I would probably have forgiven you if you had. . .'

Heron stood up. 'What are you driving at, Cathy?'

She closed her eyes in despair. 'I came here early this morning,' she said faintly, 'I came on purpose to let you seduce me, I came in and saw you in bed with another woman.'

Heron started. Recovering his poise, he said, 'It wasn't me. I was at my uncle's home last night. It was two friends of mine you saw. They asked me for the use of this room for a night. . .'

Cathis looked at him in amazement. 'I don't know what good you think you're doing by this,' she said. 'I didn't see the woman's face, but I saw yours clearly enough.'

'How could you see it?' Heron's normally clear-thinking mind had been thrown off balance. 'It was dark when – when I –'

'I moved the curtain.'

'The curtains weren't moved.'

'I put it back afterwards, before I left.'

'Why did you move it at all?'

She regarded him, almost curiously. A chilly calm had fallen upon her. 'That, Heron, is not the point. What is important is that you have betrayed me and that I do not wish to see you again. I think I'd better leave now.'

'No, don't go yet,' said he, suddenly active. He came up to her, closed the door, caught her wrist and drew her back into the room. She made no effort to resist this compulsion. He turned away from her and occupied himself, for a short while, without speaking, in filling and lighting his pipe. When he finally turned back to her he appeared to speak with a harsh, brash confidence.

'So, Cathy. You've seen me in bed with another woman. You're extremely shocked. You are, aren't you? You think me depraved and callous, completely faithless. All your dreams are shattered. You must feel very sorry for yourself. I feel a little sorry for you too. But wait. Think a bit. Don't you realise the hypocrisy of this attitude? Haven't you just admitted you'd come to me for the same purpose? Fornication is a crime, whoever commits it. Twenty-five lashes for a woman, fifteen for a man: that's the law; it doesn't make any difference who the offender is, whether it's you or me or anyone else. Aren't you equally guilty yourself, in moral terms? Shouldn't you stop trying to judge other people like a perfect High Priest?' He waited for her to answer.

She said tiredly, 'You're not achieving anything. You've missed the point entirely.'

'Oh, no? And what about your little love-affair with dear Sally? A lesbian relationship is a far more serious crime to enter into than mere adultery.'

She recoiled from him.

'But I don't bring that into it. I don't mind it at all. I don't blame you for your hypocrisy. None of that matters at all; it's all Priestly nonsense and rigmarole. These religious rules were only invented to make people who don't know any better miserable. Now, we both know better, don't we? That's why you came to me this morning.'

A look of incredulous disgust came over Cathis's face. Heron was not looking at her, however. His eyes travelled round the room, evading hers, while he gestured with his pipe. His diatribe continued.

'You know what's important; you agree with me. Enjoying yourself, having an interesting time, that's what matters. There's nothing wrong with having sex with two girls at once; nor with switching from a girl to a man, if that's what you like doing. Enjoying life is the best thing possible.' He fixed his gaze on her and grinned aggressively. 'Come on. Why not now? Let's do what we want to enjoy doing. Don't be frightened, there's no one about.' He put down his pipe and came towards her. His face was flushed, his eyes glittered.

Cathis had never heard anything like this before. For her, every fresh revelation of his character, every new development of his specious argument, had been like a protracted fall through an incredible abyss of horror: abyss after abyss, extending themselves below her into black infinity. But her aspect might have been taken to indicate assentience: she was very white, her eyes wide, her lips parted, her hands grasped each other tightly. Soon awareness of spiritual vileness became subdued to practical, physical considerations. Her reactions were slow. He had come up to her and grasped her firmly before she realised that she was in danger of being raped. She began to struggle in his embrace. His mouth, hot and tobacco-smelling, covered hers. She turned her head away and felt his breath on her cheeks; at the same time she thumped his back vigorously with her fists. She noticed a group of brown paint-stains on the left shoulder of his white shirt. She tried hitting the back of his head and kicking him, but he clasped her even more tightly, his hand fumbling underneath her dress, clutching at her buttocks. She was being dragged away from the door, towards the couch. Her feeble attacks could make no impression on his hard, thick, male toughness. His breath blasted against her face as if from a furnace. It did not occur to her to scream. A single expedient remained to her, one she had learned from Salla in the course of an idle afternoon's chat long ago. Bracing herself, she suddenly brought her knee up into his groin as hard as she could.

Heron gave a brief shout of pain, released her, and retreated two steps, clutching at his genitals. His face was ugly with pain and fury. Cathis realised that he would not allow her to assault him thus a second time, and that unless she escaped immediately she was lost. She was lucky. Casting blindly around for a weapon of some sort, she picked up a smooth, heavy object from the nearby work-table. As Heron sprang at her, yelling incoherently, she threw the jar of black paint at his face. Fear gave her strength and the range was very short. The jar struck his forehead with a soft, horrible thud, shattered and burst into a great treacly splash. Heron swayed on his feet, his face masked. As last he crashed to the floor like a bombed chimney-stack.

Cathis stood still, tingling. For some time she was unable to draw breath; she seemed to have forgotten how to breathe. Then, having recollected, she breathed in and out slowly, several times, wondering whether it had been to her or to some other foolish young woman that an extraordinary day's events had happened; and whether that day had lasted hours, or weeks, or years. She longed intensely to lie down and rest, to sleep. She was no longer conscious of much mental pain, only of a dull exhausted ache. But now she heard running footsteps outside and two men, Craftsmen, burst into the room. In an instant she had made the decision to keep the truth secret and thought of a plausible explanation for the condition of Heron, prone on the floor, soused with black paint and sprinkled with broken glass.

'What's happened, miss?'

'Mr. Heron was standing on the table, reaching for a pot of paint on the top shelf, when he slipped, and the pot fell down on top of him.'

'H'mm. Glass jar; nasty. Bert, go and get a couple of Doctors up here quick.'

She noticed one or two thin lines of red oozing into the shiny black expanse of Heron's forehead. It was difficult not to imagine that she had killed him. She went down on her knees and began dabbing at his face with her damp and inadequate handkerchief.

'Allow me, miss.' The Craftsman had found a cloth and started cleaning Heron's face properly. In a few moments a couple of Doctors arrived with a stretcher. Cathis repeated her story and left unobtrusively.

Heron recovered consciousness in the hospital ten minutes later, and left it after half an hour with a bandage round his head and a couple of stitches. He had sustained no serious injury. The next evening Malcom came to see him and they had a long and confidential talk.

Christofer began his course of elementary instruction on the computer. He found the mental efforts involved, particularly in mathematical analysis, stimulating and congenial. Before long he knew much more about it than Settle did. The latter, who was interested in the computer chiefly as a source of information, recognised his friend's aptitude and told him the number that would open the glass screen, having first made him promise to keep it strictly secret.

Meanwhile they found more poltergeist-like traces – objects stolen, footprints, distant noises. But they could catch no glimpse of the author of these disturbances.

On the second evening of his course, Christofer closed the screen at about half past ten and said goodbye to Settle. The night was cool, cloudy and mild. After a day spent in entirely sedentary pursuits, first in his office and then at the computer, Christofer was conscious of an unusual excess of physical energy; and also of a mental exhilaration, after an evening of intensely interesting instruction. He walked home by the most circuitous route he could think of and arrived soon after eleven, alert and wakeful.

In bed, he tried feeling for his wife's hand. It was available, though unresponsive. He made one or two deliberate overtures, and, meeting only an entirely blank indifference – which was, however, a vast improvement on the active discouragement with which she had been accustomed to meet his attentions since the earliest days of their marriage – proceeded to execute his purpose. Being, however, unlike Heron, a most inexperienced amorist, and severely handicapped by his wife's corpse-like frigidity, he had only a very limited success. At the end of it, withdrawing gloomily to his own side of the bed, he fell slowly asleep. In the early hours of the next morning he had a dream, which he forgot as soon as he got out of bed. But the end of it returned to him vividly later that day.

He was looking at the pictures on the wall of Cathis's bedroom: the birds, the flowers, the ladies. He noticed one of them particularly. A girl, with long hair, a disproportionately – as in the others – large head, a huge blue cap and a brown skirt, sat on a box. He put his hand up to this picture, feeling a desire to touch it. It came away easily in his hand and now filled his whole range of vision. The girl still smiled at him; he now recognised her as his wife. Suddenly, to his horror, he seemed to see an image of Heron's face superimposed on top of her. Heron was still smoking his pipe. He was wearing spectacles, a blue cap, and had a tense, rapacious expression on his face. To his surprise Christofer recognised Heron's cap as the one his wife was wearing, and then the two images, for a moment, seemed to merge into one that contained them both simultaneously. But before it faded away he thought: that pipe is her feet. But why should smoke be coming from the top of her feet? The baffling image disappeared. He looked round. A skeleton sat in the tree opposite and raised the gun it had been holding.

That afternoon a messenger came up to level 1 and delivered a package addressed to Cathis, who was sitting alone in her room, sewing industriously. Surprised, she examined the package, a canvas-wrapped bundle securely bound with string. A folded note accompanied it. It read, simply, 'Sorry. Heron.'

She untied the string and unwrapped the bundle. It proved to contain a pair of shoes. Obviously Heron had made them; Cathis knew that, in addition to his other skills, he sometimes diverted himself with cobbler's work. She vaguely recalled his having made tracings of her feet a year or two ago. Nearly all Habitation boots and shoes were made by the Craftsmen. These shoes seemed to her the most beautiful she had ever seen. The uppers were of soft, reddish-brown hide, without laces, and had a delicate, fretted, dog's-tooth pattern along both sides and round the heel. The sole was of solid, double-layered leather, stitched with remarkable evenness in a thick, tough-looking, light-coloured thread. It rose in a graceful ogee to the heel, a remarkably high heel, a good two and a half inches, made of some dark, polished wood, tipped with a neat leather pad. The two shoes were exactly the same size and, save for being mirror-images of each other, almost identical. In a community where the clumsy, durable men's boots and rather ramshackle women's sandals and slippers were, apart from wooden clogs, the rule, these shoes were a pair to be proud of.

There was a knock on her door. 'Come in,' she said. Settle came in. Christofer hovered irresolutely outside.

'Good afternoon, Cathis,' said Settle. 'I – hello, what's that you've got there?'

'Pair of shoes.'

'How nice.'

Christofer came into the room, tentatively, as Cathis sat on a chair, slipped her sandals off, and eased the shoes on carefully. They fitted her.

'Wherever did you get them from?' asked Settle.

'Never you mind.' Cathis's tone was not rude. As a matter of fact she was so pleased with them, irrespective of her present feelings towards Heron, that the presence of Settle and Christofer uninvited in her bedroom, did not irk her; they gratified a wish to show off her new possessions. She looked at her elegantly shod feet with pride.

But Christofer was paying her little attention. His dream had come back to him; he was wondering if he was awake or still asleep. He had noticed one of the pictures on the bedroom wall.

Cathis stood up. As her weight came on her heels she staggered slightly and they heard something like a faint, muffled click. It was too slight and momentary a sound to demand any attention.

'That's odd,' she said, 'the heels seem to have pressed in a bit.' But the shoes now supported her quite firmly. She walked a few steps.

Christofer stood, rapt, gazing at the picture. He could not understand how he seemed to be seeing two things at once. There was Heron, scowling, unkempt, bespectacled as he had occasionally seen him, teeth clenched on a smoking pipe – but there, too, was a little, immature-looking girl, no longer recognisable either as Cathis or Salla, seated on some kind of box, and smoke was coming out of her feet. Her legs were his pipe. An inarticulate terror possessed him.

He turned. They were looking at him, Settle with amused surprise, Cathis with annoyance. 'What's wrong with you?' she asked.

He opened his mouth to answer but was able to produce nothing more than a croak. His eyes were irresistably drawn down to her feet. As he had expected, there were wisps of smoke about them. For an infinity of time he fought to bring his vocal organs under control.

'Take them off,' he gasped. 'Take your shoes off. *Quick.*'

'What for?'

'Look, Cathis,' Settle had looked down. 'Where's that smoke coming from?'

'What are you all babbling about?'

'I don't know what it is,' articulated Christofer carefully, 'But I feel sure you should take those shoes off immediately. There's something wrong with them'

'Yes, Cathy, take the things off.'

'Oh,' said Cathis, who had now looked at them for the first time. She sat on the bed and began wrenching at the left shoe. It fitted closely, however, and refused, with the natural recalcitrance of all inanimate objects in nervous, hurried hands, to come off. There was an agonising wait.

'Let me give you a hand,' said Christofer.

'No, it's off. Now for the other –'

There was a bang and a puff of smoke. The light-globe shattered. Cathis screamed and dropped the shoe. Tinkling fragments of glass fell round them. Her hand began to bleed. Christofer had the sensation of drowning in some thick liquid like paint or glue. The shoe was stained black; its heel was rent open.

Simultaneously it came to the three of them that the other shoe had still to be removed. The realisation was too late. Cathis began to tug. A second later there was another, quieter detonation, and a long red gash suddenly opened itself out of her bare calf; she collapsed in a faint.

116

Christofer stumbled out of the room. Settle divined that he had decided to call a Doctor.

Settle approached his daughter. He put his hand on the shoe, intending to remove it in order to examine her foot. Blood was seeping out of it. He pulled the shoe carefully off. The sight of the underside of her heel made him turn his head away, sick. The long wound in her calf was bleeding profusely as well. The shin-bone seemed to have lost its rigidity; the foot was bent inwards at a heart-rending angle, like the foot of a broken doll or dummy. There was a widening crimson stain on the bed-spread. He took out his handkerchief and tried to bind the shin; then, more sensibly, took the pillow-case from the pillow, tore it up, and applied an unskilled tourniquet below the knee.

'Heron?'

'Must have been him. She said the shoes were from him.'

'You mean he deliberately caused that to happen to her?'

'Yes. I don't know how.'

'You mean to tell me – you can sit here calmly discussing this when you know the name of the maniac who did it?'

'What else do you want me to do, Christofer?'

'*What else?* What – well, never mind that for the moment. How is she? That's what I was going to ask. Has she come round?'

'Yes. She was unconscious for two days and nights after the amputation. Doctor Lonard took her foot off as soon as they got her to the hospital; he saw it was the only thing – oh, I'm sorry, I've told you this before, haven't I? – I'm feeling so confused nowadays. Well, we were afraid she wouldn't recover from the anaesthetic at all, but she pulled through this morning. I was with her for a quarter of an hour. The odds are now that she'll survive, unless she gets gangrene, in which case she's done for.'

'But she won't get her foot back, will she? Crippled for life. . .'

'No, she won't. But her hand's all right, at least.'

'Habitation . . . but, Settle, I don't understand about –'

'Well, you wouldn't have heard . . . It throws an interesting light on the workings of our friend Heron's mind. The Doctors know nothing of guns and bullets – I had a hard time explaining

117

to them as much as I thought right for them to know – but – anyway, from what they told me, I was able to deduce ... that each shoe had a cartridge, with a bullet in, fixed upright in the heel...'

'Yes?'

'The bang, in both cases, was the bullet going off. The first one just wounded her hand because she had got the shoe off and was holding it ... But the second one fired, as it was no doubt meant to, right up into her leg, along it, inside it.'

'But that's...'

'The result – is that the bottom two-thirds of her shin-bone and her ankle were smashed into about fifty pieces. Luckily the bullet didn't reach her knee; it smashed out of the back of her calf ... the Doctors had to cut her leg off, just below the knee. She'll have a wooden leg when she gets better.'

'Oh, *God*.'

Silence filled the room, apart from the crackling of Settle's pipe and the crying of birds outside. This conversation was taking place in Christofer's home. Salla was listening, sitting motionless at the table, her hair falling over her face. Settle's face was grey and aged-looking. His moustache gave the impression of drooping. Christofer was unshaven, with a restless, excited air; his eyes had a feverish glint.

'So, I suppose,' he said, 'she was lucky not to have both her whole legs completely shattered.'

'Quite lucky.'

'But still – why on earth would anyone want to do a thing like that? And how could it be done, anyway?'

'Your first question is – well, as I said, I went to see her this morning. I was with her for most of yesterday and the day before, but she wasn't conscious then. I didn't say much; she did all the talking. She was in pain, but calm and lucid. She gave me some information about her relationship with Heron – and about her earlier one with you, Mrs Clerk.'

Salla gave no sign of having heard.

'What happened, among other things, was that Heron attempted forcibly to take her virginity – to rape her, in other words.'

'*What?*'

'But she succeeded in repulsing him physically. She said she threw a jar of paint at his forehead and knocked him out. And she kneed him in the groin.'

Salla sniggered. 'Heron wouldn't enjoy that,' she said.

'No. It must have been a deeply humiliating experience for him.'

There was another long pause.

'I feel rather out of my depth,' said Christofer weakly. 'You mean – while all this was going on no one else knew? Didn't she say a word? When did it happen?'

'Six days ago. Now – as regards your other question: I can't say how it was done. We all know that our artistic friend is highly competent at mastering any kind of technical procedure. Also, it is virtually certain that either he or Malcom or both are, for some unspecified reason, engaged in clandestine activities in the Library. I know at least one box of ammunition was missing the other day. I've cached all the rest of the stuff in the computer annexe, where I'm sure they can't get at it, but I can't be there all the time.'

'So he may have found materials to make a couple of explosive devices?'

'Yes ... there's also the question of how the things were timed.'

'I remember – that's right – hearing a click, though I disregarded it at the time ... One just can't imagine what those two may have stumbled across in the Library. I wish I could stop them, but there's nothing I can do without letting the Priests and the Clerks know about the computer. I hope they'll come out into the open and tell me what they're up to. Why should I mind, whatever it is? It might be worthwhile seeing what we could find out about explosive substances in the computer's reference system.'

Outside the clouds were gathering; it had become dark in the room. Salla got up and went out. Christofer went to switch the light on.

'I can't believe this is happening,' he said presently. 'Us ... sitting here and discussing it so calmly. Settle, you don't seem to feel *anything!* This man has attempted to rape your daughter, and made an attack of – of – unthinkable, appalling malice, spite, violence. He's left her maimed for life ... You *are* sure of this?'

'Yes, I am.'

'And – and you don't feel anger?'

'Anger? no. I wish him to be punished for his crimes, but this shall not be done by me. That would be an act of personal revenge. And I've told you why we can't appeal to the Clerks or the Priests.'

'So – what are you going to do?'

'I shall refuse to meet him until he shows signs of repentance, which looks extremely unlikely, I admit.'

'*Repentance?* So in fact you're going to do nothing at all?'

'Christofer, you aren't taking a balanced view of this business. Don't let your feelings for Cathis, whatever they are, distort your judgement. Her behaviour has not been perfect. She's been reckless, wilful, and blind. She had abandoned all conception of obedience to authority and decent behaviour.'

'Yes, but –'

'In effect, she made herself extremely vulnerable to people like Heron. That's what our rules are for, to protect the weak. And, in addition, you mustn't let yourself be blinded to Heron's good qualities.'

'He hasn't any.'

'On the contrary: he is a gifted and creative artist, the best in the Habitation. He has a great deal of generosity and an enormous amount of physical courage. He climbed the outer wall, remember, at every possible risk and small possible gain to himself.'

'All the same –'

'Christofer, what are you thinking of doing? If it seems a good idea to you to kill him, put that idea out of your head. He is a human being, with good and bad qualities like the rest of us.'

'I wasn't thinking of murdering him. But he ought to be punished. He *must* be punished. He must be made to regret his crimes. There is no possible hope of repentance until he does.'

'What are you going to do, then?'

'I don't know. I haven't had time to think it out.'

After a few more silent minutes Settle rose. 'D'you fancy

coming back for another go at the computer?' he asked. 'Take your mind off things.'

Christofer assented. On the way back to the Sphere Settle began to speak.

'Duelling would be a good way but as you'd agree, it's not likely to be successful. Neither of us could defeat him in any form of combat. Unless – yes, that's a thought –'

'What?'

'It's true that Heron can do most things, but there's one thing he can't, at least not very well. He can't handle a bow; you've seen him, haven't you?'

Christofer was not deceived by the apparent light-heartedness of Settle's subsequent fantasies, but, not being very imaginative himself, he listened to them with interest.

III. ii. CHAPTER OF ACCIDENTS

Effacing himself as nearly as possible, Settle fingered his torch and waited for the quiet footsteps to approach the chamber. It was quite dark, but for a faint, strengthening gleam of light, which swung up and down irregularly from one of the mouths of the four passages. Settle recognised the slow, heavy tread: it was Malcom's. He controlled his breathing as much as he could and silently rehearsed the words he intended to say. Outside, in the forgotten region where the sun shone and the winds blew – Settle had been standing by himself in that same place for more than an hour and a half, pondering a distressful interview with Cathis – it was late morning, the day after his visit to Christofer's home.

The intermittent light grew, and Malcom, a dark shadow behind his torch, entered. Settle switched his own torch on, into Malcom's face, and had a brief vision of it, flat and white and strained, before Malcom's torch came up dazzlingly into his own eyes. For a moment the two men's torches attacked in opposite directions like weapons. Then Settle spoke:

'Malcom.'

'Settle.'

'May I ask what you are doing here?'

'You may.' Politely Malcom turned his beam down from Settle's face to the ground, and approached him.

'Why have you been entering the Library without my consent? Why have you been removing articles from it? Where have you taken them?' The firmness of Settle's tone surprised them both.

'I'll tell you if you first tell me something. You remember Cathis found a key, which you kept safe? Have you still got it? Have you kept it safe?'

'Yes – I think so.'

'Where is it?'

'Just a minute – you haven't given me any justification for

122

your conduct yet. Why are you stealing from me? The Library is the Librarian's property.'

'I haven't stolen anything. All the things you've missed are still here. Where's the key?'

'Malcom, I could have you arrested and jailed. I want some justification from you, and if I don't get it I'll go to the Clerks and have you proscribed.'

'Very well. Here is my justification.' Malcom brought his torch up to Settle's face; Settle started back; Malcom immediately drove his fist into his stomach. As Settle doubled up, coughing, Malcom quickly snatched up a femur from the floor and brought it down hard on Settle's head. It broke in his hand and Settle tumbled to the floor, unconscious. Malcom picked up Settle's torch, switched it off and pocketed it. Then he dragged Settle out of the Library into his apartments and locked the door on the inside.

When Settle recovered, fifteen minutes later, he was aware only of an agonising, throbbing pain in his skull. Slowly he began to recognise other, different pains in his body: a great, constricting ache over his diaphragm that made breathing painful and difficult; a curious, disagreeable pull on his upper lip; an itching tightness at his wrists and ankles; two hard objects digging upwards into his armpits; numb bruises at his right elbow and shoulder; and a sensation of tiredness and weakness at his knees. Cautiously he opened his eyes, and felt an increased stabbing into the top of his head. He found himself in his own sitting-room, standing upright, on some kind of support. The room was in some disorder. He realised that he was leaning against the closed door, his hands bound behind him, his ankles secured together too, and his armpits supported by two invisible pegs or spikes driven into the door. He saw Malcom sitting in an armchair with a pistol in his hand. He could not move his head, because something was pulling his moustache upwards and outwards.

He stared at Malcom in mute, crucified interrogation.

'Awake, I see.' Malcom came up to him, reached under his arms and removed the two spikes, so that his weight now came on his sagging legs. He felt a horrible pull on his upper lip as his moustache grew tauter, and hastily stood upright.

'The reason, Settle, for all this, is that I wish to obtain the key that was found in the Library, in order to gain access to the upper levels. I have good reason to believe that this key will open the door at the top of the ramp. Where is it?'

Settle said nothing.

'I have given your apartments a quick search, but you have probably put it away in some safe place and I don't want to waste any more time looking for it.'

Settle continued to regard the man who stood below him: the light, receding hair, the expanse of grey sinciput, the thick, heavy nose, the determined eyes, the solid, bulky shape.

'If you do not tell me, Settle, I shall torment you until I receive a satisfactory answer. If the key is with your stores in the computer room, I will need to know the combination that opens the glass screen; and I will go and check it before releasing you. If it is not to be found on this level at all, you will have to tell me where it is and wait for me to fetch it.' He paused again.

Settle remained dumb.

'Very well. You have observed that your moustache is fixed. You cannot see, but it is fastened to the door on either side with two large, round-headed tacks. I have hammered them in firmly and they will not be pulled out or allow your moustache to escape. The thing you are standing on is a jack from the Electricians' workshop. It's used for raising and lowering heavy objects. Thus, by pressing this lever down with my foot – so – I can raise you half an inch; and by pressing the other, so, I can lower you the same distance. The ends of your moustache, however, remain fixed. You understand? I shall lower you until you give me a satisfactory answer, or until some other means becomes necessary.'

Settle gazed at him. 'I've forgotten where it is,' he said.

'I don't believe you.'

He depressed the lever. There was a muffled click and Settle sank. He depressed it again, and again, and again, and again. Settle was now standing erect, his head back, like a soldier on parade. His moustache was tight but not yet unendurably so. He now found it difficult to look down on Malcom. He noticed some cobwebs, and a small crack in the plaster, in the cornice of the wall opposite. His head still hurt him frightfully.

124

'I tell you I don't know where it is. I've forgotten.'

Another click came from beneath his feet and his heels left their support. There were more clicks.

'Try to remember, Settle. How are you feeling now?'

Settle stood desperately on tip-toe, his neck bent at an angle apparently approaching ninety degrees. Sweat glistened on his face. His moustache was two strong grey ropes attached to his upper lip. He now felt a strong inclination to reveal the whereabouts of the key to Malcom, but he had been telling the truth: he really could not remember having done anything in particular with it. He remembered Cathis's finding it and entrusting it to him, and his own undertaking to look after it, but nothing after that; and the various physical anguishes which were now afflicting him were not conducive to any methodical exploration of memory.

'I *can't* remember. I'm trying. Please – stop. If you stop I may be able to.'

'You're lying.'

And now Settle seemed to experience pain for the first time in his life. His exhausted toes and ankles were on fire with effort; his neck was almost snapping. He heard another click and his lower lip was pulled upwards. It occurred to him that one more depression of the lever would be sufficient to rip his whole face off; lower lip, nose, eyes, cheeks, forehead, would be left dangling like a rubber mask, while he, collapsing, presented a soft, blank, pink surface for Malcom's inspection. He could see a spider floating six inches above him, suspended from the ceiling.

'Ah, stop, for God's sake Malcom stop, oh, stop.'

There was another click and Settle became incapable of coherent thought. His tense, lean body twitched convulsively. A low, gargling, choking noise came from him. Malcom could see little of his features now, except for the jutting chin and the enormous, pink, wet protuberance of the underside of the lower lip, higher than the nose. Settle could no longer remember what he had to do to obtain relief. He knew that the key was important somehow; he could remember where it was; but he could not connect these two facts. They danced around his mind like elusive, brightly-coloured balloons. He seemed to hear a tearing noise – the muscles in his lip were rupturing. If he had had his eyes open he would have noticed that, with slight pinging sounds, the outermost hairs in his moustache – the ones under the most strain – were either breaking or coming out at the roots. Malcom observed this.

'It looks as if your moustache is coming out at last, Settle. Well, I never liked it. Have you anything to tell me?'

Settle was now unable to speak at all. He made no answer but a low gargle.

'You deserve to be congratulated for your courage, Settle.'

Malcom pressed the lever again. With an unpleasant ripping sound the two whiskers tore off and hung dangling. In a faint, Settle subsided slowly against the door. Quickly a new moustache grew; a red, irregular moustache that dripped out of the raw patches of torn flesh, into his mouth and down his chin. Malcom filled a glass with water and poured some of it into his mouth and the rest over his face. Settle choked, vomited a little, and revived.

'I have plenty more jokes better than that one, Settle.' Malcom returned to his seat and picked up the pistol. 'Don't try to get away or I'll shoot you in the leg. Do you want to go on with this?'

Settle could feel no pain in his lip, only a strange swollen numbness. His other physical discomforts remained considerable. However his mind was now clear. 'It's in my pocket,' he whispered tiredly.

'What's that?'

'In my left trouser pocket. I didn't get round to putting it away and I've been carrying it around ever since.'

Malcom sighed. 'I see. In fact I suppose I should have expected it. You incompetent fool.' He came across and extracted the glittering key from Settle's pocket. 'Thank you.'

'Why do you want the key?'

'So I can explore the upper levels and gain access to whatever weapons there are there. I want to put an end to this messing around.' He looked down at Settle thoughtfully. 'You know, I really do prefer you without that moustache. You'll have a nasty scar on your lip, but you'll look much more like a real person and not like something out of a nightmare.' He put his hand up to one of the hanging ends and fingered it absently, much as Settle had been in the habit of doing.

Settle shifted to look up at him.

Malcom paused, surprised. He frowned, and examined the dangling hair closely, parting the individual strands.

Settle made an inarticulate noise in his throat.

Malcom turned and looked down at him, shocked and disbelieving. On Settle's face was an expression he had never seen before: a frightened, abject, surrendering imploringness.

'Settle. This – this *moustache* – it's got wire in.'

Settle nodded.

'Is that it? Is that what it's been all this time?'

'Yes,' Settle whispered.

'You have been parading your – your – your moustache as if it held itself up – and all this time it's been nothing but a fake?'

'I'm sorry. I can't say anything else.'

'*You're* sorry? You're *sorry?* Is that all?'

'What else is there?'

'You – you – why, I don't–' Malcom was dark red. Rage gleamed in his eyes. 'You *cheat!* All these years, all this time – you *fraud!* You fraud! You're not true at all!'

'Oh, God.'

'Is that all you can say?' His voice had risen, for the first time in Settle's acquaintance with him, to an uncontrolled scream. 'Do you realise what this means, you liar?'

'What does it mean?'

'Deception; hypocrisy; lies – Habitation! Settle, I'm going to –' He picked up the pistol from the table and fired at Settle's head, but his hands were shaking so much that he succeeded only in shooting off the upper half of Settle's right ear. Instantly the amount of blood on Settle's face – his lip had been bleeding steadily all this while – seemed trebled. The Habitation Librarian, a sprawled, ridiculous scarecrow, long arms and legs tied together as if intended to be stuck on a pole in the middle of a field, winced slightly but made no other movement. 'Go on,' it said, bubbling through the blood in its mouth.

Malcom raised the gun, steadied his hands, and took careful aim. 'You deserve to die,' he said.

'Perhaps.'

A moment later Malcom lowered his weapon. 'No. I won't kill you now, you nauseating infant. Or perhaps – no, I won't. Some other time, fairly soon.'

'Thanks.'

'Shut up, you fraud.' He strode back to Settle and kicked him on the knee-cap. Settle gasped in pain. 'I'll put you out now.'

'Put me out...'

'Yes. I found some stuff in the Library.' He studied the instructions on the label of a large brown bottle, and half filled a small syringe. After wrenching Settle's arm from behind and pushing up the sleeve, he emptied the anaesthetic into an artery. Quickly Settle slumped into oblivion. Malcom put the equipment back in his jacket pocket, wrenched the door inwards without regard for the untidy, gory heap it swept out of the way, and walked out. He allowed the front door to close and lock behind him. On his way out he remembered that he had forgotten to get the computer-code from Settle, and that it was now too late to think of doing so. He did not let the omission vex him. He opened the upper-level door with the key; Heron joined him later.

At the end of the next day, tired but happy, Heron came down to level 2. He passed Settle's rooms; the door was not locked, but there was no sign of him. He entered the Craftsmen's workshop and passed through to his own room. Apart from a few black marks on the floor, there were no reminders of the fracas that had taken place there just over a week ago. He filled a pint mug with milk, drank it, spread a heel of a loaf with butter, chewed and swallowed it in a few mouthfuls, urinated into his wash-basin, washed his hands under the tap and was ready for bed. He threw off most of his clothes and turned out the light. Outside the sky was cold and clear; a bright new moon had appeared; its white rays fell through his window. He gazed heavenwards for a time, marvelling. Then he shivered, closed the curtains, got into bed quickly and fell asleep.

Christofer, who had been waiting in the outer workshop, now came in, as silently as Cathis had done on another occasion. He waited for half an hour, listening to Heron's breathing. After this he switched on a torch and shone it tentatively towards Heron's sleeping face. Heron, a sound sleeper, was not disturbed, even when the beam fell full on his closed eyelids. Christofer took a bottle of chloroform from his pocket (his position as Forestry Clerk gave him access to supplies of this precious fluid, doled out in grudging quantities by the Clerks in charge of the stores). The Foresters occasionally used it for immobilising trapped animals. He poured some of it on to a very small pad and held this in front of Heron's nose. Heron's breathing slowed slightly. Christofer tried shaking him gently; then less gently. Heron slept peacefully on.

He knew before he had opened his eyes that his circumstances had altered drastically. He had an unusual sensation of coldness in the lower half of his body. He was neither lying nor standing. The first thing he saw when he opened his eyes was the moon. He was near to a large wall-window, much longer than that of his own room. The moon looked enormous. After staring at it, fascinated, for a few moments, he let his gaze wander over the dark-grey shadows and silvery glints that delineated his surroundings. Then he rigidified, horror-stricken, as several facts burst on him simultaneously. The room was the Craftsmen's workshop, he was at the far end of it among the pottery throwing-wheels and bins of clay, he was naked from the waist downwards, and he was bound fast to a large round flat surface. A man, a shadowy motionless figure in the moony mist, stood before him, holding a bow and arrow. A loud tick came from somewhere at regular intervals. These observations spun and wound in his mind like threads, round and round until they formed a thick rope, a choking noose of vivid imaginative conjecture. His eyes bulged and he tried to let out a scream, but found himself tightly gagged. He squirmed and writhed, with small, ineffectual twitches.

The outline of the man in front of him was familiar to him, and he was on the point of recognising it when it spoke.

'Do you hear me?' asked Christofer. 'Nod, if you do.'

Heron nodded convulsively.

'Heron, it has been made known to me that you were responsible for the attack on Cathis Librarian. I believe you were the maker of the shoes she received, and you had purposely made them to explode when she put them on. Do you deny this?'

Heron had become tense and watchful. He made no movement.

'Shake your head if you deny it – no, don't bother, because I won't believe you.'

Salla had entered at the far end of the room; she heard these words. She had been returning from a late evening with a new acquaintance of hers, a girl, aged seventeen. Coming past the Craftsmen's workshop in the dark, dimly-lit, deserted passageways, she had seen that its door was open and, a moment later, had heard her husband's voice, quick but in a tone of high-pitched, nervous resolution. She went in and listened, first in astonishment, then in horror.

'Cathis's father has told me he intends to take no revenge against you at all. I don't think he's forgiven you, but you've escaped scot-free as far as he and she are concerned. I saw her this morning and told her what I intended to do, and she tried to persuade me not to. But I just can't – I cannot accept that you should not be punished for your wicked, your abominable crimes. So what I shall do, in a couple of minutes' time, is to shoot an arrow through your genitals from a distance of twenty yards. You have seen me use a bow and you know I won't miss.'

At this point Salla slipped out of the room and walked away as quietly as she could, breaking into a wild run as soon as she believed herself out of earshot.

'This clock ticks loudly every ten seconds,' concluded Christofer. 'You may expect to feel the arrow in exactly two minutes from ... now.' The clock ticked.

Christofer had retreated to the unlit regions beyond the moonbeams. He flexed his arm-muscles and began to strap the leather sleeve on to his bow-arm. The clock ticked.

Heron was a pale figure in the moonlight, spreadeagled on the target. His upper half, clad in a jersey Christofer had thoughtfully put on him, was a light brown colour. His belly and legs were a pallid white. His penis was quite distinct, a pale spot beneath the black smudge of pubic hair. The target on which he was fixed consisted of the top of a stout old wooden table, circular in shape, about six feet in diameter. Heron's wrists and ankles were tied with wire-cored rope – another commodity to which Christofer's official position gave him access – and he had made the four lengths come together diagonally on the reverse side of the table-top. The clock ticked.

Christofer raised the bow, fitted an arrow, and bent it once or twice. He waited silently, while Heron's hair began to lift itself up – the clock ticked – until it stood on his head, more or less vertical. His moustache bristled. Christofer knew theoretically about the physiological effects of extreme terror, but he had never before encountered any of them in reality. More surprises were to follow.

The clock ticked. The blood had drained away entirely from Heron's working face, which could now be seen clearly, even in the dim light and at the distance at which Christofer was standing, as a shade of green, ghastly and unreal. The clock ticked again; four more times.

With a rush, a sudden erubescence, Heron's blood returned to the surface. It seemed likely that his muscles were making frenzied, unavailing efforts to snap the ropes and escape. Christofer saw the ropes gouge deeply inwards. His staring, bulging countenance was a darkening mauve. A tide of pink spread down from his waist to his feet. A great, pulsing vein stood out on his forehead, casting a black shadow. The clock ticked.

The blood-pressure was evidently reaching a dangerous level. Christofer was slightly alarmed: it was no part of his plan for Heron to die; he had anticipated great fear, but not decease through apoplexy. However, relief came. The vein writhed like a snake; the nostrils in the purple face flared blackly; and a brilliant crimson gush issued from them. Soon Heron's jersey was mostly a dark red, while scarlet trails ran down his stomach, into his groin, along his legs; and descended to the desk-top, on which the table rested, and thence to the floor, trickling loudly, in thick, dark drops.

The clock ticked. Christofer told himself that he would have to do a disagreeable amount of cleaning and wiping, but also that this outburst had very much lessened the danger of a stroke. He raised the bow again and examined the target. The target seemed to have altered. Perplexed, he peered forward, screwing up his eyes. The clock ticked again, and it became clear to him what was going on. A wave of amazement and loathing swept over him.

Heron's bloodstained organ had erected itself.

Later, when he had leisure to reflect on this phenomenon, there seemed to him to be two possible, but equally implausible causes to assign to it. Either, in spite of the blowing-off of the nasal safety-valve, his circulation had been sufficiently constricted by the bonds for its seething, near-apoplectic turmoil to cause a distension of the blood-vessels similar to those observed in hanged men; or, in spite of himself, his sexual nature had responded, in ghastly, involuntary fashion, to the perverted bizarrerie of the situation; or these two factors may have been combined. For the moment, however, Christofer was lost in shocked astonishment. Then he heard the clock tick, and remembered that he would have to shoot in ten seconds' time. There was no longer any question of Heron's penis being impaled since it was now upright, and Settle, as Christofer recalled, had cautioned him against shooting Heron in the stomach, but the pouch of the scrotum was just visible. Christofer never forgot the sight that confronted him as he raised the bow for the last time: the livid, jactitating, blood-bespattered body; the distorted, inhuman features with their bushes of pale golden-grey; and, at the centre, the immense, tall, unnaturally distended pillar of carmine and white.

Blood dripped, unabated, in the silence, for an infinite extension of time.

The clock ticked.

Heron's sanity, overloaded far beyond breaking-point, collapsed – as irreparably as Settle's toast castle had done – at the moment when Christofer aimed at a place six inches below his left testicle and shot accurately. The twang of the bow and the thud of the arriving arrow echoed in the room, as Heron fainted.

After quitting the Craftsmen's workshop Salla ran down two flights of stairs, out through the empty level 4, where only the night doctors still kept watch, and out into the open, moonlit Circle. She ran on for a quarter of a mile without thinking where she was going. After a few minutes, out of breath and with a pain in her side, she stopped and tried to think what to do. In all her experience of her husband she had never previously known him to make any firm, decisive action; she had despised him as an effete coward. But the awareness that he was now about to implement his talk of retribution filled her, not with admiration, but with a cold horror. She shrank from going back and trying to persuade her husband against castrating Heron, yet she desperately wished somehow to prevent this happening. She decided to go up to the Library and tell Settle what was afoot, not having heard about his afflictions of the day before. She ran and walked back to the Sphere, up to level 1, into Settle's apartments. His front door was not locked. She switched the light on, called 'Settle? Are you awake?' and looked into the sitting-room, the kitchen, the bathroom, and Cathis's room. She opened another door, wondering where Settle was, reached inside for the light-switch, failed to find it and entered. Then, simultaneously, she felt a light, momentary obstruction like a piece of string against her breast, and heard someone enter through the front door. She called out again, 'Settle?' and stepped back.

This saved her life: for the huge axe-blade, purloined from an outlying farm, which Malcom had placed above Settle's bed-room door, fell at that instant; and instead of passing through Salla's skull before slicing her head, neck, torso and pelvis into neat longitudinal halves, it merely, as it were, cut a slice off her. All she felt at the time was a rush of wind and a curious sensation of cold pressure travelling swiftly down her body. This, for a moment, she disregarded. Her head was turned so she did not see the axe-blade. The man who had entered was not Settle but Malcom. On seeing her he stopped, aghast.

There was a pause.

She began to speak incoherently about what she had seen.

He stared at her, hypnotised. 'Do you know what's happened to you?' he asked.

'No – what?' She moved towards him, but immediately fell to the floor because something was wrong with her right foot. Still feeling no pain, she followed Malcom's gaze towards her own body. Then she was gripped and locked in the embrace of a

133

horror so unnerving, so appalling, that movement became physically impossible.

Blood seemed to be spouting from her, all over her, like water from a colander. From head to foot, all, *all* was dyed a thick bright red. It looked as if she had been bathed in blood. She rolled in a pool of blood. She could feel the hot moisture on her skin; blood had soaked her clothes through and through. The taste of blood rose in her mouth; she felt that if she were to be sick she would vomit pure blood. The axe-blade, cutting the arrest of her movement in the poise of turning, shearing through her clothes effortlessly, had sliced a patch of flesh off her right shoulder (without damaging the bone); performed a smooth mastectomy on its way down her body; shaved another, larger area off her hip, this time including a portion of hip-bone; opened a great, long, shallow wound in her thigh, terminating a shattered kneecap; and finally truncated her right foot cleanly. Her toes, with a two-inch chunk of foot and sandal, still stood on Settle's bedroom carpet on the other side of the axe.

The blood's crimson rose before her eyes with a dancing roar as she felt the first intimations of physical agony. Its stifling halitus filled her nostrils. She wished to faint, but was not able to. She was aware of Malcom bending over her anxiously. Pain seared into her. Her throat unfroze and she began screaming.

Cathis awoke in the early morning.

She felt quite comfortable. A narrow sunbeam, filled with motes, fell through the room across her bed; the white hospital curtains glowed with the gold of early sunrise. The pain in her right foot was only the mildest of reminders; later it would rise to a dull grinding ache, suffused and shot with an itching, stabbing torture, centred on the amputated stump; but now it was quiescent. She had brought herself to control the urge to try to soothe or scratch this foot, for it was no longer there. It was the first time for a week that she had not been conscious of a greater or lesser degree of physical anguish, and she was unreflectively happy simply for that reason, enjoying the brief respite while it lasted. She had deliberately postponed, for an indefinite period, thinking about the events with which she had been involved.

She stretched out carefully in the warm bed. A couple of Doctors were talking outside her door. She listened inattentively to what they were saying. They were shocked and confused by the succession of injuries and maimings that had of late been emanating from the Library. After the mysterious mutilation of Cathis's leg, followed by battered, moustacheless Settle, had come the reporting, by Malcom, of injuries to an unnamed girl. Stretcher bearers had gone up to the Library at his summons – this had happened last night – and while they were getting over the shock of finding Salla lying unconscious, having apparently been attacked with a carving-knife by a madman, Malcom had disappeared. Since then all kinds of rumours had begun to spread.

Cathis vaguely realised that this conversation was of particular importance to her, but, preferring not to worry about anything at the moment, she turned over on her side and dozed off.

She was awakened, as usual, by the motherly nurse who entered with towels and hot water on a tray. After the exchange of morning greetings and the sponging, her breakfast arrived; with it came Christofer, tired-looking but determinedly bright and cheerful. Cathis had a weary awareness of the new day's demands and exactions descending on her. Her hand and foot had begun to hurt. With an effort she sat up and faced him.

With some diffidence he told her how he had frightened Heron last night. His tale aroused conflicting emotions within her; she said little, except to implore him to take no more revenge. Then, remembering the Doctors' conversation, she asked him to go out and see what might have happened to her father.

Five minutes after he had left, the nurse came in to straighten Cathis's bed. When this was done, she announced: 'There's another gentleman to see you, miss. Shall I send him in? He was very particular that he didn't want you disturbed.'

'I'm all right; he can come in.'

The man entered. He was evidently another hospital patient, for his face was heavily bandaged. What could be seen of it was grey and lined. He walked stiffly and slowly, stooping.

'Good morning, Cathis,' he muttered hoarsely, through a mouth almost completely covered by bandages. She now saw that there was a great deal of dried blood, or what resembled blood, on his black, shapeless, dusty clothes, especially in the regions of his chest and shoulders. But in spite of this strangeness there was something familiar about him.

'Good morning, sir. Sit down. What can I do for you?'

'Bless me, Cathis, what have I done now? What's wrong?'

'Nothing's wrong, except that I don't know your name.'

'Habitation,' he muttered, 'am I that unrecognisable? I suppose I must be.'

'Should I know you, sir?'

'Cathis, I'm your father, Settle Librarian.'

She had recognised him at that instant, even before he had identified himself. 'Daddy!'

He came up to her and kissed her. They embraced awkwardly, Cathis half in and half out of the bed. They both disturbed their wounds in doing so, setting up agonising throbbings and reactions; but neither of them paid attention to bodily pain.

Cathis was crying. There were tears in her father's eyes as well.

'Oh, Daddy! What's happened to you?'

'I'm sorry, Cathy. Forgive me. Everything that's gone wrong has been my fault ... I can't tell you how sorry I am.'

'But what's *happened*?'

He told her, relapsing partly into his former, accustomed flippancy of style for the recounting. She listened with growing horror. As far as the incident itself went, Settle appeared to be little more affected by it than if it had happened to someone else. 'After all, my dear,' he said, 'you must admit that there is something funny in the idea of a man being crucified by his moustache. I know it was me, and I know I'm your father, but you needn't close your eyes to the humorous element.'

'I don't see anything humorous in it at all,' she replied sadly. 'Didn't it hurt?'

'Well, yes, it did. But how are you now, Cathy?'

'Better.'

'Good.' he went on to describe how the truth about his moustache had been revealed to Malcom. For some moments the jocularity of his manner wobbled. 'It was a fake, Cathis. Since your mother died I've – I've assumed a pose. It lasted long enough – till yesterday. But it's gone now. This is me, your father, talking to you at last.'

'How old was I when she died?'

'A few hours.'

'Why don't you ever talk about her? Oh, forgive me, Daddy ... I suppose you loved her and thought I was responsible for her death.'

'That's a clever thing to have said, my dear, but it's quite wrong. As a matter of fact I couldn't stand her. When she died I felt only relief, and guilt for feeling relief.'

'What about me?'

'I just didn't know what to make of you, Cathy.' He took her hand. 'You cried such a lot – you were a visitor, a little alien. I felt I never had any idea what to feel about you. You were so difficult to control...'

'Oh.'

'I can see now how you must have regarded me, and I blame myself entirely.'

'Still,' she said, 'I behaved very wrongly.'

'If I'd done the right thing from the beginning – well, never mind, or at least I'll try not to mind. Oh dear – Cathy – my dear – please forgive me.'

'I forgive you, Daddy.'

'Thank you. You aren't the only one, but that's a start . . . thank you.'

'What do you mean?'

'Well, there's Malcom. He took the discovery of the truth very hard. But he's a criminal now. He'll have to be reported to the Clerks.'

'What do you think he means to do?'

'I'm not sure. I don't think he knew himself, until – wait. I know when it was – it was the moment when he saw through my faking – when he saw the wire in my moustache . . . Oh God, that sounds so silly, but really it was really, really bad. I've a strong suspicion – in fact I know. It's too late now to beg his pardon. That was the critical, the fatal moment. He hates me now.'

Cathis sank back again, stupefied. She said, faintly: 'What do you think he's going to do?'

'I'm not certain, and I become more worried every time I think about it. He has the key to the upper level and access to an unspecified number of weapons of possibly enormous power.'

Cathis closed her eyes.

'Are you tired?'

She nodded, wincing as a current of pain travelled up her leg.

'Well, goodbye then. I'm off to see the Senior Clerk. I'll come back and see you this evening. Goodbye.'

'Bye,' she answered faintly.

He kissed her forehead and went out. As the door closed behind him it occurred to Cathis that she had forgotten to tell him about what Christofer had told her.

Settle went off to say goodbye and give his thanks to the Doctors who had attended him. He did not meet Christofer, nor did any of them realise that he was still ignorant of the events which had taken place in his rooms on the previous night. He went up the stairs to the second level, where he sought and gained an audience of the Senior Clerk. The interview lasted an hour. The Clerk, whose first name, little heard, was Jerome, the effective ruler of the Habitation, was an intelligent man, but even so Settle had great difficulty in conveying the truth to him. A number of distorted rumours had already reached him, chiefly from the Doctor's secretary, of the drama unfolding in the upper levels. Settle had much to add to these reports. He took the Clerk on a short tour of the computer, entering it by the lower entrance in level 2, which was situated, concealed, at the south end of the Great Hall. The Clerk was much impressed. They climbed the ladder up to the trap-door – Settle with great stiffness – and debouched into the annex on the hidden side of the glass screen. Settle gave a short demonstration. They returned to level 2. The Clerk's scepticism was much weakened and Settle made several requests. These included an official pledge, from the President himself, that the computer and the Library should be assured of full protection against whatever form the Priests' reaction to these startling disclosures might take; pardon for himself and for the Scribaceous and Anagnostic Society for having concealed matters of grave import from the Clerks' notice; the proscription and arrest, as soon as possible, of Malcom Electrician, for disobedience to the Librarian's personal authority and malicious assaults upon the Librarian; and the establishment and mainten-ance of a small corps, in order to defend the Library and the Librarian against Malcom, and to capture him. After some discussion these were all granted. Times and dates were fixed. In return, however, the Clerk insisted on being informed of the computer-opening code. Concealing his misgivings, Settle told him and they went back to check it. Then the audience was at an end. Settle left him and ascended the flight of stairs to level 1. At this point he belatedly realised that he would run considerable risk in going alone and unarmed up to the level where Malcom was probably still homicidally at large. He turned back and decided to stay with Christofer until the bodyguard had been organised. He went back down, out of the Sphere, arrived at Christofer's home and knocked on the door. After a minute, no one having answered, he went in. He felt hungry; indeed, he was almost fainting with hunger. He had eaten one small meal at the hospital; apart from that, nothing at all since his last breakfast, two days ago, before he had been caught by Malcom. He found some cheese, and a loaf and butter, and fell on them voraciously.

'What are you doing here?'

Christofer stood in the doorway.

Settle apologised, realised that Christofer also had failed to recognise him, and introduced himself. Astonished, Christofer came into the room. He was very pale; he had just come straight from meeting his wife. He took a bottle from the cupboard and drank deeply from it.

Explanations followed. Settle listened impassively as Christofer told him about Salla. 'In the hospital,' he concluded, 'I came across her, lying in a room on a bed all by herself, and all wrapped up in bandages – apparently it's incredible that she's still alive at all, considering the amount of blood she's lost – and smiling like an imbecile. You can't imagine how horrified I was. I called for a Doctor, and a man came. I asked them what she was doing there. They told me. No one knew who she was. I told them my name and said she was my wife. They kept on asking me stupid questions. But eventually I got it out of them that her accident had been reported by Malcom –'

'Malcom?'

'Yes – late the night before. They let me speak to her – I tried to get her to say something back – but it was hopeless. She's lost her wits completely. The shock of the wounds, I suppose. Then I wandered off, I don't know where. Suddenly I found myself face to face with Heron. I put my hand on my gun. But he just said, 'Hello, Christofer.' He had an odd, vacant look on his face and he never looked at me – just went on twiddling his bouncing wheel on a string – he seemed preoccupied by that. I couldn't think what to say. I suppose he's planning some new trick to play on me...'

'Why should he?'

'Oh, of course – you don't know about that yet. That happened last night as well. I carried out one of your suggestions.'

'Say that again.'

'I did what you suggested – you remember, the last time we

140

were here. I thought then, and I think now, that we had to take revenge on him somehow, for what he did to poor Cathis.'

'What did you do?'

'Pretended I was going to – with a bow and arrow.'

'You did that? You *did?*'

'Everyone seems to find it very difficult to believe.'

'You – castrated him?'

'No – I decided that would be a bit too severe. I only pretended I was going to. But it must have been a most unpleasant two minutes for him, all the same; and it was pretty odd for me as well.'

Settle's head was bowed. 'What have you done to him?'

'Nothing. He's in perfect health. Afterwards I untied him, cleaned up all the blood and shit – he must have voided his bowels with panic – wiped him down, and put him back to bed.'

Settle's grey, bandaged, ravaged face was set like stone. 'I can only hope you're right. Otherwise I can see no end to the harm I have done.'

'But I can't see Heron forgiving this kind of insult.'

'No. He said nothing alluding to it? Nothing at all?'

'Nothing at all.'

'You said his eyes were vacant.'

'Yes; do you think –'

'Don't ask me what I think!' Settle groaned. 'I don't know! All I know is that I've wrecked everything!'

'What–?' Christofer was startled by this uncharacteristic outburst. He looked at Settle and was shocked at the expression on his face.

'I'm like a disease. I imagine Salla was caught in some kind of trap meant for me. That's why Malcom knew what was going on. I've betrayed Malcom. I've betrayed my daughter. What's happened to Heron and Salla is my fault as well. I've been false to myself. And if Malcom has decided that the best thing to do is to destroy the whole Habitation with whatever he finds up there, then I've betrayed everyone else – the entire human race. If we're all done for, it's me who's responsible.'

'Are you sure about that?'

'Malcom? No, I'm not sure, but it's quite possible. It would have been better, far better, for all of you, if I'd never been born.

'At any rate, you've not betrayed me. And I think you're much exaggerating your own guilt,' said Christofer presently, aware of his own ineffectiveness.

'I'm not exaggerating. I ruin – everything. I wither everything I put my hand on. My Librarianship has been a disaster . . . and there may be worse things to come.

'How do you know?'

'It's only a feeling . . . as if we're groping along a narrow, treacherous road . . . There's a fog of violence and evil all round us. There's no way back . . . and I'm sure we haven't got to the end of it yet.'

They went on with their meal.

'In the meantime,' Settle said presently, 'and that means today, I would be very grateful if you could come up there with me and get things sorted out. This afternoon?'

'Certainly.'

They finished their meal and went up to the Library. Settle was relieved to find that his apartments, though resembling an abbatoir, had not been plundered during his absence. They buckled down to the task of expunging Salla's gore.

Settle spent the next day in the computer annexe, with the glass screen securely down, trying to put together, in his mind, a programme for the systematic extraction of information from the computer. But his mind was abstracted and he made no headway. In the evening, with full ceremony, he presented a long statement to the judiciary counsel. Issuing from the Librarian, it was accepted *nem. con.* and Malcom was summoned to appear before the ecclesiastical court on charges of professional disobedience (an uncommon and severely punished crime), robbery, and malicious assault; or, in the case of his failing to appear, he was proscribed as an outlaw, to be arrested at sight by all Habitationers. Memorandums to this affect were sent out for publication by all heads of professions.

Later in the evening, Amiss Priest visited him on invitation, at Christofer's. He said that there was little active hostility among the Priests to the new discoveries as yet, probably

142

because they had small conception of their importance. He imparted also the encouraging news that the Chief Priests were considering, and were likely shortly to agree, on making over the recently-discovered projector for the Librarian's own use.

The next day, as planned, the corps of twelve men, mostly junior Clerks and Priests under Amiss's direction, presented themselves at the Library. Settle gave them his instructions.

A week later Settle was informed by the Clerk's secretary that it would be necessary to reopen the Library School. All pedagogical work in the Habitation was undertaken, *ex officio,* by the Librarian: in practice this amounted to instructing a handful of small boys, aged between eight and twelve, in the rudiments of reading, writing, and arithmetic, at intervals of about two years. The boys were without exception Clerks, Doctors, or, occasionally, Priests. Settle dusted the small schoolroom on level 1, and exhumed his supply of shabby, cracked slates, dry, blackened glass inkwells, grubby parchments, and worn quills. Shaking his head over them, he sent off a request for fresh supplies to the Craftsman. The next morning, as he was finishing his breakfast, the five scared children turned up at his front door.

The days dragged by. Settle's mornings were now often occupied with teaching. In the afternoons and early evenings, attended by a reassuring bodyguard, he continued with his exploration in the hope of finding some other, unknown means of access to the upper levels. Another detachment, headed by Amiss, explored in different directions. One or two more firearms turned up. The unknown areas of the Library diminished rapidly. One day the depressing possibility that the computer might contain a complete plan of the Library, and the other levels as well, occurred to Settle. He hastened to ascertain; and found that it did. After five minutes' manipulation of the console, there appeared on the screen before him, in bewildering detail, the original diagrams and architectural specifications for the Sphere. Presently he managed to isolate and enlarge the plans of the Library and the upper levels. The Library appeared a great deal smaller than the vast, gloomy labyrinth to which he had become accustomed.

In the hospital Cathis's recovery was slow and painful, while Salla, who was a strong, healthy girl, made good her blood-losses and somehow avoided gangrene. Her wounds healed. Unlike Cathis, she had had to undergo no further amputation, and it appeared likely that the remaining half of her foot would serve her moderately well for walking on. Her mental condition, however, was less promising. She spent long periods, seemingly unaware of the undoubted pain her wounds must be causing her, smiling or frowning into vacancy; at intervals, fully awake, she addressed inquiries to imaginary, absent visitors, with whom she sometimes carried out sustained conversations. She seldom seemed aware when Christofer or any other friend visited her. In lucid intervals, when an observer could suppose she knew where and who she was, her talk was disjointed, repetitive, foul, miserable, self-pitying, vengeful and blasphemous.

The spring was always a busy time for the Foresters, as for many others. What with this, and previous neglect of his work, Christofer was kept very busy. He had little time for visiting his wife, and none for Settle. His fear of reprisals from Heron slowly diminished as the latter continued to pay no unusual attention to him. But Christofer continued to carry a gun at all times.

In fact Heron bore Christofer no animus at all, for he retained no memory of the intense psychological torment to which he had been subjected. On the morning after it he had awoken late from his drugged sleep with a headache, a nose full of dried blood, a puzzling collection of weals at wrists and ankles, and the consciousness of having escaped from a most horrible nightmare. However, in spite of this subconscious censorship, the experience had left a deep and irremovable impression on him.

All this, while Malcom pursued his inscrutable, incalculable policy in the hidden, unattainable reaches of the upper levels: there was a feeling of enigma, a veiled fear, a source of continual, increasing apprehensiveness, like a black thundercloud descending slowly from a mountain-top.

Settle had tried leaving notes and messages for him; they were never touched. He posted his men, day and night, in strategic positions; they went in threes in regular patrols as often and quietly as possible, down the main alleys and tunnels. The skeletons had all been removed. He had examined the drawings of the Sphere, and incidentally absorbed a great deal of interesting information about the structure of the Habitation, but without finding any practicable way of getting up to level 0 without Malcom's knowledge. The staircase and lifts, it seemed, had originally climbed from the bottom to the very top of the Sphere. There were two more levels above level 0, though 1 was not very large and 2 amounted only to a single room, in which was the entrance to the central column. This column, he gathered vaguely, was more than twenty miles tall. Its functions were to provide a link between the Sphere and the solar power-station at the top, and to aid the peripheral condensors in collecting moisture from the atmosphere. Settle, in common with everyone else, knew vaguely what electricity was and what it did, but it had never occurred to him to wonder about the source of this mysterious power. The station was a huge reflecting saucer, perpetually tilting and sliding in a heliotropic oscillation, supported and positioned by twenty-four Kernevel-Hitchcock anabatic/inertial AV2 gravitors; at least, so the plans said. He wondered if the red, fixed star had anything to do with this power-supply. The power was sent down the column in the form of an infra-red beam . . .

But there seemed no way of penetrating upwards. There had originally been only the central staircase and lifts, with things called escalators – Settle frowned – connecting the levels at various points. But it seemed that the escalators had all been torn down immediately after the insurrection; there was no sign of what had happened to the Library escalator; all that remained in its place was the ramp. Settle went to have a look at the central staircase in the Library foyer. Above it, the ceiling was slightly lower than elsewhere but smoothly and indistinguishably homogenous. Someone had evidently made a careful job of concealing the existence of the upper levels. He had no equipment for cutting metal plates and planks. Other possible entrances, such as might be afforded by air-vents, drains and sewage-pipes, power-cable tunnels, and the like, he had speedily rejected as impracticable: small, confined, and inaccessible.

As the days went by his peace of mind became less and less. He was a victim of anxieties, frustrations, illogical and contradictory fears. He had an intense dread of seeing Malcom again, and an intense longing for the period of inaction to be ended. He wished to explore the computer's resources more thoroughly, but was unable to adhere to a coherent plan for doing so. He was hopelessly aware of the impossibility of effectively cordoning so large a maze as the Library. The morale of his men lowered daily. They made no complaints to him, but he soon saw that they regarded the whole affair as an incomprehensible waste of time, and himself as a lunatic. His ear vexed him continually and he could not restrain himself from rubbing at the swollen lip beneath its bandages. He slept fitfully, and was troubled by indigestion. But beneath all the shambles and the superficial confusions, the frustrations, the worries and the loneliness, lay the unceasing consciousness of his own guilt, intransigent, huge and ominous as a massive geological fault.

Ten days after the establishment of the Library guard, the youngest of its members, a boy of eighteen called Michal Clerk, was found in the ramp-room, lying on the floor, dead, with a small black hole in the back of his neck and a large red one in this throat. The murderer, however, was not Malcom as was instantly assumed by all and added to his catalogue of crimes, but Heron, who had been visiting Malcom secretly since the time of his proscription. That day, having slipped easily past the negligent guards as usual, he threaded the Library, ascended the ramp carefully, and tapped on the door, which Malcom promptly opened. Heron entered level 0, drawing a new yo-yo from his pocket. He did not look directly at Malcom.

Malcom was pale and a little flabby after a week and a half of confinement, but he looked fairly cheerful. In this he contrasted sharply with Heron, who exuded an air of insecurity and tension. He consistently avoided Malcom's eye; his movements were clumsy; his nails were severely bitten; his eyes were sunken, heavily-shadowed and red-rimmed; the set of his mouth seemed to have loosened. He was more untidily dressed than usual. His forehead was a little higher than it had been and grey hairs had appeared among the dark blond ones. 'How are you getting on?' he asked when he was safely inside.

'It's been disappointing on the whole, but I've found one or two new things.'

Heron looked about him as he flicked the yo-yo. Level 0 was surprisingly light and fresh after the choking gloom of the Library. Coming up for the first time – this was his third visit – he had been surprised by the sight of thick green leaves, the pleasant smell of flowers and foliage, and the murmur of bees. There also seemed to be a great deal of light. Then he realised that as level 0 was situated near the summit of the Sphere its wall sloped inward much more than on lower levels, thus leaving, beneath its obliquity, an area too low for a man to stand comfortably. Long ago, in this area, extending the whole way round the level, soil had been laid and shrubs planted; and since that far-distant time it had become riotously overgrown. The rest of the level, that is to say the area around its centre, had originally housed the Habitation's administration. No administration of any kind had taken place during the Committee's last days and the level had been left in disorder. There was a huddle of the mobile, modular wall-partitions and doors, some stacks of sturdy plastic chairs, and a number of desks and tables. There were also more skeletons, but these Malcom had irreverently put to one side in a jumbled pile.

'Has Christofer's wife been here?'

Malcom made no answer to this question. Without showing any impatience he said, 'This is what I have found on this level.'

'This' was another small arsenal; three pistols, a submachine gun, a solitary cylinder of some kind of gas, a battery of foam and water fire-extinguishers; the most valuable item in the assortment was a cardboard box containing half-a-dozen hand-grenades.

Heron glanced at this pile and then sauntered off towards the centre of the level. Here, where the main entrances and exits had been, there was a large square hole in the floor. Its sides were plated and smooth; only in one or two places the end of the sawn-off concrete girder, or a tangle of wires, protruded. It was about two and a half feet deep. At the bottom was a lattice of smaller, rusty girders whose evident purpose was to bear the ceiling of the level below. Above, there was a similar square hole in the smooth ceiling; a rope dangled from it.

There were no skeletons in level 1, but Malcom had found plenty of weapons. There were two small, mounted cannons with gleaming black two-inch barrels three feet long; invisible from the outside, their tiny muzzles poked out through artfully-contrived embrasures in the glass wall. These had been designed specifically to command the two-mile range of the Habitation's Circle, but had never been used in earnest. Their shells were minute, twinkling, pointed hollow half-kilo cylinders that could be held comfortably in the palm of the hand; there was a generous supply of explosive for them, sachets of fissionable gelatinoids contained in three reinforced-plastic containers. There was a metal crate containing six finned rockets, and a long tube angled on a tripod which was their launcher: a very much more destructive weapon than the cannons, but not adapted for use from inside an enclosed space. There were a few small cardboard boxes full of pistol and rifle ammunition, more small-arms, and five rifles, showing signs of considerable use, in a rack on one side. There were three greasy submachine-guns, and clips of ammunition for them, which Malcom had promptly taken charge of, and cans and drums of oil, of different sizes and sorts. Heron was especially pleased with the powerful telescope, once he had mastered its working. He found that from the height of this level the distant mountain-tops were visible above the lowest parts of the outer wall. Malcom had already entered the thick-walled radio and television office. The Habitation had been installed with the most up-to-date tele-communicatory equipment, now unused for centuries and still in perfect condition. He ran his hand tentatively over the banks of dials and switches, and his grey reflection looked out at him from the blank television screens. In one corner there was a record-player and a pile of records. He looked at their coloured sleeves curiously and read the bewildering words. There was a clock, still going, apparently quite correct. There was an audiovisual

148

three-dimensional reproductor and recorder, with several shelves of cassettes. It had never occurred to him to connect the book-cassettes in the Library with a means of producing sounds, let alone solid-looking shapes, and so he passed this by. There was nothing that seemed to resemble a projector. There were, of course, a bewildering number of spare parts. The most valuable find of all was a tea-chest full of books and leaflets, printed on paper in readable type, and not perished by age. They were instruction manuals and textbooks, and they dealt chiefly with the various kinds of equipment that the last defenders had left in the upper levels.

Some time later, Heron slid down the rope again to level 0, where Malcom was getting himself some lunch. He cut off some large hunks from a loaf which Heron had brought, and forked some slices of pickled beef on to a plate from a small barrel that stood among the rest of his supplies: crockery jars of water – untouched, for he had found a connected tap – a pile of cans and plastic cartons of preserves, left by the last occupants of the level and presumably still edible, which he was saving – a box of dry biscuits (bought) and a tub of apples (stolen). Heron had brought down a rifle and some cartridges, and was thoughtfully turning over the pages of a little book about rifles and shooting; Malcom was occupied likewise with a manual about the cannons.

After a time Malcom folded up his leaflet. He said, chewing: 'What are people saying?'

'Oh, all sorts of bees – I mean, all sorts of rumours are flying around.'

'What rumours?'

'Let's see. Some people think that you are responsible for all the things that have happened, others blame it on Settle ... the labourers and clods always think of the Library as somewhere where black magic is practised anyway, of course. I heard an apprentice potter tell another apprentice that Settle had to cut off his moustache and both his ears in some kind of magical rite. Have you seen Settle?'

'Do try and keep to the point, Heron. You know I've been up here all the time.'

'Settle won't be able to get his moustache back then. Mine's going grey too. We're all getting old.'

'Can you tell me anything else?'

'Cathis and Salla are recovering.'

'What have the people heard about them?'

'Nothing about *me*, I assure you. Some idiots have told others that you and Settle cut their legs off with a meat-axe when they were found in bed together. Salla's gone crazy, I think.'

'What about the Clerks and the High Priests? Aren't they doing anything?'

'No, they're leaving it all to Settle and his policemen.' Heron giggled. 'A lot of use they are.'

'I suppose Settle's the only one who understands the position fully.'

'That's right, unless you count the skeletons, but they have all gone now. If Settle does catch you you'll probably be executed . . .'

Malcom was deeply sunk in thought.

'I suppose they just expect to starve you out. You can't last up here for ever.'

'No. You're right. It's not satisfactory . . . We've found some useful things, and there may be more, but I don't want to be stuck up here if nothing works. . .'

'I'll have to go back. I need some more black paint.'

Heron bit an apple and took a couple of cartridges from his pocket. Chewing, he extracted the magazine from his gun and pushed them into it. He replaced the magazine, pushed the safety-catch, put the gun to his shoulder, squinted through the dusty telescopic sight, and fired at a large rhododendron on the other side of the room. The report echoed; the flower jumped into a shower of scarlet petals; and the bullet ricocheted loudly three times, first off the glass wall behind, then off the ceiling, then off a leg of the chair on which Malcom was sitting, before losing itself somewhere.

'Careful, Heron,' said Malcom, startled. 'I don't think that kind of weapon is meant for indoor use.' He looked at Heron's face for a few moments, seeming to notice it for the first time. 'Are you all right?'

'I don't feel very well.'

150

'What's wrong?'

'I don't know. It's been like this for two weeks. I've hardly slept at all. I have the most awful dreams. Something's gone wrong with me.'

'Are you worried about crippling Settle's daughter?'

'No. The bitch deserved all she got for what she did to me . . . I don't mind about that at all. It wasn't till several days after that I woke up with something dreadful – but I didn't know what it was – I couldn't remember. And it keeps coming back to me. At times I can't see where I am. There's a feeling of being . . . tied down. D'you think I'm going crazy?'

'I've no idea.'

'Oh – yes, and there's another thing.'

'What?'

'I can't get an erection any more.'

'*What?*'

'You know what an erection is, don't you, Malcom? Or haven't you ever found out? I tell you I can't. Or at least, whenever I look at a girl, whenever I think about having one, and my prick starts to expand, I feel a horrible nausea. Once or twice I've actually vomited. As for going to bed with anyone. . .'

'Have you been to see a Doctor?'

'Come on. What use do you think that would be? The Doctors don't know much.'

Malcom grunted, and fell back to reading about the cannons.

There was a pause.

Heron picked up the rifle and sauntered across to the ramp door. Like the glass of the screen enclosing the computer annexe, this door appeared black and opaque from the outside, but was transparent, though slightly darkened, from the inside.

'Aha,' he said. He opened the door very slightly, poked the rifle through it, aimed, and fired. 'A good weapon,' he said.

'What have you done?'

'There's one silly little policeman who won't be on the lookout any more,' he said, grinning.

Malcom came to the door and looked through it. 'You fool!', he said. 'They'll all think it was me!'

'Well, I'll be off now. I don't want the Chief Priest to catch me climbing the wall.'

'Wait a moment...'

'Yes?' prompted Heron.

'I feel – I'm not sure why, but I feel that it would be very useful to get the people a bit more worried than they are. I don't like this continuing calmness.' He rubbed the back of his head as they stood in the doorway. 'You are right to consider the possibility of my perishing alone up here without having achieved anything at all.'

'What do you want me to do?'

'Spread rumours. That'll do for the time being. Ideally one would like to see – stir up a bit of emnity. Tell as many idiots as you like about the history of the human race and what happened to the founders of the Habitation. Make them think – yes, that's the way – get them going on the same lines: the computer, the Library, technology, and so on, are abominations, the Librarian's brought curses on himself for meddling with them, they ought to be destroyed altogether: that sort of thing.'

'Do you want the computer destroyed?'

'Not particularly, not as an end in itself. The main thing now is to get people split up into factions. I think you'll be able to start that without too much difficulty, and once it's started, it'll accumulate of its own accord.'

'Certainly. I'll have a try. I'm not quite sure what you're getting at, but it should be fun. I don't know why destroying things should be so much more fun than creating them, but that's the way it is.'

In the days that followed, the waiting game continued. The infection of suicidal madness spread rapidly, skilfully and unobtrusively disseminated by Heron, while its encysted source remained undisturbed in the upper levels of the Sphere. Heron found that with an effort he could exclude all irrelevancies from his speech for periods of up to half an hour, so as to give during that time the impression of being a man in ordinary control of his wits. His hearers, thoughtfully selected, all swallowed the poison more or less eagerly. He was naturally careful not to implicate himself in the machinations attributed to Settle and Malcom.

Settle had been plunged deeper into depression by the discovery of the murder of Michal. He carried out his scholastic duties properly, but in complete abstraction. He saw his daughter three times a week and was further depressed by her weakness and the evident slowness of her recovery. His spirits were given a momentary lift by the ceremonious delivery of the book-projector, with the Chief Priest's compliments, but as soon as he had taught himself how to use it, the unclassified diversity and immensity of the literature available overwhelmed him like a deluge. It was evident that the coacervation of the Library's resources into one plain, manageable receptacle available for everyday use was likely to be many times more difficult and to take many thousands of times longer than he had anticipated. Hard on this dismal reflection came the realisation that this would in fact not have to be done by him, for it had been done already. The computer was the ideal receptacle. Its circuits contained, presumably, a duplication of the whole Library, but systematically ordered and available at the touch of a button. This thought was not cheering. In former times the irony of the fact that he had begun his search with the sole aim of finding a projector, and that now he had been presented with one the search had rendered it superfluous, would have made him smile; but now it was demoralising. The Library had, after all, turned out to be so much complicated futility. And, as the Librarian, who was he? What use had he been at the most critical point of the Library's, and indeed the Habitation's, history? What progress was he making now? He found himself thinking more and more about Malcom. Unlike Malcom, he did not believe that the Habitation was ineluctably doomed to a meaningless extinction; but now, confronted, in the person of Malcom with an immediate, irreducible force of destruction, he felt he fully understood and sympathised with all those who had yielded to the attraction of despair.

A week and a day after Michal's murder, Amiss made Settle come out of doors for a morning's walk round the circumference of the Circle. On their way down they met Christofer, who had visited his wife in hospital and was coming up to the Library. At their invitation he fell in with the idea of a walk, agreeing with Amiss how startlingly nervous and worn Settle looked.

'I hear that Malcom's murdered someone,' said Christofer as they left the Sphere and emerged in the misty brightness of a warm spring morning. The bird-song fell on Settle's ears most agreeably; he had not been out of doors for more than a fortnight. In spite of himself his stride lengthened briskly. The pain in his lip was almost gone, for most of the time, and he had removed the bandages. His ear, half-healed, was an ugly, distorted sight, though not nearly as bad as the huge scabs on either side of his lip. But he had given up looking at himself in the mirror, so the repulsiveness of his injuries did not bother him. He nodded in affirmation of Christofer's statement.

'But what's this about you?'

'What's what about me?' asked Settle, amused.

'I was having an informal conversation with the Forester yesterday. He gave me some surprising news. It's reported that you, well, that you have been engaging in witchcraft of various kinds; and the effects of this have been a variety of unusual injuries for you and the two women who have been your, shall we say, your helpers.'

'Indeed? Why should I practise witchcraft?'

'The devil has spoken to you through his abominable oracle, the computer. The computer, it seems, had been hidden for a good reason.'

'What reason?'

'Why, because it's evil, of course. It has given you and Malcom its evil commands and Malcom is now its slave.'

'Who says this?' asked Amiss suddenly.

'I don't know. No one in particular. I questioned the Forester about his sources. He was evasive. He doesn't believe more than a quarter of it himself, but that quarter is enough to make him uneasy. And he's certainly right to be uneasy.'

'But someone must have told him that,' pursued Amiss.

'No particular person. These are only hearsay and rumours flying around, getting wilder and wilder all the time.'

'Oh, well,' said Settle, 'it's a fact that some rather odd things have happened recently and are still going on. We must expect a certain amount of talk.'

There was silence among them for about fifty yards. They walked on to where the belt of trees loomed like a dark green wave beneath the white gleaming wall. They turned in a clockwise direction, so that the brilliant striped bubble of the Sphere was on their right.

Settle said: 'What do you think of all this? About what's going on, and what's happened? Do you think we're wasting our time?'

'No,' said Christofer.

'Come, Settle. Malcom Electrician is a criminal. He has tortured you and murdered Michal. He deserves the worst punishment a Clerical court can give him.'

'You mean – the Loony-Bin?' said Christofer.

'Certainly.'

'But no,' Settle broke in again. 'That's not what I'm talking about. I mean – life in general. What are we doing here? What's the point of it?'

'Well, you know,' began Christofer vaguely, but Settle interrupted him. 'It's odd, but I think I feel closer to Malcom, in a way, than – I haven't seen him since he tortured me, but since then I think, I feel, a deeper understanding of how his mind works, than I did before. I don't know how, exactly, but I can see what he thinks. He thinks he's found out the right answer to those questions. He thinks that we're not doing anything at all, that we are purposeless, pointless, futile. Even though the stores are going to run out before long, he still thinks it's worth his while to bring the Habitation to an end, or to try to, as soon as possible. We, I, we can have no idea what he's found up there – there are no notes in the computer on the quantities of arms left. There are water-pipes, and power lines leading down from the solar station at the top, and it's quite possible he'll be able to sabotage those. If he cuts off the power, we're done for. There's nothing we can do! There's no way up to the next level. He can do exactly what he likes, until he runs out of food. We're stuck. We're bogged down.'

'. . .So?' prompted Amiss.

'It's just that my whole life, everyone's life, seems to be lived in a similar situation, that's all. In fact, what's happened, what Malcom has become, is a good illustration of the way life works.

155

We are born, we live, and we die. Death's waiting for us just like Malcom. It is beyond our control, and inevitable.'

'That wouldn't worry you if you had faith,' observed Amiss.

'Oh, faith. Faith. Yes, religion would be a very good thing, if it made any sense.'

'But –'

'No, Amiss, I don't want to argue with you now. Hear me out, if you please. Now, I don't believe that men, that humanity is fundamentally evil, and I don't want it to be put an end to.'

'No,' said Christofer.

'But it ... I don't know ... Habitation! Why does everything have to go wrong? Why has humanity bungled so many times? There's a blight – a failing – every good intention withers – every good is corrupted in the end. The only way to avoid regressing is to stand still. The Habitation has stood still for centuries. And as soon as I try to give it some small advance, it runs straight into disaster. The Society – I don't care what you say, Amiss, but the Clerks did suppress it, and I know the Priests approved of that – but it was *good*, in intention at least. And now look what's happened to us: dissolved, maimed, shattered. And it's mostly my fault. I ruined everything. But it's not only me who's at fault.'

'The thing to do will be to put it right – catch Malcom somehow – and carry on from there,' said Amiss firmly.

'We can't catch Malcom, and if we could things would be just the same. It's not only him – it's a principle, a failing, a human infirmity that he stands for. It's almost irrelevant that he's probably going to murder us all by and by. He's a symbol. If we remove the symbol, the reality would still remain ... It's unconquerable. Malcom is permanent.'

'He's *not* permanent. He's mortal like the rest of us. What's got into you, Settle?'

But Settle was prevented from answering. Christofer looked up and said:

'What's that?'

He pointed upwards, past the central column, into a wide patch of blue amongst the slow-moving, silver and grey cumuli. 'Can you see it?'

156

'What can you see?' asked Settle, who was slightly short-sighted.

'A small black dot in the sky.'

'Where?' asked Amiss.

'Just – here, where I'm pointing.'

'Where – oh, yes, so there is.'

'I think it's moving, slowly.'

'A black dot, you said?' asked Settle suddenly. 'Is it getting bigger? Can you make out the shape? Is it a man?'

'A *man*, Settle? What would a man be doing in the sky?' Amiss was amused.

Across the fields Christofer hailed a group of Foresters at work on sawing up a recently felled tree. They hailed back. He pointed out the unidentified flying object. Puzzled, they stared up at the sky. Then one of them saw the tiny black shape. He indicated it, gesticulating, to the others.

'I still can't make out what it is, but it's getting closer,' said Amiss. 'It certainly isn't a bird.'

'If it's a man – well, we'll see,' said Settle.

'What makes you think this is a man?'

'I've seen something like this before, Christofer, when I was about six. I didn't say it was a man. It was an angel.'

Christofer gasped. '*You've* seen an *angel?*'

Amiss screwed his eyes up and strained his head backwards. The object had now come very close, in the angle of visual range, to the column, and the infinite vertical perspective was bewildering. Huge, silvery, graceful, it hung over them, advancing and receding like an hallucination. Amiss staggered and regained his balance.

'It *is* a man,' he said. 'At least –'

Christofer noticed that the day had become very warm, windless, and almost silent. The leaves in the hedgerow no longer seemed to rustle; the birds were hushed. Distant, attenuated shouts came through the still air as news of the apparition spread rapidly, but faint, diminished as if in a dream. All over the Circle men and women halted and stood stock-still, as if stricken by some communal catalepsy. It was now quite clear that the object in the sky was of human form.

As if his ears were stuffed with cotton-wool, Christofer heard Settle's voice, a ghostly mutter:

'In the Library records there are several references to angels coming –'

They felt their awareness of distance, proportion and dimensions become confounded. They could not tell whether the thing was flying towards them – or towards the left – or the right – or upwards – or downwards. It seemed to float. But it was growing.

'Premonitions – omens of disaster –'

The angel approached. Suspended in an ocean of sunlight, burning like a star, he rushed onwards. They now saw that he was naked. His bright golden hair streamed behind him – upwards! He was descending! He was flying down into the Circle! A thrill of supernatural terror ran round the Circle like an electric current.

Faster and faster, falling like a missile, he came. For the briefest of instants, before he landed, his face was clearly visible. But no one could say afterwards what expression they read on it.

The angel arrived. There was a tinkling crash, startlingly distinct like an articulated word, as he disappeared through the roof of the great hothouse. This, an area of several acres in the south-east quadrant of the Circle, walled and roofed with double layers of thick yellow glass, was not far away from where Settle, Amiss and Christofer had been halted, so that when they, in common with every other Habitationer who had beheld the visitation, began to run towards the hothouse, they were among the first to arrive at a door. The two Glaziers on duty there were as scared as the rest of the rapidly growing crowd. Assuming the authority of a head of a profession, Settle entered the hot house, his two companions close behind. The guards submitted thankfully, made no move to prevent them, and followed. After them, through the rich, golden humidity, poured the whispering, excited, fearful crowd. Settle's cloak brushed the tea-bushes as he advanced to the invisible place above which the yellow panes hung down in brilliant, jagged splinters.

They passed the tea and found themselves opposite a jungle of huge tomato plants bearing hard green clusters of baby tomatoes. Settle left the main path and plunged into a narrow lane through them. His first thought, as he approached the spot where the angel had disappeared, was that a lot of tomatoes must have ripened in one place, as if in the sudden summer of a divine heat. Half expecting a fiery, superhuman figure to rear itself up amid the green, feathery leaves, he pressed on through the last few plants. He was totally unprepared for what he saw. The world died away all around him as he looked.

The diffused splashes of red that he had seen ahead of him were not tomatoes. The angel had disappeared completely, swallowed up and regurgitated in a huge red dripping explosion. Settle stared, mesmerised, at a smashed paste of flesh, blood, bone, muscle and viscera. There was a hand, clenched and bloody. A capriciously preserved eyeball had adhered to a tomato-leaf. These were the only signs of the shape that had formerly belonged to the great green and red morass, which seemed to expand and open before him like an engulfing maw. A buzzing drone came from it; flies were circling over it and walking on it. The tainted air was nauseatingly hot. He fought to keep his reason from falling off its slender tight-rope into the expanse of receptive pulp. He remembered vividly the task of cleaning up Salla's gore from his hall; he remembered the stink. Vomit rose in his throat.

PART FOUR

'I was sick, and so were quite a number of other people, and there was a period of considerable chaos, a crowd of people milling aimlessly around, breaking the tomatoes. The smell was quite appalling. People were coming into the hothouse all the time, and of course they all tried to press forward to find out what had happened, and all the people who had seen the angel were being sick, or trying to get out, or both. After a time a bunch of Clerks in uniform arrived and sorted things out. I'm afraid the tomatoes have been just about ruined, but I won't be able to eat a tomato for some time again anyway without feeling sick, so this will not be a crippling deprivation.'

'Daddy: Christofer told me that you said you'd seen an angel before. Is that true?'

'Yes. It was when I was a child. But the reason why I was shocked today is that the last time, the angel simply flew overhead. He didn't come down and smash. One doesn't think of angels as smashing. Also, there are several references to angels in the Librarians' records. None of them ever seem to have come down, in the Circle itself, before.'

'Do you think it was a real angel?'

'How could I tell, Cathy? Anyway, angels are usually regarded as omens of something catastrophic about to happen. It was true in my time, anyhow – it was in autumn, and the next winter was extremely severe, and a lot of people died of cold and lack of food, including your grandmother.'

Cathy changed the subject.

'Has anything else happened up in the Library?'

'No.'

'It seems rather futile to me to sit and wait and do nothing.'

'And to me; but there is nothing else to do except sit and play with the computer. Amiss is coming up this afternoon to have a go.'

'I can't believe you couldn't make a way through somehow if you tried.'

'Well, you can come up when you're better and show us how.'

'Do you think you could ask Amiss to come down and see me?'

'Yes, if you like.'

Four days later Salla discharged herself from the hospital. Her wounds were not yet healed, but vigour had returned to her body and she was able to walk, after a fashion, with the use of a stick. Her mental health, however, was in a very poor state. Sitting in the sedan chair, which Christofer had reluctantly ordered to take her home in, she was silent for the first half of the journey; then she began to harangue him about a hairbrush which she said had been left in the hospital. His repeated assurances that he had remembered to pack the hairbrush in her bag had no effect. She made loud, insistent demands to be taken back to the hospital to fetch the brush. Christofer, who was already sub-consciously braced to deal with some exhibition of this kind, determinedly ordered the chairmen to continue in the direction of their home. At this his wife became hysterical and began to throw herself from side to side so that the chair was in danger of overturning. The chairmen stopped and remonstrated with Christofer. He took a firm grip on himself, then acted as he had seen the nurses do to calm her in hysterical moods, slapping her cheeks as hard as he could and holding her shoulders tightly. She went sullenly limp. The journey continued. He took her hairbrush from the bag and showed it to her. She insisted that it was not hers. He turned it so that she could see the side on which her name, SALLA CLERK, was clearly inscribed. She snatched it from his hand and hurled it over the hedge, and passed the rest of the journey curled up on the seat, her arms round her left leg, her head resting on her knee, weeping miserably. When they arrived at their destination the first thing she did, while Christofer paid the chairmen, was to clamber hastily and clumsily upstairs, her right leg dragging stiffly, to her bedroom. She opened the door of her wardrobe and looked in the place where she had hidden the pistol, with its one remaining cartridge. Finding it gone she sank to the floor and wept afresh.

The dust-cloud of perplexity and suspicion that Heron had been doing his best to raise, naturally received a fillip from the arrival of the angel. After that the status quo remained unaltered for some time. Malcom remained aloof; Amiss made an enthusiastic attack on the computer's scriptural resources; Cathis continued quietly to recover; Salla moped, chattered vacantly, and occasionally smashed pieces of crockery; and Heron made one more visit to Malcom, but was subsequently deterred by the occupation of the ramp-room by a permanent guard, armed with fire-arms as well as bows and arrows.

Eleven days after the arrival of the angel the disturbed momentum of the Habitation's existence was again adversely affected. In the middle of the morning, while the sun shone and a light breeze rippled the grass and pressed the green tree-tops, a loud, muffled, high-pitched detonation was heard. It came from the direction of the Sphere. As the men in the north-east quadrant turned their heads wonderingly, some of them heard a high, shrill whistle. There was a small spurt of mud in the middle of a ploughed field, where a Farmer and his two sons were sowing. They halted in surprise. Immediately there was another, much bigger fountain of mud and pebbles, with a core of white flame; a bang; and an irresistable blast of mud, broken stones, splinters of metal, and punching, scalding wind. All three of them fell. After a short time the elder of the two boys got up, crying, with a scratch on his arm, addressed his father and brother and ran off into the farmhouse.

On level 1 Malcom, who had not bothered to aim the cannon for his first shot, pulled the lever marked 'eject.' The empty propellant-case dropped out. He looked out through the wall, chose a small, ivied, red-brick house for his target, and turned the direction and elevation-adjusting handles until the house was neatly framed in the telescopic sights with their delicate black X. The heavy, black cannon responded to his directions as sensitively as a horse. A red light and a green light shone on the dashboard before him. The green light had come on when he had pushed the plug, on the end of the flex, into a power-point on the floor and tripped a switch close by it; the red, when he had inserted the shell. He sat back comfortably in his chair and pressed the glowing red button. The cannon shouted. He felt a slight vibration through his chair. His ears were singing as he observed the target burst in a cloud of red dust. When this cleared he saw that the house was partially demolished, and on fire. Two more shots sufficed to level it to the ground.

On the evening of the next day, Heron, looking unusually smart in a clean shirt and tie, newly shaven and with his hair brushed and slicked, came up to level 2. He found his way through unfamiliar, dimly-lit passages to a wooden door, on which he knocked. A servant opened it. He told her his name and asked for an interview, and was presently admitted. She showed him into a small room with a north-facing wall-window, where the man he had come to see was finishing a plain-looking evening meal.

Tomass Priest was a small grizzled man in his late fifties, with bright eyes, a slight squint, and quick, energetic movements. Heron told him he had come to talk about the recent signs of divine displeasure with which the Circle had been afflicted: the angel, and the mysterious thunderbolts that had destroyed a house and killed two people, an old woman who had been in the upper floor of the house and had not been able to escape in time, and the younger of the two boys in the field (the father had suffered only a broken arm.) He said he spoke as a former member of the Librarian's misguided Society, who had come to see the error of his ways. The Priest listened gravely. 'Go on,' he said.

The Priest had doubtless been informed of the discovery of the computer. Did he approve of the stand his seniors had taken on this issue? Did he not rather, like Heron himself, feel deeply concerned that such abominations should continue to be tolerated? He must have heard rumours of the corrupt practices and perversions that had been in the upper levels by the idolatry of the computer, and know of the hideous mutilations, the horrible results that had come to pass. Finally there had come the unmistakable signs of God's anger.

Tomass took all this in. Heron was a fluent talker and could usually be persuasive on any of the few topics that interested him. Tomass was not a particularly clever man. His naive, fundamental belief in God was softened by no civilised admiration for the products of the mind, for human skills and achievements. This limitation, which he shared with some of the other Priests, had not been dangerous as long as the culture of the Habitation had remained static and stagnant; but, as Heron had shrewdly realised, out of all the Priests Tomass most resembled in mentality the original insurrectionary Priests who had brought about the suppression of rational thought. He was, whenever serving in a Priests' court, an unsparing advocate of the Ejector-Seat and the Loony-Bin, as well as the other more barbaric forms of punishment. It was probably this propensity that had prevented his preferment to a more senior post in the Church hierarchy, thus leaving him, in spite of his advanced age, in an unbefittingly subordinate position. He was not married.

They talked for half an hour. At the end of it Heron had said enough to give form to what had previously only amounted to nebulous suspicions and dislikings in Tomass's mind. The latter agreed that the best thing to do would be to find out how many other Clergy were similarly disposed – he had an idea that at least half of them were, to a greater or lesser degree – and would back him in a demand for the High Priests to withdraw their sanctioning of the computer, and to order the return of the book-projector. The two men rose and shook hands. Heron left the level well satisfied. He went down the staircase spinning his newest yo-yo absent-mindedly.

Suddenly he stopped. For five seconds he stood still. Then he went on his way, grappling eagerly with the implications of a brand-new inspiration.

Nine days after leaving the hospital Salla went out of the house of her own accord, having become vaguely conscious of a strong desire to tell Heron something. She wandered towards the Sphere and up to level 3, and found Heron in his studio. She came in without knocking. He was carefully sandpapering a large wooden disc.

'Hello,' she said.

Heron jumped. 'What have you come for? I'm afraid I'm not feeling in the mood just now.'

'I came to tell you something, but I've forgotten what it is.'

'Bad luck, What do you think of this?' He held up the wooden disc proudly. It was about an inch and a half thick, and nine inches in diameter. 'Nice bit of work, eh?'

'It's *important,* but I've forgotten.'

'Bet you can't guess what it's for?'

'I know what I came for.' She sat down on the sawdusty floor and looked up at him craftily. 'Have you got a pistol? Christofer's taken mine – either him or someone else.'

'You want a pistol?' Heron put the disc down on the work-bench. He had perceived that Salla was very far from being in her right mind. This, however, did not strike him as a reason for refusing her one of the two pistols he had obtained from Malcom's arsenal, with a plentiful supply of ammunition; it acted rather as an inducement. 'All right. Here you are.'

Standing behind her so as to be out of her line of fire, he pressed the heavy, cold, black thing into her hand. 'And some bullets.' He gave her a heavy little square cardboard box.

She refrained from pulling the trigger. 'There was one bullet left in my pistol,' she said.

'You've got some more bullets now, you'll be able to shoot a lot of things.'

'Yes,' she said disconsolately, 'but Cathy hated me ever since I shot the cat.'

'Do you want anything else?'

'No. I just came to tell you –' She glanced at him. The crafty, vacant look had left her eyes, which now held an expression of simple, troubled earnestness.

'Buzz off now, there's a good girl,' he said.

Her eyes glistened, unobserved. 'To tell you – it's very important. Christofer –'

'Bye, bye.' He stood her up and steered her out of the door.

'Tell you – what? What was it?'

'I don't know.' He went back into his studio and shut the door firmly. Salla was left standing outside. She put her new possession in her pocket and moved away listlessly.

Whether this donation was the effect of dull thoughtlessness or diabolical subtlety on Heron's part, its results were as bad and traumatic as he could have possibly hoped for. After another short lull, during which Malcom refrained from carrying out any further target practice, and the dissident movement of Priests gained supporters in secret, the Habitation was galvanised into a state of shuddering panic by a succession of motiveless murders.

Murder and violence were not unknown to it during the long period of tranquillity; but two deaths in suspicious circumstances in ten years, and one plain obvious murder in fifteen, had been approximately the average rate, deaths by misadventure being very much more frequent. The uniformed Clerks, who were the nearest thing to an executive police force maintained in the Habitation, were a lax, undisciplined, part-time body, seldom called upon to perform any kind of duty in this relatively crimeless society, which explains why the Library Guard, mostly drawn from the Uniformed Clerks, was so unconscionably inefficient for such a long time. Small misdemeanours, moral insubordinations, petty infringements of the laws of property or safety-procedure, were dealt with by the heads of the twelve professions, who, except for Settle, wielded great power in their own domains. Serious crimes were only very occasional: the molestation of a girl, a man lain in wait for and knifed by a personal enemy, an accusation of witchcraft or sexual deviation (two equally rare, obscure and abhorred infractions of moral law). These were dealt with by the Clerical court, whose judge was the President of the Senior Assembly and jury a convocation of Clerks and Priests, who seldom failed to reach a unanimous verdict. The President would occasionally be called in to arbitrate in a professional case, and sometimes, in a disagreement over an abstruse point of law, the Librarian would be consulted.

The rapid accumulation of violent events after the spring equinox of the year 32 (the thirty-third year after the installation of the previous Chief Priest) was something quite untraditional. For this reason the Habitation's social corrective mechanisms were not capable of dealing with it. Thus the burden of trying to cope with the troubles was thrust upon the few individuals whom circumstances had involved at an earlier stage, who had the intelligence to be fully aware of the problems, and the social conscience to be sufficiently concerned.

Salla quickly tired of shooting blackbirds and pigeons. She killed two cats, a sheep and a cow, before her fundamental antipathy towards all forms of life, apart from herself, led her to select human victims, mostly children. By this time, after a series of lengthening absences, she had left home for good. Her first victim was a little boy of four, shot through the head and body five times outside the front door of his family's house. The noise was heard by the boy's mother, who came to the door. She was six months pregnant. The shock caused the baby to miscarry and deranged the woman's mind.

This was the signal for the start of a reign of terror. News of it reached Christofer in the afternoon of the next day – twenty days after the arrival of the angel – by which time another attack had taken place. That morning a ten year old girl had been shot twice in the stomach, through a glass window. She was discovered, still conscious, after half an hour and died two hours later. On hearing the news of the first murder, Christofer, who had not seen his wife for more than two days, jumped to the correct conclusion and assumed her to be the murderess. He argued with himself for some time, and the argument ended in a reluctant decision to inform his head of profession, the Senior Clerk, of his suspicions.

Children were locked away, gathered together in groups, and carefully guarded; shutters were put up and doors barred; those who had bows put them at the ready; armed patrols went out; and Christofer, feeling himself a probable target for Salla's next assault, walked warily and kept away from open windows, with one hand constantly in his pocket. During the next week the Sphere and the Circle were both searched, thoroughly and systematically. But Salla seemed to have disappeared from the Habitation completely, as if she had been drawn up into the sky and was hovering in the form of an invisible, noxious, death-striking pestilence-cloud. The only place left unsearched was the region where the other dormant evil waited – the levels above the Library. But the guards had been vigilant, and they all swore that Salla could have made no attempt to join Malcom, who gave no more sign of his abiding presence, except to fire five shells one morning at the outer wall. They all exploded innocuously without making any dint in its wide white smoothness. But Salla was still an active force. There were two days on which no murders were reported; then a Farmer's wife and her baby were shot dead, again through an unshuttered window. The baby was at the breast when it happened; the same bullet killed them both. On the same day Salla shot another woman. But, apparently growing cocksure, she fired only one bullet, which grazed the woman's skull, knocking her out. She recovered later and described her assailant, positively identifying her as Salla.

The doom-laden days came and went. There were three on which no trace of Salla was seen or heard of. On the second of these, Malcom's shots sounded from the top of the Sphere and crashed against the impervious, echoing outer wall, frightening, ominous, yet curiously inconclusive and isolated, like a roll of thunder sounding offstage in the wrong part of a play. Then Salla struck once more. A toddler, a little boy of three who had managed to wander out of the cottage where his grandmother dozed, was found dead with nine bullet-holes in him. He was the only child of Amiss and Becka Priest.

Cathis heard about these happenings chiefly through Amiss, who used to come down to the hospital as often as he could and was now her most frequent visitor. He found her a very much more receptive pupil than Settle or Christofer, and in a fairly short time succeeded in bringing her to acceptance of and belief in God. She had suffered a profound change of heart during the slow, painful weeks that had followed her maiming. This had been shown first in her forgiveness of her father and increasing respect and friendliness for Christofer (in which the action he had taken on her behalf towards Heron had also played an appreciable part), and then in a deeper concern, such as was now plunging Settle into a bewildered stupor, for the previously disregarded world of spiritual values. A sense of its absoluteness and fixity was entering into her long before she realised it. She clearly perceived the misguidedness of her former conduct. She also, while yet feeling some admiration for it, saw Christofer's act of revenge on Heron to have been wrong, and his arguments in its favour incomplete, long before she understood why this was so. When she began to talk to Amiss her conversion was rapid.

On the day of the murder of his son, a meeting having been arranged for the later part of the morning, she ate her lunch alone, wondering what had become of him. In the afternoon a grim-looking Christofer arrived. They talked for twenty minutes. At last she said, now more calmly:

'Well, any time you're feeling bored, there's something you can come and help me do.'

'Oh?' said he.

'You see those things?' She pointed to the floor beside her bed. They were a pile of thick, polished wooden sticks. Some of them had a round head, to which had been attached a leather cap. All of them had a strap, with a buckle, at the other end. 'Have you guessed what they are?'

There were, as a matter of fact, fewer of them than he had thought at first sight: about a dozen. 'No, Cathy. What –?'

'Don't laugh – they're wooden legs. I've got to choose one and learn to walk with it.'

Christofer did not see the potentially humorous side of the idea of a girl having a wooden leg till a long time afterwards; he gave no sign whatever of wanting to laugh at that moment. 'Yes,' he muttered, 'I suppose you have.'

'The Doctor says my stump will soon have healed well enough for me to try it out, but I'll need someone to lean on.'

'I see. I'd be delighted. Shall I come down tomorrow – no, sorry, I can't manage tomorrow – three days' time? In the morning?'

In the cold grey twilight of the next morning, while it was still early and the dew was thick and white and the trees were black, dripping shadows, Heron, reaching the fringe of the wood, was not surprised to find Salla lying at his feet in the soaking grass. One leg was twisted underneath her. Nearby was scattered the smashed ribs of a water-cask, and a considerable quantity of fallen, looped rope. He realised, in a dreamlike way, what had happened. The pulley, a simple but effective contrivance that he

172

had fixed on the outer wall for Salla's benefit, so that she could fairly easily ascend and descend from her secret hiding-place, which was the observation room he had discovered at the top of the wall – how long ago? – was ruined; and Salla must have had an accident. The cask, filled with water, had formed the counter-weight that had enabled Salla to pull herself up and down the wall, although her leg was crippled.

She lay before him. She was filthy. Her hair was a tangled mat. Her face and hands were white, wet and dirty as paper. He bent down and felt her pulse. It was still going, very faintly. He considered briefly, then took the pack from his back, opened it, rummaged and produced a small bottle of rum, which he opened and inserted into her mouth. He stood back. She coughed and gagged. Her eyes fluttered and opened. They focussed on him.

'Heron,' she whispered.

'Morning, Sally.'

'I remembered what it was.'

'What what was?'

'What I wanted to say. I was coming to tell you. That's when I slipped.'

'Oh?'

'I saw you that night – before I went up to the Librarian's room.'

'You saw me? Where?'

She began to shiver violently. Her teeth chattered. 'You were – tied up – in your Craftsman's place. Christofer was there.'

Heron frowned.

'He had a bow and arrow. He said –'

The long-submerged unspeakable memory was re-emerging from its hiding-place, hideous as a sea-monster or a drowned, bloated corpse returned to the surface, limbs puffy and rigid, eyes sealed, hair awash, face putrescent and black.

'He said he was going to shoot you through the balls. Did he?'

Full recollection came to him. He closed his eyes, almost fainting anew at the horror of it. He gave no more thought to Salla. He staggered away like a drunk, unaware of his frequent collisions with trees and branches that whipped his face.

Twice he stopped and vomited. And soon, as he rambled

involuntarily back to the Sphere, his nausea began to change, freeze and slowly shrink into a cold, corrosive, brain-searing hatred.

Two hours later Salla was captured.

She received an immediate, summary trial by the President and a hastily-convened jury. The trial lasted less than five minutes. The gag was not taken off her, and there would have been little point in doing so. She was sentenced to death by Loony-Bin; the sentence, said the President, to be communicated to the people and carried out at sunset. She was taken out on a stretcher and an official crier went to the market-place to announce the good news.

In the afternoon Christofer heard that the murderess had been caught at last. He left his desk and went to obtain permission to visit her, which was presently granted. He went to the small, windowless room in level 2 which occasionally served the Habitation for a prison, gave a password to the sentries and went in. Salla sat on the floor in a state of suspended animation, her back against the wall, her legs stretched straight out before her. She had been washed and her hair was combed, but no one had thought it worth the trouble to splint her compound-fractured leg. She wore a single garment of rough sacking. He saw how white she was, thin and starved-looking. There were a large number of grazes, scratches and cuts, deep and ugly, on her limbs. He spoke to her; he sat down beside her and took her hand. Her countenance remained quite blank. He stayed with her for fifteen minutes and then left, longing for her and his ordeal to be over.

Word of the execution spread, as usual, with great speed. As evening came on groups of people left their homes, large and small, and converged on the Sphere. A dense crowd flowed into level 4, down the stairs and into the insalubrious depths of level 7, where it filled the small, dim gallery from which led the dismal Bin-corridor. A few dispersed light-globes glowed. There was, however, a general atmosphere of excitement and relief, a subdued revelling in the lifting of the terrible burden of fear. Christofer, coming down with Settle, found it hard to resist this feeling, and after a time abandoned himself to it. Settle was attentive and appreciative as usual, concealing his despondency.

There was, indeed, much to appreciate. It is natural for executions to be popular spectacles, but this manner of doing to death was much more than a crude form of public entertainment. The sinister black shape at the end of the bleak passage, the solemn splendour of the Priests' vestments, the formal liturgy of the Chief Priest's address, the grim, muscular anonymity of the masked executioners, the slow steps of the final procession up to the Bin, the writhings of the victim, the victim's disappearance, and the clang of the replaced bin-lid, all combined to produce a ritual, though short, of great dramatic impressiveness and symbolic profundity, overwhelmingly reinforced by the total, imponderable, impenetrable obscurity of the victim's fate. What happened to binned people after they disappeared was as hidden as the future; their departures were as final as death. For very many simple folk who believed the Priests' teachings, the idea of Hell was simply a dark hole into which one was pushed, and many of these actually located it in the lowest levels of the Sphere.

The ceremony took place.

Salla, sitting on the floor, seemed to have realised what was going to happen to her. She bounced and squirmed incessantly. At the end, being unable to walk, she was carried to the Bin by two executioners, who held her hands and feet. It was generally known by this time that her right leg, the one that had received the axe-wounds, had been broken in at least two places. Christofer wondered again, pointlessly, about his wife's thoughts and feelings; and about the sensation of the splintered ends of leg-bones jarring.

The Bin was opened. The restless, grey-clad cipher that Salla had become disappeared slowly into it, obscured by the tall forms of the executioners. The Bin was closed.

In a mood of frightened exhilaration the audience made its gradual exit. 'Well, that's that,' said Settle to Christofer, who was light-headed, almost giddy with relief. He had unconsciously straightened his back and felt two inches taller.

'Yes,' he said. But they were both wrong. It was the end of her life; the assumption that the Loony-Bin would be invariably fatal to those it consumed was not to be disproved. After a while Salla died. She lay on her face in darkness. Her heart ceased to beat; her blood halted; her lungs stopped. A few hours later her muscles locked as *rigor mortis* set in. Only her hair and nails grew on, undisturbed. But, although she *was* dead, her career was as yet some way from its conclusion.

When Settle and Christofer arrived in level 1 they were alarmed to find the Clerk, with two subordinates, waiting for them. The Senior Clerk very rarely came on his own errands. They went into Settle's sitting-room. Wasting no time, the Clerk produced a parchment document, which he told Settle to read. Settle read it out.

It was a letter from Tomass Priest, addressed to the Chief Priest, the Senior Clerk, and the Librarian. It stated that the computer was evidently abominable to God, since its discovery and use had been attended with such evil omens. The undersigned members of the Church profession saw no prospect of the present troubles ending while the idolatry of the unsanctified creation continued. They recommended that the computer should, if possible, be destroyed, and if not possible, should be closed and declared permanently prohibited to all members of the Habitation. It was signed by four Priests – Amiss's name was not among them – and a dozen or so X's, with 'Tomass Priest, his mark,' 'Jonest Priest, his mark,' and so on, beside them.

Settle laughed. 'Idolatry of the unsanctified creation, eh? I'd like to meet the fellow who invented that phrase.'

'Settle,' said Christofer, 'this seems to me a lot more serious than it looks. Isn't that so, sir?'

'It is so,' answered the Clerk. 'Tomass, you note, can't write, but the man who delivered this letter mentioned him specifically, probably on orders, as its author.'

'Not all the Priests are with this,' observed Settle.

'No. Many of them are, but none of the High Priests, who agree with us that the computer is a beneficial thing, especially after your friend Amiss told them about finding the Scriptures in it. I wonder if Tomass's group have been informed of this? . . . But I don't think it would make any difference to their attitude.'

'I'm sure that's right, sir,' said Settle. 'But – all the same – what is the possible danger of this kind of nonsense?'

'The danger is that these Priests have been quietly disseminating all this nonsense, as you call it, in the Circle for the past few days. They have a firm grasp on the minds of the uneducated. It is to you gentlemen that I owe the knowledge of what happened the last time the Priests took it into their heads that knowledge was evil.'

'Habitation!' said Christofer. 'Do you think that may happen again, sir?'

'Quite possibly.'

'Yes,' said Settle, 'I see. Am I correct, sir, in thinking that there is nothing much you can do about it, and that you have realised this?'

'Precisely. They are disregarding the express command of their own head, the Chief, who is the only human authority to whom the Priests are accustomed to hold themselves accountable. We've had a little trouble over taxes and tithes with them before now, for this reason. But rebel Priests are unlikely to pay any attention to our own orders when they have disobeyed those of their own Chief. The only way to stop them stirring up trouble, in that case, would be to inflict some kind of punishment on them, and no kind of punishment seems to be practicable. We can't imprison them, flog them or hang them. The bodies of the Priests, you understand, are sacred, whatever the circumstances.'

Christofer re-read the letter thoughtfully. 'I notice, sir,' he said, 'that they don't say what they'll do if their demands aren't met.'

'Yes. That is one of the most favourable aspects of the business. I have a strong suspicion that they themselves have no clear idea what they will do. We need not send any reply to this letter for some time. In the meantime, however, we must decide what to do.'

'I'm afraid I can't think of anything at all to do just at present,' said Settle.

'Are you then in favour of acceding to their opinions?'

'No, Habitation, no, not at all, sir. Are you?'

'Very well. Since the computer is part of the Library it is in your official province, and I have no wish to overrule your authoritative pronouncement. As I said, we have some time to spare. You must use that time to find some third alternative.'

'Very good, sir.'

'There is one other thing. You have had a number of Clerks at your disposal, for the Library guard, with the aim of catching Malcom Electrician, for some six and a half weeks now. They are being employed at considerable expense and no public benefit. I wish this man to be caught, but the treasury is not prepared to subsidise an indefinite siege.'

'Sir –'

'That is all I have to say. Good day to you both.' He went out, followed by his two men.

Heron spent that day at work on his latest project, his hands occupied, his mind brooding on insanely imaginative and artistic schemes of revenge. He went down at sunset with everyone else and watched Salla's disappearance. On the way back another delightful idea struck him. After a couple of hours of thought it had evolved into what seemed to him a feasible, watertight plan. He went to bed and lay awake for several hours. In the early morning, before dawn, he got up, dressed, and went out of his studio. He returned half an hour later, heavily burdened, without having drawn any attention to himself.

For Christofer, too, the night passed sleeplessly, haunted by erotic images, uneasy memories of Salla, and worries for the future of the Habitation. He got out of bed early, feeling exhausted, with a bad headache, and went for a walk around the Circle before arriving at his office. The day flowed miserably on. He came slowly back in the evening; his headache was much worse, and he was feeling more weary and emotionally drained than ever before in his life. It occurred to him that the dreadful events of the last few days had exacted a much heavier toll on his emotions than he had previously realised. He drank a glass of water and went to bed, aware as he did so of the curious sensation that the parts of his mind were slowly sliding away from each other, in different directions. For some moments he had difficulty in remembering who he was.

He lay restlessly awake for a short time, then sank into a deep, welcoming oblivion, and was not conscious of being disturbed as the night progressed. He slept for about twelve hours. Towards the end of that time, even before waking, a faint consciousness of something amiss began to trouble him; like the sound, in an empty mansion, of a distant tap dripping somewhere, far, far away, beyond a vast, silent complex of deserted rooms, passages and staircases. But this had no effect on him. His mind floated upwards through a clear warm lake of dreams. He felt his wife's hand.

At this, the awareness of an unidentifiable incongruity struck him slightly more forcibly. But the last few days had disappeared from his memory, in a temporary amnesia brought on by fatigue and delayed horror, and again he was easily able to disregard it. He stretched and lolled in the warm bed, drowsy and drugged with sleep. He pressed her hand interrogatively. The response was favourable; at least, she did not immediately snatch it away. He moved up to her. She lay motionless. On placing her in Christofer's bed several hours ago, Heron had taken the precaution of adding a few hot-water bottles. Thus, at least superficially, Salla had been warmed up sufficiently for her husband's illusion to be sustained.

She was naked. He put his hand on her soft breast and stroked it gently. Something about the feel of this breast – a slight lack of pliancy and resilience – might have given him an additional warning. But by now the pressure of his sexual desire, after weeks of frustration, had made him deaf and blind to all extraneous considerations. He moved up to her and slid his hand between her smooth warm thighs. They parted amiably enough. He heaved himself on top of her and kissed her mouth, without noticing that no breath was coming out of it. He did not open his eyes, or he would have been alerted by the expression on her face. He continued caressing her breast, back and plump bottom, agreeably surprised by her tractability and readiness to please, which was much greater than it had been for a very long time. It should be remembered that he had never slept with anyone but his wife, and so had no conception of the normal reaction of a healthy heterosexual girl to erotic stimulation. He did not know that women can have orgasms.

He found her vulva and inserted his member. He really ought to have realised at this point that something was terribly wrong. Instead of the hot clasp of the vaginal sheath, there was only a slackness, a soggy, squashy coldness. But a perverse madness had gripped him as firmly as he now embraced his wife. He fucked her with a blind, abandoned determination. The distant trickle of anxiety had grown terrifyingly; the waters were racing and swirling. He was wide awake now, and knew that if he allowed himself to think consecutively for two seconds he would remember something intolerable. The memory battered at his consciousness as if at a flimsy door. He clung to the yielding woman as if for protection against it. Amazingly – he himself was astonished afterwards – he managed to bring himself to a climax.

This happened. His gasps of satisfaction were not entirely whole-hearted. And something was wrong, terribly, terribly wrong.

He opened his eyes.

He stared at his wife's face. The expression of agonised, paralysed malignancy he saw, a few inches away from him, made him shrink back in horror.

'Sally? What's the matter? Have I hurt you?'

She made no answer.

'Sally –'

He wondered why her face was so fixed; and why her body, pressed against his, now seemed so still.

'Are you –'

He looked at her. The curtains were drawn. He listened to the loud wild callings of blackbirds and thrushes in the wood. The room was light. He saw that she had only one breast. In place of the other was a seamed, livid mass of scar-tissue. The intolerable realisation hit him like an enormous steel club.

'You're dead,' he said aloud.

The sound of the birds went away. There was a confused, roaring, semi-articulate sound in his ears. A choir of desynchronised voices wailed and groaned. His mind's eye was aware of an odd flickering light, an unimaginably rapid strobe effect of grey and white flashes. His arm held the warm softness of his wife; his hips, belly and thighs pressed hers; his erect penis was still inside her. It was inconceivable that she should be dead. But she had been binned. He had watched her disappear into the Loony-Bin. She must be dead. That might be true, but it was not acceptable.

'Dead.'

His mind reeled. It now seemed to him that the conditions that had previously guaranteed his peaceful, day-to-day existence, the accepted premises about life that made for mental stability, were in reality less strong than the frailest of cobwebs. He tried to think of the Library, of Forestry administration, of the Senior Clerk, of Cathis and Settle, but they all snapped off into nothingness. A great broom was brushing the web away. He cowered like a spider, tossed and jolted as the strands parted. There now seemed only a few left; only two – only one. Screaming inaudibly, he hung on the end of an infinitely attentuated thread of sanity, a tiny, brightly illuminated object in the middle of an immense black void.

IV. ii. CONFUSION IN PROGRESS

Half an hour later Settle turned up unexpectedly at Christofer's home and was much perplexed to find Salla, naked, sitting at breakfast with her widower. The table was laid for two, but Christofer did not appear to be eating anything.

Settle tried to think of something to say.

'Hello, Settle,' said Christofer. 'Want some breakfast?' His speech was slower than usual, and slurred, as if he was drunk.

'What's happened, Christofer?'

'Eh?'

'What's *she* doing here?' Settle's hair had lifted itself on his head. 'Isn't she dead?'

Salla stared at him maniacally.

'Dead: dead: dead ... She *isn't* dead.'

'How did – what – why – Christofer!'

'Yes?'

'Have you gone crazy too?'

'I'm not crazy,' he mumbled, raising an empty cup to his lips, and swallowing its imaginary contents. 'It was a dream. I must say, though, I like her this way. She's easier to get on with alive than dead...'

Settle could bear no more. He ran away.

Cathis said: 'Dad, you're the Librarian! It's for you to *decide* what happens to the Library! *Don't give in.*'

Settle left the hospital five minutes later. He walked vacantly through the crowded market-place, under the gateway, and out into the bright sunny plain of the Circle. His thoughts were marching round and round in a circle like a thirsty man following his own tracks in the desert. He had just told Cathis the reason for his coming to Christofer's house, which was that he had that morning received a formal memorandum from the Clerk, to the effect that the Library guard would be disbanded at the end of five days even if Malcom had not been captured by the end of that time; and that he thought it likely – as usual, the Clerk did not disclose the source of his information – that the Librarian would receive a fuller statement of the demands of Tomass's party within the next two or three. That was all. It added little to what Settle knew already, but the sight of the message, the crabbed, uneven black letters on the dingy parchment, the disconcerting precise and dispassionate wording, had had a paralytic effect on his powers of constructive thinking; and now, after coming to Christofer for advice and finding him and his wife together, coherent thought had deserted him entirely. He was still dazed by what he had seen. The idea of going back to that house and trying to ascertain Christofer's mental state filled him with numbing dismay. Amid the rest of his confusion he was aware of this cowardice and despised himself for it.

Malcom had withdrawn into an impenetrable citadel, full of deadly, inscrutable purpose; he, Settle, was to blame for the poisoning of their friendship; he had done nothing to save his friend from the quicksand of intellectual despair that had engulfed him; if anything, his antics and frivolity had served to push Malcom deeper; and if the Habitation was destroyed, that would be his, Settle's, fault. Cathis had been hideously wounded: again, an effect of his lack of sympathy that had raised a barrier between them since her earliest days and encouraged her waywardness. Heron had been harmed by his folly – the torture inflicted on him by Christofer had been originally a whimsicality of his, Settle's, devising. Salla was actually dead: caught, in all probability, in a trap intended for himself; but before dying she had murdered others; and even from death she seemed to have been able to return to torment her husband. And now, latest of all, Christofer had collapsed. The Scribaceous and Anagnostic Society was labouring under an inexpiable curse. And the effects of the curse were reaching out, slowly but fatally and unstoppably as a radioactive leakage, to contaminate the health of every level of Habitation Society. There was no end, no end at all, to the evil he had done. A procession of unbearably vivid images circulated unendingly through his brain: the Library skeletons – the symbolic collapse of his toast castle – the nihilistic message so clearly inscribed in the angel's pulped corpse – his daughter's smashed foot – the upright axe-blade embedded on a gory carpet with five toes left beside it – the two whiskers dangling – the hole in Michal's neck . . . Blood and ruin, death and madness, all, all, *all* was owing to him. The Habitation Librarian, the founder of the Scribaceous and Anagnostic Society, the enlightened promoter of adult literacy, the man who had thought to raise the human race from its placid, stagnant trough, had succeeded only in inflicting on it damage beyond repair, beyond estimation, beyond comprehension. His guilt was infinite, irredeemable. And he could think of nothing at all to do. If there was a Heaven and a Hell, as Amiss believed, then he was surely damned.

A new conviction struck him. Hitherto he had been accustomed to think that no worse could be possible, that he had plumbed the depths of the profundity of evil. The sense of a withering blight that attacked everything he touched, the repeated collapses of people, of values, and of ideas with whom and by which he had tried to share and lighten his ever-increasing burden, had led him to believe, on several different occasions, that he had descended to some kind of bottom. He now saw, however, that no bottom existed. The abyss was infinite. However far he had come, whatever worse remained to happen, there could be no limits to suffering and disaster as long as life itself remained. Some people had been killed and wounded, true, but worse, much worse, could still happen. This perception did not cheer him at all. He longed to reach some kind of conclusion. It occurred to him that perhaps he wanted to die. But the idea of suicide had no attractions for him. He did not know what he wanted. He wanted an end to violence and misery; but Malcom's chosen method of ending them horrified him. He wanted life, not death, and the prospect of life was ruined ... He tried desperately to pray, calling on God to help him. Nothing happened; he had not expected anything to happen. He had no faith in God. For one terrible moment the temptation to despair, to abandon all resistance and mental effort, to go home and surrender the computer and then to consume a bottle or two, or three, assailed him.

He put it behind him. At length he turned and went back to the Sphere. His mind was as confused as ever. He hoped vaguely that he would be able to think of something soon.

When he arrived the insight was confirmed. It was now noon and Heron had spent a busy morning. He had, as a matter of fact, been hiding in Christofer's bedroom, having remained there all night, when the latter had given entertainment to the disastrous delusion that had, for the time being, demented him. Heron had intended to kill Christofer as soon as he had become aware of Salla's proximity; but the plan had succeeded so much better than he had hoped that he had restrained himself from stabbing him through the bedclothes, fascinated and incredulously anxious to see how far Christofer would carry the performance before discovering his mistake. Eventually Christofer had dressed, carried Salla downstairs and quickly gone through the motions of preparing breakfast. Settle had come in shortly after, whereupon Heron stepped into the next room. On Settle's retreat, Christofer dropped a fork on the floor with a loud clatter. Then he too got up and wandered out of the door. Heron, prompted by some incomprehensible impulse, picked Salla up and set off back to the Sphere with her, carrying her on his back. Being encumbered, and very tired, he was not able to go fast. He met several people who recognised Salla and backed away in fear. By the time he arrived at the Sphere a small crowd was following him. He paid them no attention. He went boldly up to the Craftsmen's room, which happened to be empty; it was still quite early.

When Settle left the Hospital he was too much absorbed in his own woes to notice the undercurrents of uneasy excitement on level 4. It was a market day; a large number of people had seen Heron entering the Sphere with his burden, and more were arriving all the time, wishing to know why affairs were at a stand-still. Market affairs were forgotten by all; the influx continued. All kinds of ghastly rumours were flying around. After a time between four and five hundred people had gathered in the Public Hall opposite the market. No official cognisance had yet been made of this unconvened assembly. Suddenly Tomass Priest, who had happened to come down the stairs and seen the people, but had not thought of finding out from anyone why they had congregated, decided on impromptu action on his own account. He hastily sent for his robes and himself found two of his lieutenants, to whom he explained that he was going to seize this opportunity to address a substantial portion of the populace.

A solemn hush fell as the small but splendid procession entered and made its dignified way to the stage. The level 4 Hall was a much wider space than the Great Hall of level 2. It saw a public assembly three times a week, for church services, but otherwise it had little official use. The general feeling of uneasiness gave way to a confident, though slightly puzzled, expectancy as Tomass mounted the steps to the stage and took his place at the podium.

The sermon he preached lasted twenty-five minutes. He was a vigorous and lively speaker. His audience may have been somewhat surprised at first to hear no word of explanation for the reappearance of the recently-binned woman, but they soon forgot all about this in the spell of his oratory. In picturesque language he enumerated the disturbing incidents that had taken place in the last few weeks: the angel, the aimed thunderbolts that had smashed houses and killed men, the scourge of Salla's murderous insanity. He went on to mention the rumours they had heard concerning the disfigurement of the Librarian and his daughter and the secret activities of the Scribaceous and Anagnostic Society. He spoke on roughly the same lines as Heron had done at their first meeting.

The latter, meanwhile, had gone up to his room, dumped Salla in a corner, and picked up the latest piece of equipment he had constructed. It was of course another yo-yo, black and red, but his conception of the 'bouncer' had by now mutated into something very different from its original embodiment as an amusing, slightly childish toy. This yo-yo was nine inches in diameter and weighed nearly ten pounds. It was made of oak, rimmed with iron, and ferociously studded. The cord was a twenty-foot length of highly flexible, woven-steel wire, which Heron had had great difficulty in obtaining. Its most alarming aspect, however, was not its size, but the fact that the rims of both the discs were bristling with the angled, protruding, half-inch points of sharpened steel nails. The wire was led clear of the spikes through a short length of swivelling tube. Its free end was attached to an ingenious thing like a half of a metal gauntlet, designed to protect his hand from the spikes, although he had perfected the necessary art of keeping it in motion without having to catch it between throws. He now carefully shortened the wire to six feet by winding it over a couple of very small hooks on the inside surface, fitted the hand guard on like a knuckleduster, oiled the central axle and the fittings of the tube, and began practising with it. It was very much heavier to wield than he had expected – astonishingly heavy – and he found difficulty in simply keeping his balance. However, he perservered, and soon felt himself acquiring control over it. After a while his right arm was feeling very tired. He took the yo-yo off, smoked a pipe or two, picked up a pistol absent-mindedly, put it in his pocket, and drifted out in a reverie.

In a minute or two he found himself on the fourth level, at the back of the crowd which Tomass was addressing. He listened uncomprehendingly till he realised what Tomass was talking about. Heron made his way to the front, put away his pipe, and joined him on the platform. Tomass nodded to him, still unaware that Heron's reputation of respectable citizenship had taken a severe blow quite recently, and went on haranguing the crowd. There was no doubt now that it was responding to his words. He succeeded in giving form and definition, as Heron had done for him, to the nebulous but powerful feelings that recent events had inspired. By the end of his long sermon his audience, four-fifths of it, was feeling a strong, religious resentment against the computer, the Library, the Society, and Settle. He concluded with a prayer extempore:

'Oh God, who seest and knowest the minds of men, Thou who art aware of our manifold sins and wicknesses, Who hast uncovered our hearts and examined our souls, Who art filled with righteous and insupportable wrath for the crimes and abominations with which this Habitation, this Thy excellent and glorious handiwork, is become defiled, have mercy upon us, Oh most righteous God, we pray; suspend Thy just anger; put not upon us the grievous burden of thy rebuking; avert Thy awful and intolerable gaze; and turn our sinful hearts into the ways of repentance and humility. We acknowledge our faults, we are dust in Thy sight, we are hopelessly astray in sin, we are evil and corrupted and worthy to be destroyed; yet forgive us, Oh Lord, forgive us our iniquities, and amend the errors of those set in authority over us, for the sake of thy blessed Son, yours faithfully, amen.'

'Amen.'

The congregation opened its eyes and unclasped its hands. Scattered murmuring broke out. Heron, now alert and excited, asked Tomass for permission to make another speech, and took the podium. Silence fell, but before he could speak another loud voice came from the back of the Hall, where a band of police, twenty or so, had unobtrusively made their way in.

'This gathering is not authorised. You must all return quietly to your normal business. Tomass Priest is preaching unlawful heresy. Heron Craftsman is a criminal who has stolen the body of an executed woman. Both of them are under arrest. The Chief Priest and the Senior Clerk together command you to disperse.'

The crowd stirred and rippled angrily. Confused voices were raised. The Priests and attendants, all except Tomass, became pale and uneasy. Heron shouted back: 'It is not we who are the heretics, but the Clerk and the Priest themselves, who have allowed the Librarian's wickedness.'

'Silence!'

'You have no authority over us!' yelled Tomass. 'People of the Habitation, do you mean to allow this –'

Heron's voice was lost in the roar of the crowd as it surged back onto the men in black uniforms. They retreated. Heron saw the Clerk in command of the party turn and speak to one of the men carrying bows. The rest were armed only with clubs, which they grasped nervously. Thinking quickly, Heron drew his pistol. The archer brought his arrow up to face him and bent his bow; the arrow disappeared behind its point. Heron fired. The shot echoed, the man collapsed, the arrow flew up to the ceiling and stuck. At these astounding and magical effects the whole assembly froze, except for Heron, who jumped down from the platform, pushed through the crowd, made a run for the nearest exit and escaped before anyone could think of trying to stop him. He reached level 3, dived into his room, collected Salla and the yo-yo, and staggered out again up to the Library. There were no guards at the top of the stairs; all the available Clerks had been ordered down to deal with Tomass.

Heron's pursuers came running up the stairs. Soon the immemorial stillness of the Library was being violated by the sounds of shouts, screams, crashes, running, skidding footsteps, and the occasional muffled shot. Only about a third of the Library guard had come up again, and even these had no more than a limited knowledge of the maze. They dashed in in a disorderly manner, courageously overcoming their fear of the dark, turned a corner or two, and immediately became hopelessly lost in the black labyrinth. Heron, on the other hand, threaded his way through fairly easily in spite of his load and weariness, manoeuvred her slowly up the ramp, gained admission from a surprised Malcom, and deposited her. He had realised what difficulty his pursuers were having and was determined to make the most of it. He took three hand-grenades, plenty of ammunition for his pistol, and the yo-yo. Fifteen minutes later the entirety of the Sphere felt the vibration and muffled noise of a large explosion.

Settle came back, sunk in gloom. He found a couple of demoralised guards in the foyer, heard their pitiful story without comment, and began a round-up. After half an hour the rest of them were all found. Two were dead. One had been shot, the other, a victim, the first to Heron's yo-yo, had had most of his chest minced off. Of the other half-dozen most were uninjured. One was surprised to find he had lost a finger from his right hand. Before that time, however, Settle had come out into the ramp-room, found it deserted and full of black smoke, and seen that the computer annexe was a black, gutted shambles. That looks like the end of the computer, he had thought dispassionately. What next?

Christofer also had spent the morning wandering aimlessly around the Circle. He had once passed within a few paces of Settle, but neither had noticed the other. His discovery of his wife had shattered the firm crust of his self-confidence; his wits, if not scattered, were shaken and disorganised. Inconsequent images and preceptions flowed and eddied in his brain. The few hours that had elapsed since the event had served to increase rather than allay the horror it had induced. An elusive vision of

Salla's dead face floated before him like some ocular defect; whenever he tried to focus his attention on it, to attempt seriously to consider the thing that had happened to him, it floated away, out of the range of contemplation, and a deadly nausea came over him. Other memories, however, that he did not wish to recall, obtruded persistently, cavorting and careering with the random motion of gas molecules.

After several hours' distracted peregrination it came to him, like the appearance of a star amid a swirl of dark-grey cloud, that Cathis was still in hospital and that – he made an intense mental effort – he had said he would visit her that day. He turned abruptly and made for the Sphere.

Cathis was peacefully asleep – it was early afternoon – when he arrived. He paid no attention to the signs of disturbance on level 4 and went straight to the hospital. He stood outside her door for five minutes while he recollected what he had come for, and then entered without knocking. The room seemed very quiet and peaceful. A short strip of sunlight lay on the floor before the window. Her faint, regular breathing was the only sound. A slightly dishevelled rose stood in a jar on the table by her bed. Two petals had fallen from it. As he stood over her it occurred to him for the first time, not irrelevantly, to think that she was not totally unappealing physically. Her face was rounded and calm. Her fair, downy eyelashes lay on her cheek, almost invisible. Her lips, pink and delicate, were slightly apart, not compressed into their habitual thin firmness. She was wearing a green cardigan over her white nightdress; the sheet and blankets had been pushed down below her breast. The fingers of one small white hand were curled round the bedclothes, their grasp relaxed and forgotten. Her soft hair, quite long now, lay round her head on the pillow. Christofer was aware of a peculiar scent in the room, delicate, attractive, feminine. He picked up a fallen rose-petal, examined it, and replaced it carefully. He restrained an impulse to pass his hand over Cathis's forehead or down her cheek. Instead he picked up her hand and pressed it gently.

She woke and blushed to see him; but then, remembering what Settle had told her, questioned Christofer insistently about the presence of Salla's cadaver in his home. Christofer was

190

extremely reluctant to answer, and when she began to force him to describe what had happened, he fainted suddenly.

From his vantage point at the top of the ramp, secure and unseen behind the closed door, Heron watched with moody satisfaction as Settle and his men picked over the scrambled wreckage of the computer's interior. After some time he turned away and went up to level 1, where Malcom sat on the floor, surrounded by a litter of explosives. Heron lay down, feeling more exhausted than ever before in his life. He had not had more than six hours' sleep in the last seventy-two. For a time he lay, uncomfortable and idle, fingering the gory spikes of his yo-yo.

Malcom said: 'Well, then, Heron, what's been happening?'

Heron gave a slow, somewhat involved, and frequently elliptical account of the day's events. At the end of it Malcom nodded gravely. 'Yes,' he said.

There was silence for another half-hour, while Heron muttered and wriggled on the floor, and Malcom continued to tinker, absorbed and assiduous, with the bomb he was in the process of constructing.

Heron got up, suddenly aware that he was hungry as well as tired. He had eaten nothing that day. He went to the provision cupboard. It was empty.

'Is there nothing left to eat?' he asked.

'No.'

'How's the bomb getting on?' Heron appeared to have noticed, for the first time, what his companion was doing. The bomb was a contrivance by which Malcom hoped to be able to explode the entire stock of gelatinoids simultaneously, providing a blast sufficiently powerful to demolish a structure much solider than the Habitation. He intended, as soon as he was satisfied that it would work, to shoot his way out of the Library, take the bomb down through the levels to the seventh, and there set it off. However this simple plan was still a long way away from being put into execution.

'Not very quickly, I'm afraid,' he said in response to Heron's query. 'The detonator is making a lot of unexpected difficulties and the materials I've found up here are barely adequate.'

Heron wandered off, found a staircase, and ascended to the

opmost level of all. Level 2 was a small circular room whose roof was a shallow dome, most of which was glass. In the middle of the room was a round, windowed enclosure which was the base of the column. Heron had been up the column already. He was debating, in a feeble sort of way, whether to go up and look at the mountains again, or to lie down and make another attempt to go to sleep. Weighing up the pros and cons of these two alternatives occupied him for a long time. Finally, wanting sleep more badly than he had ever wanted anything in his life, he made his way down to the warmer levels. It had become dark; Malcom was still working with great single-mindedness. Heron lay down on the floor, choosing Salla's belly for a pillow. During the course of the night he did at last go to sleep. He slept for about twenty hours.

When it was quite dark outside Settle stood up, switched on the light, and went to his mirror. He stared at his reflection and examined the injuries. His ear had healed well enough. It was no longer at all painful, but it was undeniably horrible to look at, a small, distorted, puckered, purplish excrescence like some kind of vegetable, protruding about twice as far as the undamaged ear on the other side of his head. His lip was still stiff and hurt sometimes. No hairs had grown from the great, pink, shiny expanse since the moustache had been torn off. What with the long, swollen scar across his scalp, his face was grotesque, to say the least; but it was not this that worried him. He contemplated it thoughtfully. There was no doubt that it was an old man's face that stared back at him. The brown eyes were tired and sunken as a ghost's. The gaunt cheeks had fallen and become lined. There were new, grim lines about his mouth and bristly jaw. The skin underneath his jaw had also fallen, and was hanging in limp folds. With a shock he noticed that the hair above his ears, which had certainly been black the last time he had looked at it – but when was that? – was now grey.

He turned from the mirror with a sigh. He considered having a meal, remembering that he had as yet eaten nothing since breakfast. But he did not feel hungry. He drank a glass of water and went to bed.

The Senior Clerk had already sent carefully worded messages, signed by himself and the Priest, to the other nine heads of professions, concerning the threatened rebellion of Tomass's party. He urged them not to allow their own people to become affected and forcibly to emphasise their own adherence to the policy of the established and divinely appointed government. Tomass's opinions were strongly denounced. All unauthorised public assemblies were prohibited. By the time these communications reached the heads, however, a public assembly had occurred spontaneously and Tomass had seized the chance offered to him.

When Heron fled the damage was exacerbated. For a few moments the crowd was immobilised and shocked; but the Clerk in charge of the armed party, being entirely unaccustomed to tense situations and necessities for quick thinking, lost his head and took the worst possible measure: he ordered his archers to shoot a few arrows at the Priests on the platform, in the hope of frightening and subduing the crowd. The twanging of the bows broke the stillness with as much force as an unexpected thunderclap. One robed attendant fell with a crash, an arrow in his neck. Another man was shot in the hand, another, who was not even on the platform and had nothing to do with Tomass, was shot in the shoulder. The archers were nervous and aimed poorly, not liking to aim at men. But the one death was enough to alienate the crowd beyond hope of reconciliation. With a roar it swept back on to the policemen. Most of them fled; those who remained were trampled down.

Ten minutes later the Clerk himself came down to find the Hall empty except for a handful of dead or unconscious policemen and a dead Priest. He took charge, gave the necessary orders, found and questioned the surviving police, and then, after reflection, sent a herald out with a proclamation. A free pardon was issued to all those who had been in the riot. Tomass was named as responsible for it. He was proscribed and a large reward was offered for his capture. But again these measures, though prompt, were too late. By the end of the morning, when Settle was returning and Christofer was still wandering around the Circle, Tomass was established in a house in the north-west quadrant, with fifty devoted enthusiasts encamped in the front garden; it was now no longer feasible to think of arresting him or capturing him.

The nine heads of professions had all responded to the Clerk's advice. In the afternoon normal work came to a standstill, as the entirety of the population became caught up in a welter of speeches, circular letters, memorandums, rumours, arguments, threats, appeals, accusations, denunciations, counter-denunciations, sacrifices, auguries, prayers and lamentations for the dead. Both sides blamed the other for all the evils that had taken place. Few of those not directly concerned could tell for certain whose side it was right to be on. In the evening Tomass sent an ultimatum to the Senior Clerk: the computer was to be destroyed, and so was the Library; the whole of level 1 was to be sealed off as abominable and polluted ground; and the Librarian was to be put on trial for his crimes before an ecclesiastical court. Otherwise, the ultimatum stated, the True Priests, being filled with righteous anger and the power of the spirit, would not hesitate to remove the corrupt and secular government of the Habitation; the ultimatum ended on a note of aggresive naivety by hinting at the gravest personal consequences for the Clerk himself, should the demands not be met. All the latter did in reply was to send the information that the computer had now been destroyed.

Night fell slowly.

The next day dawned. In the morning all was the same. Tomass, who also was suffering from insomnia, addressed an audience of several hundreds, sacrificed an ox, and sat down to dictate another ultimatum demanding the immediate execution of Settle and his daughter and all the other non-Priestly, non-Clerical Habitationers who had acquired the ability to read and write, the resignation of the Senior Clerk and the Chief Priest and the incineration of all literary material contained in level 1. The Clerk made no reply to this. The all-pervading atmosphere of doubt and mistrust remained, hugging the Circle like a cloud of dense, heavy gas.

PART FIVE

V. i. RESISTANCE

It was only in the hospital, in the room where Cathis lay, that a precious fragment of peace was to be found; or so it seemed to Christofer, when he came in the morning. He found her sitting up in bed, looking down at her legs under the bedclothes with an expression of great determination on her face.

'Hello, Christofer,' she said. 'Come in, come in, come in. You're just in time. I'm going to get up and I need your help.'

'What for?'

'Walking, of course.'

'Oh. Cathy, have you–'

'Come over here and sit on the bed. That's better. Now – if I can –' She pulled her legs from under the bedclothes, and drew back her nightie so that the stump was exposed. They looked at it.

'Habitation!' muttered Christofer. Conflicting emotions, more violent and extreme than he had ever felt before, were rushing to and fro in his mind, contending like winds in a blizzard. Something was shrinking, disappearing, dying. Something else was growing like a tree. What were they?

The stump lay among the folds of the blue counterpane, inconceivable and unreal as a nightmare. On the one side was the healthy living foot with the pink toes; on the other, termination, truncation, absence. They both had the feeling that the other foot should still remain in existence somewhere, and that, should it be found, it would only be necessary to attach it to the stump to make the living limb as complete as before.

Christofer looked at Cathis's face. It was cheerful, her eyes were bright.

'Now, Chris dear, would you mind stretching and picking up one of those wooden ones? Choose one that looks a suitable length.'

He obeyed.

'Now, give me a hand with getting it on. That's right. The strap fits – you see.'

Christofer's fingers touched the naked stump as they placed the artificial limb in position and fumbled with the buckle. He began to tremble.

'What about a pad? Don't you need one?'

'Oh, yes, there's one here.' But she made no move to reach down to pick it up. She leaned slowly back on the pillow, laying her hands by her sides. Christofer, facing her, was left holding the stump.

His feelings were whirling round and round like a centrifuge; he felt that he was almost falling to pieces under their pressure . . . he made himself examine it. It was soft and warm, not hot, to the touch. He opened his eyes. It was much darker than the whiteness of her leg; a light, warm, reddish mauve. The flesh was seamed. There were two small red weals in it; he found out later that these had been the holes from which the short black threads of rotting blood-vessels had hung. There were about three inches of shin left below the knee.

'Can you bend your knee?'

The stump twitched in his hand, and moved a little.

'That's all.' Her voice was very quiet. 'But it can bend all the way if you press it.'

He pressed the short length of flesh and bone gently and her knee bent. There was a long pause, tense as a violin string.

'Christofer.'

'Yes?'

She said huskily: 'You don't find it too – awful? too ugly and deformed?'

'No, well – no, of course not.'

'Do you. . .'

'Yes?'

'Never mind.'

'It is – well, ugly, but it makes me – I don't know if you – that–' Christofer's throat was dry and his tongue seemed to fill his mouth. He avoided her eye. His hand began to caress the stump.

'Lots of things – lots of things I'll never be able to do again.'

'No, but –'

There was another silence.

Suddenly Christofer lowered his head and kissed the thing he was holding. He put it down and took her hand. She had turned bright red. Her eyes met his. He had a sudden keen awareness of the absurdity of the situation, tried to prevent himself from smiling, and was unsuccessful. She smiled too. He heard himself chuckling and she giggled. Both of them abandoned themselves to mirth.

'Well,' she said, wiping her eyes on the sheet.

'Cathy, I love you.'

'I had an idea something like that was coming.'

'May I kiss you on the mouth now?'

The kiss was interrupted by more laughter. They drew apart, then back together again.

'I feel fine now,' Christofer said presently. 'Everything's fallen into place. I've recovered, I'm all right now.'

'Oh? Oh yes. Well then, you can tell me, if you don't mind, because I'm extremely curious. And what's been going on outside? The Doctors and nurses won't tell me anything. I kept on hearing some great commotion going on outside my door and I had no idea why. What's been happening?'

'Never mind that for the moment. Tell me what happened to you – that is, if you don't mind.'

For a brief moment a hideous cloud of phantasms rose up again before him, nauseating him, veiling his sight, swarming around him like huge insects. He took a firm, deliberate grip on his new-found self-confidence and they subsided. He told her in as much detail as he could bear to recall, but as delicately as possible. Finally he turned back to her and tried to grin.

She said nothing.

'Heron was there at the time. I saw him, but it didn't seem to matter then what he was there for. I put some clothes on and took Salla downstairs ... I think...' He tried a few different words, collected his thoughts and resumed. 'You see, I couldn't bring myself to believe that she was dead, after all. I persuaded myself – half-persuaded – that she was alive, in one of her sulky moods. I kept on telling myself I had to get breakfast for us. I sat her on a chair in the kitchen and put a few things on the table. Yes, that's right. Then Settle came in and said something and went out again. Then I felt so awful – how can I say it? As if the air was full of some thick, heavy black liquid like treacle, pressing on me, crushing me, in my lungs, pressing on my eyes and blinding me. I tried to get away from it by going out. Then I dimly remembered I was supposed to have come and seen you. So I did.'

'How do you feel now?'

'Not perfect, but much better.'

'Thank you for telling me.'

'Now, what about this wooden leg of yours?' He came back to the bed with an air of brisk determination.

After midday they were both standing, side by side, at the bright glass wall. The ninth leg Cathis had tried had seemed satisfactory. They had not ventured out of Cathis's room. Christofer had continued to wander round the Circle in a distracted state after leaving her the day before, having recovered from his faint; and had passed the night in a secluded ditch. In the early morning, somewhat calmed after a night in the open, and conscious of the eccentricity of his appearance, he had returned home to wash, change, eat and shave. Then he had set off for another visit to Cathis. During all this time he had remained entirely in ignorance of the momentous schism which was now threatening to tear the Habitation apart. So he was as surprised as she was to see an odd-looking procession advancing out of the Circle, towards the Sphere. There seemed to be a large number of people, many with packs on their backs; some laden carts; they recognised the Farmer and the Forester, robed and dignified, striding deliberately forward in the fore of the procession; there were ambling pigs, cows and slatted crates with the heads of chickens protruding from them.

They looked further; another, similar procession was advancing from another quarter.

The air outside looked unusually thick and misty. After a while they saw the reason for this. In the distance smoke was rising above the green tree-tops. There were flames, too, pale in the sunshine. Several houses were burning.

The dramatic, instantaneous change occurred in the middle of the morning. For a time the same all-pervading air of bewilderment and indecision had remained. Then as it seemed, everything suddenly became plain. In one moment, all over the Circle and throughout the Sphere, people were made aware of what the alternatives were, and whose side they were on: Tomass's religious party, or the established government. To both sides the opposing creed now seemed equally loathsome, and apparently within a matter of moments the Habitation divided itself into two hostile camps. This was at about ten o'clock.

It was soon seen that, although the heads of professions had all agreed the Clerk's proposals and had exerted the utmost influence over their own people to bring them into the government side, Tomass's party was in a considerable majority, of at least two to one. This awareness quickly led his supporters into acts of aggression, undirected and haphazard but nonetheless very alarming. Everyone, especially the young, seemed to have acquired a telepathic sensitivity as to whether or not a stranger they might chance to meet was on their own side or not. It was lucky for Christofer that he had arrived safely at the Sphere before the attacks started. A Clerk carrying messages from the Senior Clerk to the Glazier was met by a small band of rebels, aged eighteen and under; his papers were torn up. The same band met another messenger, who was also deprived of his messages, but then carried and thrown into a nearby pond. A third was beaten and stripped naked. An old man, a Farmer, who had stubbornly insisted on going out as usual, not being able to bear the idea of neglecting his fields, was set upon, clubbed, and left unconscious. There were other incidents, of which the culmination came at about half past eleven, when a crowd about thirty or forty strong surrounded a lonely cottage which contained a young Waterworker and his wife and their two children. They were allowed out, but the crowd stoned them as they fled, and set fire to their cottage.

A little before midday the heads all met and agreed to ask Tomass to let them withdraw safely with their remaining adherents to the Sphere. This was a timely request, since he was now virtually in control of the Circle. Their eight-strong embassy met him. He allowed no exchange of arguments, berated and menaced them for fifteen minutes, and finally granted their request ungraciously. They were spat at and one of them was kicked in the back as they made their way through a lane in the hysterical crowd. Half an hour later the Heads led their nervous and demoralised processions into the Sphere. By the time they arrived, their houses were mostly on fire, having been first plundered of all remaining possessions.

In the afternoon Christofer went up to level 2 and proffered explanations for his absence. His explanation, that he had been prostrated with grief following his wife's execution, was accepted. His colleagues brought him fully up to date on the recent history of the Habitation. He went to the Forester, who was annoyed at having been deprived of his secretary at a time of crisis, and did his best to mollify him. He now found himself extremely busy, and had no time to visit Cathis next day. She was now walking for ten or fifteen steps at a time, undeterred by painful stumbles.

At five o'clock on the day of the retreat to the Sphere, Heron woke with the warm early evening sunlight in his eyes. The humming of bees came up faintly through the hole in the floor. Nearby he could hear the sounds of Malcom's patient tinkering. In spite of cramped aches in his neck, back and buttocks, a dry throat and a dull feeling of emptiness in his stomach, he felt relaxed and peaceful. He lay with his eyes open, his head propped on Salla, admiring the gorgeous panorama of the evening sky.

'Malcom?' he said at last.

'You've slept well.'

Heron turned his head slowly. His neck was agonisingly stiff. Malcom did not appear to have moved since he had last seen him.

'How's it going?' he asked.

'Quite well.'

'What's for supper?'

'Nothing. I've told you, there's no food left.'

With an effort Heron sat up, realising how horribly hungry he was. 'Nothing? But didn't Settle cook anything?'

Malcom made no answer. He sat, cross-legged like a tailor on the floor, surrounded by screws and components, making some minute adjustment with a small screwdriver. The containers of explosive stood by. The orange light fell over him; the metallic parts twinkled; his big, pale face shone like an August moon.

'What shall I have to eat? I'm *hungry*.'

'There is nothing to eat.'

Malcom resumed his work. Heron stood up slowly and paced round the room, trying to rid himself of the cramp. He groaned, yawned and stretched. He came to the hole in the middle of the floor and looked down into the emerald brilliance of the shrubs below. A hopeful thought struck him.

'What about those bees? Is there a hive anywhere?'

'Yes. I've eaten all the honey there was, that could be eaten.'

Heron swore. He went to the east part of the wall. The circle was green and tranquil looking. The smoke from smouldering houses rose in thin blue lines. The outer wall gleamed warmly through the haze. It did not occur to him to wonder why so many houses should have caught fire. He was thinking only of his stomach. His eyes lighted on Salla.

'Have you a fire here?' he asked.

'Yes. Why?'

'What about her? She's mine, remember, but you can have some of her if you want.'

Malcom was not shocked. 'That's a thought,' he said. 'An excellent idea, in fact. What part of her?'

'I think it would be best to keep her together as much as possible,' said Heron thoughtfully. 'I rather fancy a nice leg.' He grinned, licking his lips. 'Let's have a knife.'

Cutting Salla's right leg off below her pelvis was a messy, tedious task. The knife was sharp and the cold, dark-red flesh parted readily, but the thigh-bone, intractably hard, resisted Heron's attempts to saw though it. Malcom watched with interest. Heron began to curse. Finally the knife blade snapped.

'You should have found a joint and cut through there,' said Malcom. 'What about breaking it with a bullet?'

Heron took his pistol out. 'No,' he said, 'wait ... of course.

Stupid of me not to have thought . . . Just a moment.' He went and fetched his yo-yo. 'Now – watch this.'

He cast the yo-yo downwards three times. Flesh and bone seemed to crumble like cake before the advance of the whirling nails. A thick red spattering rain fell around them. The hip, knee and ankle disappeared and Salla's leg lay in three pieces.

'Very ingenious,' said Malcom, unperturbed.

'Now, let's roast them. Where's the fire?'

'There's a cooker too, as a matter of fact. Over there.'

Heron popped the two larger pieces of meat into the oven and shied the disconnected foot away somewhere. Then he went down to level 0 and considered going out, but changed his mind when he saw through the door that there were five men sitting in the room below, all of them with a vigilant look, two with pistols in their hands. His mood, at the moment, was not murderous; his thoughts were almost lucid; he had a desire for conversation. He went back up to Malcom, but got nothing more than grunts from him. Then he went up to level 2 and entered the column. He looked up it. A fragile looking staircase led upwards in an unending spiral. There was a faint sound of dripping and trickling. A cold wind blew down on him. He shivered and sneezed. There was, close by, a windowed container which was a lift, with a floor area of about two square yards. The lift was not raised by any visible means; there were no ropes or wheels; its roof was of glass. It was possible, standing in this lift, to look upwards into the empty, luminous, tubular space, encircled by the dark spiral, vertically striated by the long silver lines of the glass lights. He pressed the button that opened the lift-door and entered.

He had been up the column with Malcom, on one previous occasion. The lift had travelled smoothly and silently for three minutes, and then stopped, and the door had opened of its own accord. The room at the top – not of the column itself, but of that small portion of it through which the lift travelled – had seemed to be mostly glass wall. He had instantly been transfixed with wonder. Immediately below the Circle had sat like a wide plate; beyond it rose the mountains, range beyond range, depth after depth, height above height. Their immensity, far greater than that which he remembered having seen from the top of the outer wall, had dazed him. Low clouds swam slowly among them. He had stared at them obliviously while Malcom looked curiously at the fittings of the low, round cabin. There were doors leading out at the left and the right, and a ladder at the back of some kind of control console leading to a trap-door in the ceiling. Malcom noticed several noises: a low, pervasive humming; the faint trickling of condensation; a distant, uneven ticking; and the noise of the high-altitude wind outside, muted by insulation and double-glazing, now a moan, now a whine, now a faint roar. He gained the impression that the whole column was moving, rocking, with a steady back-and-forth motion. He tried the trap-door. It was immovable. The doors at the sides, however, opened easily at a turn of the handle, revealing short passage-ways. He went down one. There was another, larger door or hatch at the end of it. This passage was exceedingly cold, alarmingly unsteady, and the influence of the atmosphere upon it was obvious. It seemed to bounce and dip like a bird, and to echo like a musical instrument. There was a strong, freezing draught coming in at the far end. Conquering his unease Malcom had gone along to the end. The door was barred. He unbarred it and pulled down a massive lever. The door swung open inwards.

Malcom found himself standing in mid-air, horribly suspended between the sky and the wheeling earth. The bellowing wind tore at him. The column seemed to be describing a crazy circle like a pencil twiddled between someone's thumb and forefinger. He took in with detached clarity the details of the scene plunging about thousands of feet below: the tiny dots slowly moving on the white threads of roads, which were people and oxen, the red and brown squares of rooftops, the small checks of fields, the green moss of trees. He had a sensation of falling; the power of controlling his muscles had left him. It seemed inevitable that he should immediately be precipitated outwards. He thought, 'this is death.' But though his reason was temporarily overwhelmed, his limbs kept their grasp on reality. He did not fall, and after a long time, chilled and shaken, was able to retreat into the comparative firmness of the column, shutting the inner door behind him.

That had marked the limit of Malcom's exploration. As soon

as it became clear that the column had nothing to offer in the way of destructive weaponry, he had returned to level 1 and had promptly set about the task of deploying his resources in their most effective form; which he presently decided to be a large bomb. The manufacture of a detonator for this bomb, as he had said, had presented unexpected problems, and that is why he had allowed so long an undemonstrative interval to elapse. But, after studying all the available literature intensively, and dismantling most of the equipment he had found, and the failures of several promising approaches, he was now confident of producing, within a matter of days, a satisfactory device. He had given some thought to the possibility of sabotaging the power-lines that carried the Habitation's electricity down from the solar turbine, which was situated immediately above the place where the lift stopped in its upward journey. If he had been able to do this it would have certainly put paid to the chances of survival of human life on the Habitation; but there were one or two factors that dissuaded him from making the attempt. In the first place, the cables seemed to be very heavily armoured. One thing he had not found in the upper levels was a torch capable of cutting through an inch or so of steel. Secondly, he was not sure that an attempt to do so would not lead to his own death through electrocution, before he managed to sever the important cables. It occurred to him to use a grenade or a larger bomb in the column itself; but here he was restrained by a point of pride or self-respect. He wanted to make an absolutely clean sweep; and the destruction of the power-lines could not be expected to do this. He wanted to end the collective existence of humanity at a blow, not to condemn it to a lingering, miserable demise over the course of two or three winters, while the woods, the wooden houses, the fences, furniture, hay and corn were all burned up to provide a few sparks of warmth for the wretched, famished, perished survivors. Indeed, Malcom had perceived that this would be exactly the kind of end he had pledged himself to anticipate. So, a bomb it was to be.

Time passed. The light crept along the darkening floor as the sun sank. The rays of sunlight were horizontal. The furniture turned black and fire-edged. Salla lay supine like a mistreated doll.

Malcom turned his back to the light and worked on. Eventually there came a diffused brightness from the ceiling. It was a patch of sunlight; the dim, mote-filled rays were now shining slightly upwards. This soon disappeared abruptly. There was now only a dark turquoise light in the sky, with a greenish-white patch where the sun had set. A fine golden crescent moon swung lazily downwards and a couple of stars pulsated faintly.

He lit a candle. The cooker ticked faintly in the darkness like a robot, and the air was filled with a succulent, ravishing smell. Heron returned. 'A beautiful sunset,' he said. 'Well, is she done?'

'Should be.'

Heron, burning his fingers, extracted the two brown, spitting joints from the oven. The smell of the meat was overpowering. They both felt weak with hunger. 'There's only one plate,' said Malcom. Heron handed him the calf, keeping the thigh and ham for himself. Malcom put his meat on his plate, cut slices off with his knife, and ate them with his fingers; Heron held his in his hands and tore at it with his teeth in complete disregard of the blood and fat that spattered all over his face and clothes. The three conspirators sat or lay round the candle in the dark, each of them, in his or her own way, differently aloof, absorbed, preoccupied, obsessed, or dead. The sounds of chewing and slobbering filled the dark spaces behind them.

'Heron,' said Malcom presently.

'Yes?' The sound was indistinct: Heron's mouth was full and his face buried in the meat.

'That *is* Salla, isn't it?'

Heron gave a rather confused account of the vicissitudes Salla had undergone since her death. Malcom listened to it without much emotion.

'So you went down into the Bin, did you?'

'Er – yes, I did.'

'What was it like?'

Heron put down his much-reduced joint. His face was greasy and flushed in the candle-light. Shreds of meat and gristle adhered to it. 'Not quite as you'd expect,' he said. An unpleasant, vacant look came over his face, induced by some sinister recollection. His mouth opened involuntarily, his eyes unfocussed.

Twenty-three hours later, Settle, slumped in his seat, was listening half-heartedly to an interminable, directionless argument between the Clerk, the Chief Priest, the Doctor, the Electrician, and one or two other heads of professions. They were in the Great Hall on level 2. The President of the Senior Assembly had summoned an extraordinary convocation (a phrase of Settle's which had passed into currency some time ago). First, he had read out a long statement, written by Settle, which set forth all that he knew of the origins of the present troubles. He had listened attentively while the clerk was reading, but when the statement was over he had subsided and slumped, with the feeling that matters had now passed completely out of his control. He took no part in the ensuing discussion.

The Clerk had received, in the late afternoon, a communication which bore the mark of finality even for one so prodigal of demands and ultimata as Tomass had been. It also showed an intelligent apprehension of strategic realities. The Clerk read this out as well. It was concise and contained much less religious sentiment than its predecessors had done. It demanded that: the Library should be emptied as far as possible; all movable items should be taken from it down to the Circle to await ceremonial incineration; level 1 should be declared a profane area, and prohibited for ever; the Librarian was to appear before a special court, presided over by Tomass himself, on charges of witchcraft and heresy; the Senior Clerk and the Chief Priest were to resign from their posts, which were to be taken by nominees of Tomass's; the whole of the Habitation were to undergo a voluntary, penitential three-day fast; the people's tributes to the Church were to be trebled; the Uniformed Clerks were to be disbanded, and a new moral police force instituted, under the control of the Priests. If these demands were not granted *in toto* by the evening of the day after next, concluded the document laconically, the guard-posts that had been set outside the exits from level 4 would kill anyone who attempted to leave the Sphere.

An excited hubbub broke out as soon as the President stopped speaking. Few had yet grasped the full implications of the ultimatum. The President had let the babble continue for some minutes before rising again. Silence fell. Settle watched the slow curls of smoke rising above the altar.

'I'm sure I'm right in assuming that none among us here entertain the slightest sympathy for this. Some of you, indeed may be inclined to laugh at it, since it is undoubtedly the effusion of an unbalanced mind. I myself have the most total contempt for all that these demands stand for. But, all the same gentlemen, you must consider the likely consequences of agreeing with it, and the certain consequences of refusing.'

A surprised murmur and scuffling travelled along the benches.

'I must in fact say that, in my view, we have no alternative but to comply.'

There was a general, inarticulate sound of astonishment. All except Settle, and one or two other perceptive individuals like Amiss, sat up suddenly in their seats, whispered to their neighbours, or half-stood up to speak. Two disregarded slate pencils dropped to the floor and broke.

'Please, gentlemen, hear me for a few moments. The last two lines of that message are the most important. They mean what they say. Tomass has already put a small army of men out around the Sphere, and if they decide to besiege us here we will have no means of escaping, and nowhere to escape to. I had the four gates closed and locked yesterday to prevent the mob from following us in ... The importance of this, gentlemen, is that our food-supplies are limited. Tomass is in control of the fields and the barns. I believe he knows he has only to wait until the choice between surrender and starvation faces us.'

There was a stunned silence.

'In other words it is inevitable that we shall surrender sooner or later. The later it is, the more needless suffering we shall have endured.'

He sat down. The Doctor, in his green robe, was the first to stand up. 'I would like to know some details. How many has Tommass's side? How much food have we? How, are you, Mr. President, so certain that this is Tomass's plan? What has become of the man Heron Craftsman? And is it certain that there is no alternative – no way, for instance, of retaliating?'

The President answered calmly from his seat. 'This morning I gave orders for our side to be counted. I believe us to number four hundred and twenty' – there was a gasp of dismay – 'of whom two hundred and four, including all those present, are men. There are a hundred and fifty-four women and sixty-two children. Many of them, particularly the Farmers, acted on my advice and brought livestock and food-supplies with them to prevent it falling to the enemy, though I confess I had no thought of being surrounded and starved. Still, what with the small supplies we already had in the Sphere, we can expect to last a week; two, or even three, if we tighten our belts. But this is no use unless we – unless you, gentlemen – can think of a way of striking back at Tomass.'

Several other people stood up at once, and a fierce argument broke out. All that the Clerk had said had been accurate, although he had omitted to say that his reason for keeping the Sphere doors locked was less to prevent attacks from outside than to stop people who might wish to defect to the stronger side. The Sphere had been incommunicado since the delivery of the ultimatum. He now took charge of the argument once again, and invited all heads to speak in turn. The Chief Priest's statement was sententious, tedious and unhelpful. No one said anything after he had finished. Settle, called on in turn, declined the offer to speak. Various other heads now took their turns. Retaliations such as cutting off electricity supplies to the Circle, or polluting its water, were suggested and emphatically vetoed by the Forester and the Waterworker. A rambling discussion developed. Settle listened to it for about half an hour, hope slowly dying within him. When the same emotive sentiments, irrelevant prejudices and unnecessary distinctions had been re-expressed half-a-dozen times, he followed the examples of the Craftsman and the Weaver, and took his leave of the Assembly.

He went to his room and sat down in a chair. He now contemplated the Habitation's approaching débâcle with resignation. His own feelings of guilt no longer vexed him much; the belief, though he still held it, that his own stupidity had been the sole agency of all the disasters that had happened, had subsided like a black sediment in a jam-jar full of water. It lay at the bottom of his heart, thick and impermeable, but it no longer clouded his mental vision. Apart from the deadly threat of Tomass's triumphing, he could not rid himself of the fear of Malcom's maleficence. His presence still seemed to emanate from the mysterious levels beyond the ramp, hard and baleful as an irradiation of X-rays. Settle seemed to become more and more conscious of this as his body wasted away.

He went to his bedroom, thought about eating, again decided not to, washed perfunctorily, and went to bed. He lay awake till after one o'clock with the odd, baseless feeling that he was waiting for something.

Next day the weather turned cold and windy. Cathis's absent right foot was throbbing painfully, in sympathy with the swirling draughts that filled the enclosed Sphere. She had not seen her father for some time, nor Christofer for two days, and she still had little idea of the reason for the almost palpable air of fear and bewilderment that hung around the hospital. That morning, therefore, having awoken from a good night's sleep and eaten a substantial breakfast, she decided that the time had come for her to go and see for herself. She could now walk for quite long distances at a stretch. She went to her Doctor, thanked him for all he had done for her and informed him that she was now discharging herself.

She fetched her bag from her room and left the hospital, determined to perform the task of climbing up four flights of stairs to the Library. There seemed to be very many more people about than usual, and she was struck by how depressed they all looked. There was a great, silent crowd in the Public Hall, standing and sitting, individually and in small groups. Apprehensive, resigned, or indifferent, everyone she met had the same look of passive, expectant misery. Few heads turned as Cathis, embarrassed and at the same time intensely curious, stumped past them on her wooden leg. Only one little dark-haired girl clinging on to her mother's skirts returned Cathis's glance, cautious and wondering with a frown of innocence. Apart from the subdued whispers and muttering, an occasional burst of sobbing or petulant exclamation, the only human sounds were the wailings of babies. But there were a surprising number of animal ones. A lot of cows were mooing somewhere. Hens ran about hungrily, squawking and pecking in competition. She could hear something that sounded like a goat.

The stairs were trying. With perseverance, however, she acquired the knack, lifting her right knee high enough at each step and holding on to the baluster with two hands. She picked up speed as she went on, but even so the whole ascent took her slightly over twenty minutes. She sat down on the top step in level 1 and rested for a little while. The non-existent foot stabbed at her spitefully. Then she stood up, went in to the Librarian's apartments and found her father sitting before an empty grate.

His appearance shocked her. She had never seen such a look of utter, lifeless despondency in the dark eyes and set mouth. And worse than that, much worse, was his dreadful thinness and pallor. He looked as if he had not eaten anything for a week (in fact, he had eaten nothing for three days). His hair, what there was of it, was white. His immobile pose forcibly recalled to her the memory of the skeletons in the Library, sitting or standing in silent, perpetual vigilance. At the sound (a thumping noise) of her entry, he turned his head; it was as if a skeleton had moved of its own accord. She stood in the doorway, paralysed with horror, feeling the impulse to scream wildly and run away as if she still had two serviceable legs.

'Hello, Cathy,' he said. A ghostly smile, a feeble, pathetic diminution of his former grin, touched his lips. 'It's nice to see you again.'

His voice broke the spell. It, at least, was the same as before, if a little weakened. She thumped forward, kneeled down carefully on the floor by his chair, and kissed his cheek. He took her hand.

'How are you? You seem to be walking all right.'

'I'm fine, Daddy. But you don't look very well. What is it?'

'I'm not ill. I just haven't been feeling much like eating recently. And I've had a lot to think about.'

She stared into the black grate. He looked at her. Her hair was lustrous, her eyes were bright, and she was a little plumper than she had been. But then, he thought, she had been more or less isolated during the last few weeks, insulated and shielded from demoralising pressures. This estimate was not entirely fair, but it was made without bitterness.

'Why haven't you been eating?'

'I've simply lost my appetite.'

'Won't you starve?'

'I don't know. I feel I'm waiting for something – for some great calamity, some turning-point – and then, if all goes well, I shall be able to recover. But now I'm just waiting. I can't do anything else; I've given up.'

'Oh. Oh dear.'

'No – that's not true.' This was more like the old Settle, brisk, argumentative, animated in the pursuit of exact analysis. 'I haven't exactly given up, but I feel that everything's got beyond me. There's nothing I can do now. I started all this trouble, and I tried to control it and suppress it for a long time – but now I'm no longer strong enough to carry on with the fight. Everyone else knows as much as I do now. I can't do anything but wait . . . there may be something for me to do before the end.'

'The end? of what?'

'I don't know of what. It may be the end for us all. It may be defeat by Tomass, Malcom may do something fatal.' His head sank back against the back of the chair.

'But what's *happening*, Daddy? I've heard Tomass's name – who is he? Why are there so many people on level 4?'

'When did you hear your last news?'

'Christofer came to see me two days ago, in the morning.'

She reddened at the memory of that occasion, but Settle had stopped looking at her face.

'Very well. I'll tell you what's happened since then.' She had the sensation of being slowly overwhelmed as the apparent hopelessness of the situation was made clear. She asked questions. After about three quarters of an hour the door opened to admit Christofer, who had been down to the hospital and found her gone. Settle now left most of the talk to him, only occasionally contributing an item of information or comment to supplement Christofer's apologetic crushing of all her hopeful suggestions.

'What do you think about all this, Christofer?' she asked him at last.

'I've told you what I think.'

'No, you haven't. Have you given up hope or not? Do you see any point in carrying on?'

'Cathy, there is no struggle, only a choice between two bad alternatives.'

'What about the struggle to think of a third?'

'That's what the Senior Clerk and Settle and all the other heads are racking their brains to try and think of.'

'Then there *is* a struggle.'

'I suppose so, but –'

'But you've given up. Settle admits it.'

'Can you think of anything else to do?'

'Stop saying that! I keep thinking of things, but you won't have them!'

'Not if they won't work.'

'Are you, Christofer, still trying to work out a third alternative?'

There was a pause. Settle turned and looked at Christofer with a gleam of amusement in his eyes. 'Well, Christofer,' he said, 'are you?'

Christofer, nonplussed, said feebly: 'It's not for me to decide. I'm not the Senior Clerk ... I can't do anything.'

Cathis looked from one man to the other.

'Shit,' she said.

Neither of them had ever before heard her use such a word. Settle's eyes opened wide; he chuckled. Christofer sat where he was, blushing.

'No. I won't have it,' she went on. There was an unaccustomed, abrasive firmness in her light voice. 'You're depressed and demoralised, and you're tired of all the worries, and you want to give in. You're beaten, the whole lot of you.'

'Not me,' said Settle blandly, 'I've told you.'

'Am I right or wrong, Christofer? Yes?'

He nodded.

'Well, then. I haven't had time to despair yet, and I'm sure that there must, there *must* be another way out. How long have we got?'

'There's another Senior Assembly meeting this evening,'

answered Settle. 'If nothing positive comes out of that, then he'll surrender tomorrow morning.'

'Well, that gives us some time,' said Cathis resolutely. 'And – I've just thought of something else. I don't suppose you're going to the meeting tonight, Daddy?'

'No, no, no.'

'In that case, I'll go for you. I'll represent you from now on. All right?'

'That's a good idea, Cathy ... in fact, it's an excellent idea. It's just what I've wanted – yes, I shall resign as Librarian now. Cathy, you can take over the job.'

'Oh.'

'Get the big chain out of the drawer in my bedroom.'

'Oh! Are you–'

'Go on.'

She fetched the chain and brought it to him, and stood wordlessly as he placed it over her head. He arranged it carefully on her shoulders. They looked into each other's eyes for a moment. He stooped and kissed her.

'There you are, my dear. I'm sure you will cope with whatever you decide to do.'

Christofer put in an observation: 'The Clerk is fond of documents; it would be an idea to give her a statement of some kind, a writing saying she's now officially taken over.'

'Yes. Fetch the writing implements, Cathy, there's a good girl.'

She fetched them. Settle wrote out a short statement and signed it.

'Thank you,' said she, folding the paper. 'Come on, Chris, let's go. I want to have a look round ... You don't mind being left, do you, Dad?'

'Not at all,'

She stood up heedlessly; her wooden leg slipped, she staggered and collapsed, luckily managing to fall back on the chair.

'Are you all right?' Christofer asked solicitously.

'Yes. Can I have your arm?'

They said goodbye to the ex-Librarian and went out. For the next hour or so Cathis made a tour of the Library, asking

Christofer and the guards a great many questions. At other moments, in the privacy of the dark corridors, Christofer said things to her that had little noticeable relevance to the crisis at hand. Last of all they came out and stood at the top of the staircase. Cathis leaned over the rail and looked down the well at the lift, five levels below, motionless and unattended.

'So,' she said, disengaging her hand from his, 'your verdict on that lot is – give in?'

He considered. 'I don't think you've quite understood,' he said. 'There are two separate problems. One is Tomass, and the other is Malcom.' He expounded on this theme; Cathis thought about ways of attacking Malcom.

She looked down the shaft and up at the ceiling. There was a rectangular area there, above the shaft, corresponding to it in size, indistinguishable from the rest of the smooth, white, cobweb-hung surface except for being an inch or two lower.

'There's no way of cutting through solid steel, Cathy, 'I'm afraid.'

Cathis thought differently. 'Look,' she said. 'We don't know how many more levels there are above, but there is bound to be one, at least. Right?'

'Of course. Probably two or three. What has that –'

'It's obvious. The lift used to go all the way up, or at least as far as the level above this – level 0, I suppose we must call it. And when the Library and the upper levels were sealed off, the lift-hole, the entrance, whatever you call it, was filled in too, and it was made to go only up to this level. So the ceiling is likely to be much less strong here than anywhere else. We know where to direct our first attack.'

Slightly nettled by her confident tone, he asked, 'What do you know about it?'

'About what?'

'Metalwork.'

'Not much. But there are people who do and I don't suppose they've all gone over to Tomass.'

'Well, Cathy, I *do* know a little about it – I don't agree with you.'

They argued. He brushed away, as gently as he could, all her ignorant suggestions of blowlamps, welding-torches and laser-punches. She reminded him pinkly that they had no way of knowing how thick the covering was. He fetched a chair, climbed on it, and, leaning precariously over the open shaft, rapped the ceiling with his knuckles. The sound, a dull knock, gave no clue. Cathis suggested scraping some plaster off. He took out his pocketknife. To his chagrin, at the first pressure of the knife-point on the plaster there was a small tearing sound and the blade sank in about two inches. Both of them felt comment to be needless. Christofer cut into the ceiling tentatively. The knife met an obstacle and turned a corner. The next moment a little avalanche of dust and rubbish poured out through the L-shaped rent.

After that Cathis sent Christofer away for the rest of the morning. She stayed in the same place, leaning on the rail, swinging her wooden leg pensively. After half an hour she went down and presented her new credential to the Clerk's secretary, requesting an audience. This was presently granted. She talked with the Clerk for twenty minutes.

Meanwhile Heron had made a last attempt to escape, but the guard had been alert. Seeing the black door begin to open they had taken cover in the exits, waited for him to emerge, and then fired erratically. Heron dived back behind the door, startled but unscathed.

Cathis came back to level 1 and had lunch with her father. His meal, in spite of her impassioned pleas, was restricted to a couple of glasses of water. They spent the afternoon at work together. Settle dictated and Cathis wrote. Towards tea-time Christofer turned up again, breathless with curiosity to know what was going on. The small rent in the ceiling, he observed, had not been enlarged. They told him to be patient and continued with their composition.

At sunset Settle's attendants arrived. He explained to them that he had resigned from his office. Cathis came out of her room, nervously resplendent in blue cloak, blue mortar-board, and gold chain, all too big for her. A sweeping black dress concealed her legs. Christofer asked for permission to accompany her into the Senior Assembly, which was granted. On the

217

way down, in the lift, she suddenly burst into tears. Christofer asked for no explanation, confining himself to putting an arm round her shoulders and offering a handkerchief, for which she was grateful. She blew her nose and wiped her eyes. The lift went on. They stepped slowly out into the greenery of the level 2 foyer, where the clock, long since inactive, read 05.64.99. A shocked and scandalised gasp went round the solemn convocation as a young, unfamiliar *woman* appeared among them, dressed in the Librarian's full ceremonial attire. Trembling slightly but otherwise betraying no self-consciousness, Cathis took her place in the forming procession. They entered the Hall.

As it was another extraordinary meeting there was no fuss about minutes or sacrifices; in any case the supply of livestock within the Sphere was now far too precious for this use, however recklessly Tomass might be slaughtering animals outside. The President opened the meeting.

'The first thing to say,' he said unemotionally, 'is that our colleague, Settle the Librarian is away this evening, as you have seen. I am informed that the anxieties caused by the continuing troubles have so upset him that he considers himself no longer able to perform his duties; his powers, as he says, are passed to his daughter, Cathis Librarian, whom we welcome here today. Her official installation can wait until we find ourselves in less pressing circumstances.

'To business. Gentlemen, you have had a day.' He paused and looked searchingly round them; or, at least, appeared to do so. The evening sun was on his face. 'Have any of you any suggestions to make? I explained to you yesterday that the alternatives are acceptance of a tyranny dominated by Tomass's unorthodox Priests, or starvation. Since then I have been compelled to alter this view.' There was a stir of interest. 'But before this is explained, do any of you have anything to say?'

The heads of professions all sat motionless, except for Cathis, who shifted uneasily in her seat.

'In that case I call upon the Librarian to put her view of the situation before us.' He sat down.

Cathis silently uttered a short prayer and stood up. She ran her eye over the first few lines of the carefully prepared speech in her hand. With a strong feeling of being a spectator of her own performance, she opened her mouth, took a gulp of air, and began to speak.

'Gentlemen, it has occurred to me –'

Her voice sounded ridiculously, inaudibly high-pitched. She began again, pitching it lower, as loudly as she could.

'Gentlemen, it has occurred to me, on becoming apprised today of the present state of affairs, that the choice between the alternatives that confront us is not as stark as you may think. It has occurred to me, and I now firmly believe, that there is a third way out, a way that if successful will restore to us the fullness of our dignity, freedom and independance, a way that at first may seem terrible and shocking to you, perhaps a worse visitation of evil even than Tomass's rebellion itself, but which, if resolutely, intelligently and successfully pursued, will bring our society into a new order of strengthened harmony, increased wisdom, and rightful, rational devotion to God.'

The manuscript said at this point, 'pause.' Cathis paused. She had a sudden surge of confidence as she glanced round at the faces beside and below her. Grey-haired, red-nosed, white-bearded, heavy and pouched, veined and lined, capped, helmeted or hooded, all had a look of interest and puzzlement. The bemused scorn that had greeted her first appearance was gone. All heads were turned to her. In the benches below most of the occupants had turned in their seats and were craning backwards to keep her in view. The Head Craftsman had got up and was sitting on the book-rest, back to front, with his feet among the embroidered cushions. He smiled at her encouragingly.

'This third alternative, gentlemen, is to resist Tomass by force. I mean that we should go out and fight him.'

She had expected some kind of outcry, or at least reaction, at this point, and was prepared for it; but there was none. If anything, the bewilderment seemed increased. Cathis's third alternative was, as a matter of fact, a very bold and original conception. Organised warfare was at that time a thing of the past, unremembered and absent. Fist-fights between individuals, wrestling-matches among children, and illegal, bow-and-arrow duels that took place at very rare intervals, were the only modes in which physical combat ever found expression. The idea of employing a large body of men to fight a collective battle with another body of men was totally novel.

However, she and her father had foreseen that the heads would have as much difficulty in grasping as in accepting this plan, so she was not taken aback. 'Bear with me a few moments,' she went on, 'if you please, while I attempt to explain the implications of this proposal. When I have come to the end of telling you what I suggest, I will try to show that it is not wrong, however startling and unfamiliar; even corrupt and wicked, it may at first appear.

'You withdrew from the Circle because it had become evident that you could not live in amity with Tomass and those he has seduced. It was the one possible choice before you, although it drove you into what many have since considered a trap. And here we are, within that trap. We have insufficient food; we cannot stay here long; but Tomass will not receive us till we yield to his demands. My solution is to attempt to destroy Tomass's power over his adherents, so that they allow themselves to become reconciled with us when we remove him – by which I mean capture or kill him, together with those other Priests who have joined with him and might succeed him in authority. He is protected, however, by the great mass of the people. Yet, if we can overcome them temporarily, we will be able to capture him, and once he is in our power we will be able to forgive the common men and women in compassion for their delusions. First, though, we must fight them.'

She paused momentarily again, herself overcome with a ghastly, enervating spasm of self-doubt. The expressions on the heads' faces had not altered, but her speech now seemed bodiless, totally absurd and irrelevant to everything. But in spite of this loss of belief she struggled on. 'It is, I think, quite probable that a well-planned assault would meet with success. Though we are outnumbered by about two to one, there are some aspects of our position that, if made intelligent use of by us, are likely to counterbalance this. First, remember that Tomass's men will not be expecting an armed, determined attack, so they will not be organised to resist us and they will have no immediate access to whatever weapons they possess. Second, we have on our side a body of men that is accustomed to and proficient at

220

archery: the Uniformed Clerks. Third, we will be in a position to choose the time and place most effective for ourselves and make all out dispositions beforehand, whereas their defence will have to be summoned up at a few moment's notice. Imagine, if you will, the demoralisation, the shock and the panic that would be instilled in your own hearts by the sudden, unexpected appearance of a huge, hostile crowd, a hundred strong, unanimously intent on a maiming, murderous attack. Make no mistake, gentlemen, though –'

The feeling of doubt had passed away. A note of thrilling sincerity had entered her voice.

'Make no mistake in your seeing of what must happen. We must – that is to say that every able-bodied man we can enlist in our service must – do his utmost physically to subdue the enemy. While the necessity lasts, they must wound and kill, must shoot, stab and crush, not reluctantly but eagerly, since hesitation may be fatal, all men who set themselves in opposition against them. While the necessity lasts, I say. I hope and trust that it will not need to last long, no longer than is necessary for a selected band to force their way into whatever hiding-place Tomass may retreat to, or to pursue and catch him if he tries to flee; him and his confederates. That being accomplished, there must be no further hostilities at all. Those among us who have lost their property, their homes, or the lives of their near ones, must forgive; and we shall trust that time eventually will remove all bitterness from the people of the other side also. The man who finds he has struck down his companion or friend, or even his father or son, we will leave to accept and overcome his anguish. There will, I fear, be some such. This will be the worst of all the consequences or resistance; but once victory is achieved, we will not let the cases of individual sorrow, while we sympathise with them as best we can, cloud and blacken our lucidity of overmastering gladness at having escaped from the horrible scourge which Tomass threatens.'

She drank some water. Every eye remained fixed on her.

'This is a new thing among us. The Habitation has not seen warfare for many life-spans. We must hope that such a thing will not happen ever again. I say to you a third time, make no mistake in your understanding of what I propose. It is bad that this should happen, but the alternatives are far worse; in fact, as you have all realised, there is only one alternative, and that is capitulation. Realise also, that this is not a certain way. It is not likely, but still possible, that Tomass's men will rouse themselves sufficiently for their weight of numbers to prevail, and if this does happen we will all, almost certainly, be put to death, or worse. He will either catch us on the battlefield, in the Circle, or, supposing that we are able to retreat to the Sphere, wait for us to starve behind locked doors. You may be assured that the possibility of making a second attack, successfully, on an alerted victor, has no significance. The choice before you, then, is between the tame and cowardly acceptance of a brutal tyranny, and an auspicious, valiant attempt to repel it and risk defeat; between a passive and abject self-preservation, and a dynamic, honourable adventurousness.

'One thing more, which is the most important of all, and then I have done. You know that Tomass and his people have rebelled in the rash confidence that God is on their side, that they alone are being true and faithful to Him, that we are the unrighteous and the damned. If the fortune of battle favours them and they are able to conquer us, they will undoubtedly ascribe their triumph to God. I say what you know, else you also would have joined with them, that in this they are blindly, recklessly wrong, and that God is with us. I call on Him to give us victory. I tell you: if we fight, God is on our side. But I do not base any infallible assurance of victory on this, as they would do if they knew of our intention to fight them. The issue will depend on our strength, our speed, and our courage. God will not give us this battle as a gift; we cannot rest secure in the persuasion of His favouritism. Remember the other side is as sincere in faith, if not more so than we. God cares for individuals more than for crowds; He is with us, whether we win or lose. He is with every man who kills without hatred or hesitation, with every man who is killed, with every bereaved wife or mother, with everyone who will be willing to forgive and forget when the affray is ended.

'Thank you all, gentlemen, for your patient hearing.' Her face and voice relaxed. 'I beg you to give consideration to what I've said. I know you will. Thank you.' The last words were an exhausted whisper. She subsided into the carved seat, trembling. She coughed.

There was a short silence. Then the President said, without standing, 'Does anyone wish to say anything?'

Apparently no one did. Whatever may have been the defects of the arguments put forth, the spell of her oratory still hung over the Assembly. Many of them, illiterate heads unaccustomed to involved syntax and five-syllable words, had not grasped the entirety of it, but this did not matter much since they had all understood its purport; and the tendency of elevated literariness in formal speech, among Habitationers, was not to affront but to flatter and impress, respect for education being (until recent times) normal.

The President said: 'Since I have nothing to add to what the Librarian has said, I think the most sensible course would be to take a vote on the alternatives. I therefore ask all Members of the Senior Assembly who are in favour of complying with yesterday's ultimatum to raise their hands.'

No one moved.

'Will all in favour of any other possible course of action please signify.'

Cathis's heart leapt as the general immobility remained.

'Then, will all in favour of action along the lines the Librarian has proposed raise their hands.'

The President raised his own hand immediately. So did Cathis. Outside the broad, twilight sky was mauve, blue and green, streaked with vibrant bars of pink and amber. There was a soft pink light in the darkening room. 'Tomorrow will be fine,' thought Cathis as other hands then rose, some boldly, some more slowly.

Heron had passed the whole day since his failure to escape in going up and down the column in the lift, like a mayfly over a stream. He did not notice, by the time the evening came, when he went to partake of Salla for the third time, that the lift was now moving much more slowly, as if its power-supply was depleted. Malcom, absorbed, had not spoken a word all day.

'A splendid oration,' said Christofer to Settle. He had come into

223

the Great Hall unobtrusively and had listened to Cathis's speech, enthralled. 'And she made a splendid job of it, though I thought I could distinguish the Settle style most of the way through.'

Settle was lying angularly on his bed, with his arms under his head, smoking languidly. The bowl of his pipe reposed on his chest. Christofer sat at the table in the next room, eating.

'What's the next move, then?' asked Settle's voice.

'The heads have all gone down to the fourth level to speak to their people,' said Christofer. 'The Clerk's organising everything. He's taken charge again. They're sorting out weapons, organising companies, and so on. The attack's going to take place tomorrow at dawn. In the meantime they've put guards on the doors to stop anyone slipping out and giving the game away.'

'You seem pretty enthusiastic about it.'

Christofer came into Settle's dark, smoke-filled bedroom with a sandwich in his hand. He looked at the thin, veiled, recumbent form on the bed. 'I suppose I am,' he said thoughtfully. 'Yes. Cathy's perfectly right.'

'You're going to take part in this attack, I imagine?'

'Of course I am. We'll need everyone we can get. We're terribly few as it is. What about you? You can shoot quite well.'

'No. I'd be no use.'

'As you wish,' said Christofer, deliberately muffling the tone of his voice with a mouthful of sandwich.

'Don't despise me. I'm still waiting for what I've got to do. This isn't it.'

There was a thumping sound in the Hall. While they were still trying to recall what it meant, Cathis came in. She had changed out of her Librarian's robes.

'Cathy! Splendid! You were amazing! You've saved us all!' Christofer enfolded her in his arms and kissed her, forgetting that his mouth was still full.

'That may be,' she replied severely, 'but you can't kiss and chew at the same time.'

'Oh. Sorry.' Still holding the remainder of his sandwich behind her back, he drew his head back, manducating and swallowing hastily. They smiled into each other's eyes. On the bed Settle watched, looking rather wistful, as Cathis saw with a pang as she at last noticed his presence.

'Oh, Daddy! I'm sorry!' She made him amends.

'Well done,' he said. 'I hear you've just saved civilisation.'

'Your speech went down marvellously. They were as impressed as anything.'

She stood up again. Christofer switched the light on.

'Now then, Christofer, come on.'

'Where?'

'We're going through the ceiling into the next level. You'll need your pistol. *Come on.*' She took his hand and jerked him away. 'Goodbye, Daddy.'

'Goodbye, dear. Good luck with whatever you're doing.'

'What *are* we doing, Cathy?'

They stood in the open space outside the Library. 'I told you,' said Cathis, 'We're going up now, or at least you are. It's not very late and we mustn't waste time. I've just been down to see about organising some men.'

The men were there; five Library guards whom Christofer recognised, two with pistols, the others with bows and quivers, and a strange man, black-haired, dressed in the Metalworkers' blue overalls, with a complicated-looking piece of equipment in his hands.

'This is Jerome Metaller,' said Cathis. 'He works a torch in normal life. The Clerk suggested him. He's to come and help in case the ceiling isn't as thin as it looks.'

Under her directions the penetration into the upper levels proceeded quite easily. A stout table was brought out for Jerome to stand on; he climbed on to it, removed more of the ceiling with a knife, and cut out some steel bars with his torch. The others waited apprehensively. Christofer kept his bow ready in case either Malcom or Heron should appear above. Three quarters of an hour later there was a rough hole in the ceiling, looking as black as if it had been painted on.

At Cathis's request, Christofer climbed up nervously through the hole, carrying a torch and a pistol. He found no one; level 0 was apparently deserted. Then he saw the rope, close by him, dangling from the counterpart hole leading into the next level. He told the others about this. On Cathis's orders they all came up, as quietly as possible, followed by Cathis herself. She put a chair on the table down below and was able to climb up without help in spite of her disability. Her courage and determination struck Christofer almost as heavily as some of the other shocks he had recently received.

After a torchlight search of the level and a brief conference Christofer went on up the rope, as quietly as possible, to level 1, where Heron and Malcom were waiting for him. Without warning he felt two strong hands grasp his neck. But Cathis was on the alert below. She swung up the torch, and Mathew and Jasper, two of the Clerks, let fly simultaneously. Both of them, luckily, missed Christofer, and Jasper's arrow stuck in Malcom's shoulder. Then Cathis pulled out her pistol. Malcom saw this and released Christofer, who had fortunately retained his hold on the rope and so escaped falling through the hole down into level 1.

Then there was a burst of submachine gun fire from above, which injured no one. After it they heard the sound of hastily retreating footsteps, so they were not afraid to advance upwards. Cathis chose Mathew for the next attempt. He went up. They heard him gasp and then fire deliberately, five times, but he was evidently not under attack.

'What's happening?' Christofer called up.

'I can see one of them,' he said, 'sitting in a chair. He's got a gun in his hand. I can't seem to hit him.'

'Have another try,' said Christofer.

Mathew had another try, with the same result.

'Are you sure you missed him?' Cathis called.

'No, Miss,' answered Mathew from above. 'He's sitting in a chair about twenty yards away, with a gun in his hands...'

Christofer snorted. 'Go on, Mathew,' he said. 'He won't hurt you.' He pulled himself up the rope and approached the seated conspirator, who regarded him unflinchingly, wrapped in a blanket that shadowed the face so that only the gleam of eyes was visible. Christofer wasted no bullets. 'I thought so,' he said, pulling back the hood. 'Come on, all of you.'

The other guards were horrified at finding a woman's legless corpse, but there was no time to waste. Cathis insisted on being pulled up on the end of the rope, overriding all appeals to caution and propriety. A moment later they were all on their way up once more. Their torches showed up splashes of bright, wet blood on the floor, an encouraging sign. Following these traces, the six men raced to the staircase; Cathis, stumping along valiantly in the rear, was temporarily forgotten. They came out into the topmost level, which was brightly lit up, not by its own inert light-globes, but by the overflow from the long light-strips which were now, for the first time in centuries, illuminating the central column.

All over the Circle men and women were rousing themselves and being roused, moving to windows and opening doors, cursing quietly as they stumbled over objects in the darkness. Children clustered eagerly; dark figures crept out from obscure, leaf-shadowed corners, conversing in subdued undertones, staring upwards. Yet another portent, less sickening than the arrival of the angel or the resurrection of the binned lunatic but almost equally disquieting, had come upon them. It was as if, in the black, starless night, the moon had been taken from the sky, melted like quicksilver, and poured out in a frozen, slightly yellowish, silvery line. The darkened rotundity of the Sphere seemed to hang from it like the lead weight on the end of a bright plumbline. The people gazed at it, awed. After two or three hours, while dawn was still far away, it went out abruptly; and the few who had remained watching it went back to their beds.

By the time that happened, however, the train of events within the column had arrived at a temporary conclusion. Led by Christofer, brandishing their weapons heroically, the six hunters had charged recklessly up the spiral staircase. Cathis had remained at the bottom and tried to wait patiently as the sounds of pursuit died away above her. After some minutes she found that her father had joined her. They talked desultorily. Meanwhile Malcom and Heron made their laborious way upwards. They had found the lift out of order and unworkable; Heron's excessive use of it that day, together with the sudden illumination of the column, had temporarily drained away all the available power. Neither of them had much idea what to do. Malcom's shoulder was paining him, but Salla's rearguard action had given him time to improvise a rough bandage. In his right hand he carried a submachine gun and a leather bag of supplies and tools. Heron, staggering, carried the bomb and the yo-yo. Neither of them were able to go very fast. They had had a start, but presently the sounds of clanging footsteps, reverberating upwards through the shaft, began to reach them, and swiftly to grow louder. They peered over the rail down the shaft, but no sign of the guards could be seen; the stairs below were mostly hidden. They clambered painfully upwards. The noises of pursuit came inexorably nearer, although the hunters, somewhat out of breath, were now walking rather than running, having climbed several hundred yards.

More and more slowly, the chase continued; the distance between the two parties continued to diminish.

The hunters had now lost sight of their objective, and were thinking only of the necessity of further progress. Physical fatigue had dulled their wits. For this reason they did not think of moving quietly so as to avoid giving warning of their approach. The fugitives halted, sorted out their weapons, and waited dourly for their enemies to come within range.

Christofer was no longer leading them. He had fallen back to third place. When the attack happened there was little time to do anything. He heard a rushing, whirring sound; a black, fuzzy, spinning shape darted down from somewhere with the rapidity of a huge winged insect; and Mathew's head seemed to spring apart like some explosive liquid. A brief, red rain, minced bone and brain and blood, covered the stairs behind Mathew. It was in Christofer's eyes. He could not see.

Then, the next instant, pandemonium was released. He heard shots and screams. A stream of bullets was pouring out of Malcom's gun. He flung himself downwards, slipped on a gory step, and slithered down several steps. He stopped, collected himself, wiped his eyes and looked up. Mathew was still upright, standing headlessly above them. Christofer had a very short impression of little fountains jumping out of his back; then the body tumbled slowly backwards like a stone pillar and fell past them. The ominous whizzing sound was suddenly louder; out of the corner of his eye Christofer saw Jasper duck hastily to avoid the plunging thunderbolt. It darted past again, flicking off a haze of blood-droplets, striking and bending the rail with a horrible metallic screech. He struggled to pull the gun from his pocket while flattening himself against the stairs. He had it out, but the yo-yo was coming at him again and he had to wrench himself out of its way. He fired two shots blindly before seeking a target. An arrow soared upwards past him, but most of the other guards seemed panic-stricken; they were clattering away down the stairs. Christofer was now out of the way of the bullets. He caught a glimpse of Heron, standing braced against the tricky, powerful tug of the yo-yo, and shot once, twice, three times, before it returned towards him with effortless, pitiless accuracy. There was barely enough time for him to push himself away downstairs before it struck the step in front of him, three inches away from his eyes, with a glitter of orange sparks and a tremendous grinding clash. He went down some way, quickly and uncomfortably at full length on the stairs, then picked himself up and became aware that the din had stopped.

He stood up cautiously, trying to ignore the demands of his bruised, wounded and aching body. He called his surviving men, Jasper, Ianson, Ovel and Hugh. None of them seemed any worse damaged than he, which was somewhat surprising in view of the reckless use of automatic firearms that had been taking place. But Malcom had never made use of a submachine gun before that night – on finding these guns he had immediately hidden them to prevent Heron's taking possession of them and using them indiscriminately – and was, consequently, unable to operate it effectively. After another conference, bandaging and reloading they went on, much more warily, stepping gingerly over the headless, bullet-ridden corpse of Mathew, round and round the unending ascent of the spiral staircase.

It bored upwards within the column. From time to time there were more encounters with the enemy. Often the deadly shape of the yo-yo would reappear, there would be an exchange of shots, a quick, temporary descent and return for continuance of the chase. A sense of unreality descended on them. Christofer began to wonder what he was trying to do, whether the column and the pursuit would ever come to an end, how long it would be before the agonizing tiredness of his legs became insupportable, whether there was any point in going on, whether anything could happen to prevent the nightmare from continuing indefinitely, what time it was, what Cathis was doing, how high they had climbed, how long it would be before his men refused to come any further. They became belatedly aware of an all-pervading vibration and humming: the whole column was moving gently to and fro. There was a muted sound of wind. It was extremely cold. Water trickled faintly.

They trudged upwards. No one said anything. At frequent intervals Christofer replaced the man in the lead, whose job it was to keep a sharp eye open against incipient attack.

Sometimes they saw drops of blood on the stairs.

Time continued to pass. Christofer was now feeling liable to collapse at any moment. He called a halt. They rested for five minutes and went on.

Without warning the yo-yo appeared again. They were almost at the head of the staircase. They jumped backwards and began shooting. Another battle was joined. This time, however, there was no inexpert gunfire from above; Heron was holding the staircase by himself, armed only with the yo-yo, which was, however, a very effective weapon at close range. It was impossible for them to come near him, and next to impossible for them to remain in the same place for more than three consecutive seconds, thus ensuring that all their shooting was hurried and inaccurate. Heron stood erect, eyes bright, laughing like a god, possessed of an ecstatic sureness, a divinity of destructive power. The yo-yo sang and smote like a fabulous mythological hammer. His enemies cowered and scurried like mice beneath his feet.

'He's too strong for us,' thought Christofer. 'He can keep us off till our ammunition runs out and then we're done for.' He had a sudden perception of the enormous height they must have climbed; it seemed to extend below him like the drop from a huge, sickening precipice. There was a taste of defeat in his mouth. He made up his mind to order a retreat before their pistols became useless. His men were already ebbing away. A full consciousness of failure and futile expenditure of effort struck him in a heavy wave. Defiantly he raised his pistol for the last time, fired, missed, flung himself backwards to avoid Heron's return stroke, opened his mouth to give the order for retreat, and froze, watching the scene above him with paralysed astonishment. The others looked up too.

They were just in time. As Heron had whirled the yo-yo behind him to gain momentum for the next downstroke it had somehow passed on the wrong side of a vertical bar, probably a hand-support but with some kind of unidentifiable tackle at its base, which rose from the railing at the top of the stairs to the ceiling above. Heron had been well aware of the danger of being pulled off his feet, or of the yo-yo's becoming entangled somewhere below, and had done his best to avert these dangers, casting the yo-yo cleanly and accurately at a specific target each time, using his whole body as a counter-weight to control and redirect the difficult backswings, and, in general, operating an extremely uncertain instrument with great dexterity. But now his skill failed him. The backswing had been made on a rather longer length than usual – a matter of three or four feet – and Heron had failed to register the presence of the bar. The result was bewilderingly sudden. The yo-yo shot off to the full length of its wire in a quite unexpected direction, glanced off a metal wall, and came back like lightning before Heron could appreciate his peril. But it was now out of his control, moving in a wide horizontal sweep at the end of the length of wire leading from the bar. The wire caught him across the chest, swept him irresistably backwards against the bar, and in an instant had bound him to it securely. The others watched, aghast, while the yo-yo, no longer spinning, went on flailing round and round the lashed figure with a terrifying acceleration. The length of wire diminished rapidly. The gleaming silvery bands across Heron's chest and trapped right arm were laid higher and higher; for some reason the yo-yo was rising. An instant later Heron began to squeal. Everyone by now was expecting the full impact to be discharged against Heron's head or shoulders, which would naturally be converted to pulp; but this is not what happened. The taut, flashing wire, reaching Heron's neck just before the yo-yo attained maximum velocity, cut into it like cheese.

'Eee – ee – *eek!*'

This was all Heron had time to say. His head leaped off. Blood spouted from between his shoulders as the yo-yo stopped with a shock that shook the entire column. Spurting crimson, his head crashed to the floor, rolled flukily to the top step, and then was bouncing briskly down the spiral staircase like a marble. In a daze the men watched it disappear. It showed no sign of being about to come off the stairs. They heard the uneven thuds die away in the distance.

They looked at one another.

The memory of Heron's last truncated squeak came back to them. Simultaneously they all burst into appalled, hysterical laughter. Then all the lights in the column went out.

V. ii. RESOLUTION

Cathis sat by herself on the floor of the Public Hall on level 4, her wooden leg stretched out before her in the dust. The room, empty of people, was filled, despite the red sky of the previous evening, with the grey light of an overcast morning, as well as a plethora of abandoned possessions, blankets, boxes, bags, chairs, crockery, chicken-coops. There was a faint, stale, compound smell. The feeling in Cathis's amputated foot had returned once again; the familiar pain stabbed her intermittently. She felt very tired and slightly feverish, and was hoping that the strains of the past twelve hours had not been too much for her. In spite of her tiredness, however, and a certain annoyance at her physical feebleness which had prevented her from accompanying the expeditionary force, she felt unusually tranquil. The fact that the issues that had sundered the Habitation were now in the process of being resolved, a mile or so away in the cold drizzle falling outside, did not greatly concern her. The thought of the possibility of her own immediate death, which had come to her in the last half-hour, was now what chiefly occupied her thoughts. If Tomass were successful, it was quite likely that all those who had ventured to oppose him would be massacred, and certain that one who had deliberately taken the execrable office of the Librarian upon herself had no chance of surviving. Perhaps she would be dead by the end of the week, or the day, or the morning. She still had a pistol, but she could not run. Her thoughts slowly revolved around the eschatological subjects Amiss had told her about in hospital: death, judgement, Heaven, Hell, sin, sacrifice, God. The images of the Ejector-Seat and the Loony-Bin hovered against a vague and luridly-coloured background. If she had had the acuteness of introspective analysis possessed by her father, or to a lesser degree by Christofer, she would have observed the complete absence of fear for her own well-being from her emotions, and been self-congratulatorily pleased. She waited, neither relaxed nor resigned, but with a

233

tense, taut stillness of anticipation, on which her thoughts skated silently like drops of water on a hot iron.

۰ Nothing had come down the column till the sudden, mysterious dousing of its lights. When this had happened she and Settle had begun to move away, puzzled and anxious, but had been arrested by the approaching sound of faint, irregular thuddings. The cause of the noise came past them, rolled away in the dark, and came to a halt somewhere in the topmost level. They had found it with a torch, examined it with repulsion, and recognised the features, though much battered, of Heron. Settle had agreed to remain within call of the base of the column while she went down the stairs and the rope to show Heron's head to the Clerk, and to find what progress had been made in the preparations for the sortie. It was then about two o'clock in the morning. Cathis took little part in the continuing activity, went to bed, but could not sleep. Some time later Jasper had appeared with his arm in a sling. He had been sent down by Christofer to fetch Doctors for Ianson, who had lost part of his right hand, and Ovel, who was unconscious. Christofer and Hugh had remained in the darkness of the room at the top of the staircase, keeping guard. The medical party had come up to level 1, replaced Cathis's erection by a couple of firm ladders, and gone up to attend to the casualties.

Cathis had got up before dawn. The men were mustering in the Public Hall. A service was held there at dawn, and two bullocks were offered. Then the men were divided into three companies of about sixty each. The first of these, under the command of the Farmer, would surround and storm Tomass's headquarters, while the other two, under the Clerk, would keep attack off them for as long as possible, surrounding them in an outward-facing ring, with the aid of a small band of archers. With luck Tomass and his henchmen might be dead within a couple of hours. The Doctors had divided themselves into two parties, one to follow in the rear of the attack and one to remain in readiness at the hospital. Cathis was supposed to be acting as a reference point, a centre of communication between the various parties.

Her mind went languidly back to Christofer and whatever unimaginable situation he was now in. Even for his safety she could not summon up much anxiety. There was nothing more she

234

could do for him. She was only slightly shocked at the calmness with which she accepted this predicament; indeed, she now felt oddly comfortable. The pain in her leg had gone down again. There was a lethargic luxury in the simple pleasure of resting her tired limbs on the floor. She leaned back and the wall behind her seemed as soft as a pillow.

'Is anyone there?'

'Yes.'

'Christofer?'

'Yes.'

'Where's Heron?'

'Dead.'

'Where's Settle?'

'Somewhere down below. What are you going to do now, Malcom?'

'You'll soon find out.'

'No good locking yourself in there.'

'Oh?'

'We'll soon get that door down.'

'Indeed? I'll save you the trouble.'

'. . .What's that you've got there?'

'A gun. It shoots a lot of bullets at a time. I'll shoot you both if you move an inch.'

'Sir. I –'

'Quiet, please, Hugh ... What you are doing here, Malcom? What do you hope to get out of this game? There's nowhere left for you to retreat to now, you know. There'll be a lot of men up here as soon as the fighting ends and whichever side wins...'

'Yes.'

'What – what are you behaving like this for?'

'You'll soon find out – don't move.'

'Stay put, Hugh ... What is that you're making?'

'It's a bomb. When I've reassembled the outer casing it'll be finished. It should be powerful enough to blow the Habitation up completely.'

'How–'

'Come here. *Come here*. Right. Go along and open the door

at the end. Never mind the noises and the rocking, it's not going to fall down just yet.'

'Which way—'

'That catch – the lever on the right. There. That's it. Now don't pull it too hard.'

'Oh, oh.'

'Don't fall out!'

'Habitation. . .'

'That, Christofer, is where the bomb's going, with you and me and everyone else with it.'

'How high up *is* this?'

'Buzz off now. I've got a job to finish.'

Settle stood among the indoor foliage on level 0, watching painful evolutionary processes take their course in the Circle below. The hay stood in the fields, damp in the drizzle; the trees and little lawns were lush and wet; the winking ponds were bright with the featureless grey of the sky; and the tracks and lanes dissolved blackly beneath the heels of the knots of unevenly struggling men. He could no longer see any signs of a coherent strategy. He had brought the telescope down and watched the initial attack, which seemed to have taken place more or less according to plan. Tomass's house had been surrounded. It was too far away to tell whether anyone had got into it or not. Some of the attackers had carried torches, thin red sparkles in the rainwashed distance, but the rain would make it difficult to ignite any buildings, which would probably be just as well in the long run. There was a man lying in the middle of a field a few hundred yards away, face down in the soaking grass, with two arrow shafts sticking out of his back and one in his buttock. Presumably he was dead. There was no way of telling which side he was on, or which side was winning. The whole scene looked most unlike the stage on which the representatives of reason were fiercely contending with the forces of mania.

He looked at his watch. It said half past nine. He did not know if it was really half past nine, or whether the watch had stopped the night before. The difference between the continuation of time and the onward movement of the hands of the watch was not clear to him. He put it to his ear. He could not hear any ticks.

He put his hand on his wrist and felt for his pulse. A period of time that seemed like several minutes elapsed. He could not find any pulse at all. A man ran, limping, out of a clump of trees, making for the protection of the Sphere. To Settle he appeared to take a remarkably long time to cover the fifty yards or so in which he was visible. Settle wondered if the concept of time that had served him satisfactorily for forty-seven years had not, after all, been mistaken . . .

Everything seemed very quiet. With a sudden, intense effort he began to wind up his watch. The grinding clicks sounded very clearly. The second-hand moved on. Settle was sure that it had not always moved as slowly as it now did. Time was slowing down. He looked through the glass wall, over the outer wall on the edge of the Circle, to where faint, cream-coloured streaks of lightness showed in the lowering grey. The sky was very close. It was all about him. He rose into it, with the sensation of a slow towering, a great, majestic elevation to heights of scrutiny and leisurely power. He moved in the rainy sky like a hovering bird. Time was suspended.

'It's very close,' he said.

'What?'

Settle jerked himself out of a trance and saw Christofer in front of him, red-eyed, bloodstained, dishevelled, panting.

'Miss! Excuse me, Miss!' said the man who was shaking her shoulder.

Cathis woke up and quickly remembered where she was. 'Hello,' she said, 'what's up?'

'Clerk sent me, Miss,' said the man.

'Yes?'

'Said to tell you, we've got Tomass, but the fighting's not stopped. Fact is, Miss, that it's going on harder'n ever.'

'So . . . what time is it?'

'Nearly noon, Miss.'

'Is it bad?'

'Habitation, Miss, I'm afraid so.'

She stood up stiffly and clumsily. She looked at him more closely and saw that one of his eyes was closed and blackening.

There was a dark, creased stain on the sleeve of his wet jacket. His face and hair were wet.

'Are you all right?'

'Better'n some, Miss.'

'Well – what's been happening? Tell me.'

But before he could tell two other men appeared in the Hall and came running up to them.

'Right, now, Cathy,' Christofer said, 'tell us what's been happening.' His voice was hoarse and strained. There were blue bruises on his throat. His face was grimy and white.

'The fighting's still going on outside.' She turned to the messenger. 'Tell us more.'

'Trouble was, Miss, that they weren't as unprepared as we were told. We ran and we got to the house all right, and we surrounded it, but then a band of them charged into us.'

'But how's it going?' asked Christofer. 'Who's winning?'

'I don't know, sir. Sorry, sir.'

'Is Tomass captured or not?'

'Clerk said so, Sir.'

'Well,' said Settle, 'that's something, at least.'

'Have you got Malcom?'

'No, that's – well, that's – you see, Cathy, Malcom – oh, you tell her, Settle.'

'What we're afraid of, Cathy, is that Malcom has got his weapon ready at last. That's what Christofer says he said.'

'*Now?*'

'Yes.'

'What is it?'

'That's not important.' Christofer sighed. 'The important thing is that we must make another attack now, immediately. There's no time for any more explanations. I suppose there aren't any more men available?'

'I don't think so,' said Cathis, perplexed.

'I've run out of bullets. I came down to get some more . . . oh dear, oh dear, I think I'm losing my grip.' Christofer closed his eyes for a moment, swaying on his feet. 'I don't know what to do. . .'

'I know what you mean,' murmured Settle.

'Must we . . . go on with it?'

238

'Yes,' said Cathis.

'Yes,' said Settle. His eyes, dark and large in his fleshless face, had a withdrawn look.

'So. Up we go again.' Christofer groaned.

'Try the lift,' said Cathis.

'You'd better hurry, Christofer.' Settle's words seemed to come, a propos of nothing, like the utterances of a sleepwalker. '*Hurry.*'

And still the battle continued to rage, dispersed, inconclusive and ferocious. On both sides communications between the leaders and the forces they commanded had deteriorated to the point of non-existence. No one knew who was winning in the areas he could not see with his own eyes. Both sides felt an increasing panic. Many times men encountered, on the opposite side, enemies who had formerly been friends; and when this happened the conflict might be temporarily, tacitly ignored; but such small undeclared truces, were not sufficient to offset the general, increasingly desperate hostility.

Malcom, who had been setting the time-adjustment on his completed opus, was apprised of the re-arrival of his foes by a nervously premature shot. Christofer and Hugh came out of the silent lift. Malcom looked up and saw their pistols levelled at him.

'Stay still,' said Christofer as loudly as he could, over the loud humming.

Malcom made one or two final adjustments and stood up. 'Again?' he said. His voice and face were composed, almost cheerful, a marked contrast to the manifest exhaustion of Christofer.

'This is it, Malcom,' said Christofer, keeping his pistol steady in spite of the rocking of the floor but wondering in a lightheaded way what to do next.

'What is?'

It came to Christofer that the most sensible, practical and obvious thing to do would be to shoot Malcom summarily. He debated this for a moment. Then he said; 'Come over here, don't touch that thing, or I will kill you.'

Malcom smiled like a dead shark hanging upside down. 'No, Christofer,' he said. 'No, poor chap. You're much too late. This bomb is going to explode in thirty-three minutes. If you touch it or try to smash it or destroy it it will go off immediately –'

There was a sudden deafening discordance, a rumbling jolt and a shrill clangorous screaming as an unusually powerful buffet of wind and rain struck the column, plucking it like a 'cello string. The tiny sliver of a room swung and bounced in the huge volumes of watery air. The three men were dashed to the floor, as if overwhelmed by the uproar. The floor and the walls were shaking violently; each individual member of the structure made its own contribution in the cacophonous symphony. Malcom was the first to recover.

A short time later, the tremors having partially died away, Christofer picked himself up. He had a bashed nose and a cut lip and hand. Hugh was unconscious. A tremendous gale was hurling itself at him. Staggering against it, he saw why: the door at the end of the short passage had been thrown open. He remembered having heard a peculiar clang amid the confusion. There was no sign of Malcom or the bomb. He went up the passage. Rain drenched his face as he peered tremblingly out into the driving clouds. After a few minutes he looked down and saw, a long way beneath him, spinning wildly, madly at the end of the rope whose other end was tied to a nearby strut, a small figure like Heron's yo-yo; yet still cradling a large, dark object in its arms.

Settle heard the sound of something coming down to him: a light, clattering object. It arrived at the foot of the staircase: a steel bolt, to which was tied a tightly folded piece of paper. He unfastened the letter. It was written in an almost illegible hand, the paper was damp, there were blood-stains on it as well, but he could just about read it.

'*Settle. I dont know what to do. Malcom has jumped out of the column and he's dangling on a rope, two or three hundred feet or more. We cant hit him. We cant pull him up. Can you think of something. If we did hit him with a bullet he would probably drop the bomb, itll probably explode if he drops it. He's got a gun. The bomb is going off in half an hour, less now. He*

240

said it'll destroy everything if it does. Try and catch it if it drops. Think of something. We cant do anything. Hurry. Christofer.'

This time the sensation that time was slowing down came on Settle much more quickly. He dropped the letter. It floated slowly away from his hand. He felt that some event, something huge, momentous, was coming towards him. This thing, whatever it was, was what he had been waiting for. 'This is it,' he thought.

He went down to see Cathis, abstractedly turning the problem over and over in his mind. She read the note and handed it back to him without a word.

'How's the fighting going, Cathy?'

'Much the same, as far as I can make out. A few casualties have come in.'

'Is it safe to go out?'

'Might be.'

He went out. There was a fresh smell of wet leaves and grass. He stared upwards at the silver length of the column. It was still raining but the clouds were parting. Patches of brilliant washed blue had appeared. The drops swept into his eyes, but he had the impression of being able to see, somewhere above, a tiny black shape, infinitesimally small, which came and went . . .

There was a distant, confused noise, a low background of attenuated screams and yells, clashings and bangings. Nearer quarters were calmer; from where he stood there was no visible evidence of the conflict. Idly, aware that these were trivial irrelevancies, he considered different possible solutions to the task of catching and getting rid of the bomb. The real, imminent task that he must perform was still unknown to him, looming before his perception like an enormous dark building shrouded in fog.

He turned to see Cathis had followed him out of the grey, gleaming Sphere. Her peg-leg sank and squelched in the mud.

'Have you thought of anything?'

'No,' she said.

No, not unattractive at all, not really, thought Settle, in spite of the rings under her eyes and her pallor and her hair rats'-tailing in the rain. If Christofer wants her, good luck to him. Good luck to them both. We'll need it to get out of this mess. Get out – get out –

Then, in a blinding flash of illumination, it came. He said: 'Ejector-Seat.'

'What's that, Daddy?'

'For *me*, of course! Come on!'

'What are you talking about?'

'Have you a firearm?'

'Yes.'

'Bow and arrow?'

'In the Hall, I think.'

'Right. Wait a minute.'

He ran back to the Sphere. Cathis had hardly had time to marvel at this display of energy when he reappeared, carrying a bow and an arrow.

'Right, Cathy. Off we go.'

He set off at a brisk pace. She stumped after him.

'Keep your pistol at the ready,' he said.

She took it out. 'Where are we going?' she asked, her cheeks pink and wet with rain.

'The Ejector-Seat.'

'Why?'

'Only way to get near enough . . . and to. . .'

'What?'

'Never mind. You'd think it sounds crazy – Quick, Cathy! Shoot!'

A man had emerged from a wet clump of laurel. An axe whirled. Cathis shot. He sank down into his bush and disappeared. They went on.

'But – what do you mean – what's happening?'

'Sorry, I can't explain. *Come on,* Cathy – can't you go any quicker?'

'Sorry, no.'

'Well then – I know. Hold these.'

The bow and arrow were thrust into her hands. The next moment she found herself gathered up into her father's arms. She was astonished at his strength. They went on, Settle almost breaking into a run.

'Daddy, however, how can you do this, carry me? You haven't eaten for days.'

'I don't know. I won't be able to again, but that doesn't matter.'

'What do you mean?'

'Keep your pistol out. If anyone tries to stop us, get him. We aren't stopping again.'

Cathis could not remember ever having been carried by anyone before. She had an extraordinary sense of reunion, an unprecedented closeness and love for her father. For a time she felt as secure and as heedlessly untroubled as an infant. They came to the lonely place where the Ejector-Seat stood, a gaunt structure of steel and concrete, on a bare, rising mound. Settle put his daughter down. 'Don't ask questions, Cathy. You'll understand soon. This is what I've come to do.'

These were the last words he spoke to her. He took the pistol and shot open the lock of the door of the nearby concrete hut, entered, consulted an instrument panel and flicked several switches, came out, embraced her and kissed her. She was by now fairly well aware of what was going to happen. He drew briskly away from her, took up the bow and arrow and made his way deliberately up to the platform and the chair. He undid some fastenings and collapsed into it. In a minute or two he recovered from his faintness and waved to her.

Meanwhile there was a laboured, muttering vibration as pressure increased within the cylinder. As Cathis watched, the safety-valve began to pour out its white fountains; and with them a low whistle that rapidly rose to a high carrying scream, audible in most other places in the Circle, seldom-heard, ominous and astounding. All over the Habitation conflicts at their highest pitch were arrested and dissolved in a mutuality of surprise and fear. Few of the hearers had heard the sound more than once before, but all knew its meaning. Weapons were lowered in an immediate, automatic truce. Some men began to make their way towards the Ejector. The old men, women and children came out from the barns where they had been waiting. A small, awed crowd collected behind Cathis.

She stood fixedly in the rain. She saw Settle's scarred lips move. His words, whatever they were, were inaudible, but the expression on his scarred face reminded her of something, some part of the distant past, something long dead. Then she remembered what it was: it was the way he had looked when reciting one of his poems. But if it was a limerick she never heard it. Tears mixed with the rain on her face. The valve's thinning shriek rose beyond the range of human hearing into the infrasonic silence that preceded the climax.

The cylinder banged; the gleaming piston shot out; steam roared; the chair swept round in its huge arc, and rebounded.

Settle was flung heavily against a crushing wall of air. It battered at him and deafened him, screaming and bellowing in his ears. But the working of his mind was again superhumanly accelerated. Breathing would have been impossible; fortunately – he had leisure to note this – breathing was no longer of importance. His legs no longer seemed to belong to him; every bone in the lower half of his body must have been shattered, including the bottom of his spine; but that did not matter either. What mattered was the necessity of retaining his bow and arrow, of holding them tightly against his chest, of peering up through screwed-up lids into a blasting wind strong enough to prise his eyeballs out. To his relief he found he was not revolving as he flew. The column, a thick band stretched out obliquely beside him, was not moving about much. He swam through a formless infinity of blue and grey.

He saw Malcom's tiny figure. As he carefully brought his bow into position and bent it he recalled the story of their estrangement. He smiled inwardly as it occurred to him that if he had not lost his moustache the wind would certainly have stripped it from him by now. His clothes had almost all ripped away. Malcom came towards him. He waited for an easy bow-shot, making exact allowance for the speed at which he was moving, before releasing the arrow. It flew away from him like a guided missile. Then something left Malcom and travelled towards him, a small, black, solid-looking object, rotating like a tossed coin. Even to his perception it came very quickly. It met him in mid-air, striking his chest with a violent impact. He felt no pain, but knew that his speed must have been very much reduced. He wrapped his arms round the bomb unhurriedly and held it.

He was now able to keep his eyes open and to look about him.

He saw the expression on Malcom's face as he passed him, at a distance he estimated at about twenty yards. He wondered whether or not Malcom had recognised him. Then there was a very faint, crackling sound which died away almost immediately. Malcom was holding his gun up. Little red sparks danced at its muzzle. A bullet struck him behind his knee-cap, then two or three more in different parts of his back. He had a deep sense of satisfaction at being thus able to soak up, like a sponge, the vicious consequences of evil, the consequences of his own errors. He turned away from Malcom; he realised he was now revolving slowly, the effect of the bomb's impact. Later a last bullet struck his other knee.

He flew through the thick wet fog of a cloud. His bare skin was conscious of the cold moisture. On emerging he found himself gazing, presumably downwards, at the Habitation, now quite a long way away, and the mountainous landscapes around it. The fields and rivers, the woods and houses, the white curves of the outer wall and the small striped dome of the Sphere, all shrank away as he watched, and the supporting structures came into view: the effortlessly thin, glittering threads, the great golden pillar with its tapering cone, the sweeping shards hanging weightlessly in the void, the unending ascension of the central column. On the outer face of the wall he saw, clearly marked, a tall '1'. Habitation One, his home, slowly dwindled behind him.

He was aware that his ascent was now less steep than it had been. He was reaching the peak of his trajectory. The air no longer pressed against him. He cruised smoothly through the thin atmosphere. The earth wheeled lazily round him as he went. The sky was, if not black, a rather darker blue than before. A blindingly brilliant sun glided over and under him, sometimes dazzling him. Suddenly he realised that the bomb might blow up before he reached the ground, and that he ought to make some preparation for dying. The distant Habitation was a glittering toy.

Then, as new mountain ranges opened themselves up ahead, he saw something that caused him to doubt his own perceptions. The Habitation stood before him. He twisted his neck and saw it behind him also. He wondered if he could have flown right round the earth, or if he was seeing double, or if it was an hallucination. The sun in his eyes was an annoyance. Presently he had no longer any doubts. He was seeing two identical Habitations, the one growing slowly as the other disappeared. He had lost the control of his facial muscles but felt like frowning.

With a deep, warm, coursing flood of gladness that flushed through his whole body, he understood. Inscribed on the outer wall of the Habitation coming towards him was a large figure '2'. A number of things that had perplexed him were now set straight, including the origin of the angel. Only one thing remained for him to do now, and the two or three seconds that were to elapse before the bomb went off were quite sufficient for this. He prayed.

V. iii. AFTERMATH

But to Cathis, and to the others who stood watching, it seemed only that her father flew away into a cloud, and the cloud received him out of their sight; but a long time after there came a bright flash; and, much later than that, a reverberating boom like a distant thunderclap. Then they drew breath again and their eyes dropped from straining into the sky and they saw one another. The rain had stopped, the clouds were parting, shadow rolled away from the Habitation, and the summer sun was warm and bright. Raindrops sparkled, miniature prisms, blue, red, gold and green, on the leaves and grass. A gentle breeze blew in their faces.

And that was the end of the second Habitation war. The struggling and fighting now seemed to all an ugly, meaningless nightmare from which they had been joyfully awakened. Besides, a rumour was going round, within five minutes of Settle's triumphant exit, that Tomass and the other Priests had been captured. Cathis went slowly back to the Sphere and met the Clerk, who had had an arrow in his arm. She gave him as full an account of Settle's last words and actions as she could. He was evidently baffled by most of it, but refrained from questioning her when she told him that her leg was hurting badly again. She found herself a couch and lay down. Then Christofer came into the Hall along with a lot of other people, and sat down by her. He talked to her at some length but she fell asleep and remembered little of what he had told her when she awoke.

Finally, at yet another extraordinary convocation of the Senior Assembly that evening, the day's events were fully reported on and sorted out.

The President gave an account of the expedition, the surrounding of Tomass's house, the unexpected organisation of the resistance of the enemy, the swift deterioration of communications on both sides, the eventual forcing open of the house, the taking of several captives, the discovery of Tomass lying on a bed in an upstairs room with a paralysed left side, and the ineffective attempts made afterwards to end the fighting. The two other commanders narrated the battle from their points of view. Then the Doctor announced that he had received notice of a total of two hundred and twenty-three casualties, forty-eight of whom were dead and seventeen, including Tomass, in hospital with little hope of recovering. The rest had received medical attention and were now either in the hospital or their own homes. It was not possible yet to say how these were divided between the two sides, for the simple reason that only an impossibly small number of people would admit to having fought on Tomass's side. The Clerk stood up again to give a list of the items of damage caused by Tomass. None of these seemed irreparable. He hoped it would not be very long before the evil effects of strife had passed away entirely, and commended the Librarian for her successful intervention at the critical juncture. There was a round of applause as she stood up to reply.

Wincing occasionally as the pains pulsed in her over-taxed leg, she thanked the President for his tribute and recounted very briefly the story of the last few hours of her father's life. Then Christofer rose to give a supplementary account of his own doings. Last of all he spoke of Malcom's death:

'I can't say exactly why he decided to jump out of the column, and why he bothered with the rope; why, since he had determined on suicide and murder, he didn't jump out without bothering with the rope at all. Perhaps he faltered at the last minute, perhaps, after all, he couldn't bear the thought of dying immediately. Presumably he wanted to put the bomb well and truly out of our reach, but still wanted to hang on to the last half-hour of his life . . .

'I regret, gentlemen, that I cannot precisely inform you of the time of his death. I was a witness of Settle's last, successful encounter with him, and Settle's feat of catching the bomb in mid-air. His arrow pierced his breast and we thought he must have died soon after that, and so, having more important things to worry about than recovering his body, we left it where it was. But late this afternoon, when we went up the column once again, we saw him struggling on the end of his rope. He was still alive. We were very surprised, and we began to pull him up, but the rope was long and we were tired. The last thing we saw him do was to deliberately throw down his weapon. By the time we pulled him up he was dead. He had bled over his clothes a lot ... I am afraid he must have suffered unimaginably. But he was a criminal, he tried to destroy us all, and he was prevented only by a miracle.'

Salla was, as far as possible, reassembled, and replaced in the Bin. Malcom and Heron were taken down and buried with the other dead. There was a mass funeral and memorial service on the day after the conclusion of hostilities, and a service of general thanksgiving in the Public Hall on the day after that. At that time Tomass died unobtrusively. One of his lieutenants was beheaded as an example to the rest, who were all released. The work of reconstruction, principally of damaged buildings, had already started. Except in the homes of the many bereaved life returned to normal.

Cathis spent a couple of weeks quietly recuperating; then she began to move about, to pay visits to the families of the Library guards who had been killed or wounded, to explore for herself the upper levels and the column. After a while she reopened the school, and began to find out about the Librarian's duties. Meanwhile Christofer found himself in an unexpectedly high position in his profession on account of the number of Clerks who had been killed in the fighting. But for the moment the burden of an unusual quantity of administrative duty was falling on a depleted band of Clerks, who were all kept very busy. He could see Cathis only seldom.

Cathis fell into the habit of going for little walks by herself around the Circle, looking at the haymaking and the rebuilding of the burned houses. Everything seemed to her, especially at first, to be returning easily to normal. She saw Amiss, who had fought against the rebels and received an axe-wound in the thigh as well as a short concussion. He and his wife were planning to have two or three more children as soon as possible. Cathis wondered what he meant by telling her this. But they talked on other subjects as well, agreeing that the wounds inflicted on the Habitation seemed to be healing with remarkable speed, discussing Christofer's prospects and her own, attempting to analyse Malcom's motives. Even so, there was much about him that remained opaque to her.

As the days went by, however, a slowly increasing awareness of unease took hold of her. She asked herself, and she made Amiss ask her, what the reasons for this could be. From her uncertainly expressed answers he formed the opinion that she was worrying about Malcom's beliefs and whether or not they had been justified. The truth was, however, that she was suffering both from a lack and an excess of employment. She now spent three mornings a week in the school, teaching: a task she was enjoying. She liked her pupils; most of them were bright and fairly responsive; and she was beginning to acquire a grasp of teaching, an understanding of its problems and ways of overcoming them. It was at other times that she became depressed. She knew well enough what she ought to be doing. The Library required classification. The magnitude of this task daunted her thoroughly. It was so evidently a business that would require a lifetime, or several lifetimes, to be completed. She had no idea where or how to begin. The projector, fortunately, was still safe. She ran a few cassettes, selected at random, through it. They all seemed to her complete gibberish. She had a strong feeling that she was not by nature suited for tasks of classification and Librarianship. The thought of dealing with endless lists of gibberish appalled her.

There was a further anxiety: like Malcom, she found herself coming to have doubts about the ultimate purpose of things in general. She still believed in God; she had no teleological worries about the meaning of her own existence, or about anyone's individual existence. But the ordering and arranging of the Library's resources, she supposed, would not be a benefit for the individual, but for the community, the race. But was the race, collectively, worth considering? Was it, or was it not, doomed to a lonely, miserable demise a score of generations hence, when the first of the irreplaceable stores ran out? Was there hope for humanity or not? More importantly, was there any ultimate point in recovering the Library?

It is not to be supposed that the Librarian could have stated these conundrums to herself so explicitly. She was not fully cognisant of all her feelings. Indeed, she felt rather guilty at wasting time when there was so much that could be done. She sat in her room, browsing in the old Librarians' records and doodling on her wall; or visited Amiss; or went out for solitary walks, noting the way the people drew respectfully away from her even when she was dressed in ordinary clothes. There was only one wooden-legged girl in the Habitation, and that one was the Librarian and already a creature of fabulous legend. But one day, when the pressure of his work had eased slightly, Christofer came out with her.

'Well, Cathy,' he said as they walked along a shady lane. 'Amiss tells me you aren't feeling as cheerful as you might be.'

'No, not really,' she replied, looking down at her sandalled foot, the sun-dappled stones and the back-and-forth movement of her peg.

'Is it that?' He too looked down at the wooden thing. 'Still hurting? Or –'

'Well, no, not very often, not too much. I've got used to the thought of it.'

'Do you mind if I go on asking you things?' he asked anxiously.

'No. Carry on, please.'

'Are you upset about your father dying?'

She stopped and looked at him. 'Upset? No . . . it's odd, but I hardly think about him. I don't even think I'm sorry. It seemed – it was – so *right*, the way he died. He's all right.'

'I know what you mean. I agree with you . . . but what about the others?'

'Who?'

'The rest of the Society: your father, Malcom, Heron, Salla. All dead. Not to mention the other people, of course. But there are only the two of us left. Does that worry you?'

'Why should it?'

'I don't know.'

'Does it worry *you?*'

'Not really. I think of them sometimes.'

They turn and go on. Christofer's hand finds Cathis's. He looks at her profile. She turns her head briefly and meets his eyes. He knows now that the question he will put to her a little later on will be in no danger of meeting an unfavourable response. For the time being, however, he says:

'Well, what is it, Cathy? Will you tell me?'

'Oh, I don't know. A lot of things.'

At the end of three quarters of an hour he has a fair idea of them.

'Look at those men in the fields,' she says. 'They're carrying on just as they've always done, aren't they? There's no division any more, is there?'

'No, I wouldn't have thought so.'

'But – well – things *can't*, Chris, they simply can't go back to the way they were before.'

'Why do you say that?'

'Before – well, we were more or less content, until Malcom and Settle started finding things out. But now we won't be. A great many people besides us, besides the Society, now have an idea of what Dad found out ... You know, all that stuff, we're alone in the world, the mountains, the Habitation was built by men, the holocaust and catastrophe, and we're the last remnant of the human race, and the stores are going to run out some time. We can't keep it dark.'

'Would there be any point in trying?'

'I suppose not, but how do you think the ordinary people will react when they find out the state we're in?'

Christofer frowns. 'I don't know. I suppose they'll accept it.'

'But what then?'

'What are you getting at, Cathy?'

'Oh dear,' she sighs, 'I don't know. I'm just confused and worried ... no, not here, you idiot, people can see us! – Come on.'

They move on, hand in hand. It is a fine, windy morning. The sun comes and goes. Leaves and debris come blowing by.

'You believe in God, don't you?' asks Christofer presently.

'Yes,' she answers firmly.

'Well, so do I, now. What happened, what Settle did, that confirmed what I wanted to feel before.'

'Oh ... I thought – you and Dad said we mustn't expect miracles. But I did.'

'I don't think you should have. But the miracle came, all the same. It *was* a miracle. But...'

Cathis waits, stumping on at his side.

'You have several fears, if I understand you rightly. First, that you will not be able to deal with the Library because you are not fitted to be a Librarian. Second, that the job, when done, will turn out to have been pointless, because humanity is done for in any case. Third, the fear of some unspecified shock to people's minds when they find out the true state of affairs.'

'Yes. I suppose so. What do you say to that?'

They turn about and begin to make their way back to the shining dome. The trees rustle loudly in the vigorously tugging breeze; the white undersides of leaves flash against the light, moving greens and emeralds of translucency. The midday sun, momentarily out in a clear patch of blue, blazes amid the crowded, towering structures of the cloudscape. They face each other, Christofer's hair standing on end, Cathis's streaming out behind her. The sun stands at its zenith.

Christofer answers:

EPILOGUE: SPOKEN BY CHRISTOFER

'I shouldn't worry too much about your fitness, or lack of it, for being a Librarian, Cathy ... you don't really know enough about it yet. But you'll learn. I'll try to help you ... The most difficult business of all will be just making a start, or just finding the right place to begin. When you've achieved that you'll be able to plan out the task in front of you, and attack it piece by piece. It'll seem smaller ... Your real problem, and mine too, and everyone's, is, as Malcom said, whether or not the Library will be any use in the long run.

'Think what we must do. We must develop the knowledge the Library contains; we must find the skills that will enable us to overcome the limitations of dwindling stores and to spread out again and recolonise the earth. Our aptitude for technical invention, once the stimulus of necessity has been provided, will surely be as great as the old people's was, with the added advantage of their knowledge. Man's nature does not change. One of Malcom's mistakes, I think, was to underestimate this power. We must tell the people the truth of human history, and educate them into accepting it. There must be no more insurrections: the race cannot stand still any longer. We must go forward ...

'Malcom's second mistake, I think, was consistently to regard the survival of humanity as an end in itself. At least, he could conceive of no other end, even though he had little faith in human nature. He knew better than any of us the depths of folly and crime to which men can stoop, the suffering they bring on themselves and each other, the fatal, blighting imperfection that continually ruins the best of human institutions. There is nothing we can do about that except not to let it depress us. At the moment we are fairly well united and it is unlikely to attack us just yet. Yet even though he had no faith in mankind, he still wanted it to be preserved, until he became convinced that it stood no chance in the long run (I know all this partly from what he said and partly from a sort of diary he wrote, a confession he made, which has come into my hands). And so, the conclusion was logical enough, he determined to destroy us all, and was prevented only by a miracle.

'A miracle . . . that is the important word. It was a miracle. The event of your father's flying away into the sky at exactly the right time and place to catch the bomb and kill the enemy . . . the more one thinks about it, the more fantastic, implausible, and impossible, it seems. And yet – it happened. What one thought one ought not to pray for, actually happened . . . I find this very difficult to say. This miracle has brought me to belief and faith in God. I wished to believe in Him before; atheist ideas seemed so thin; I was very impressed by Amiss's arguments. But this inclination wasn't enough. I wanted – yes, I wanted proof, which was exactly what I knew I wasn't going to get. But what looked like proof came. Miracles don't come for the asking. But – oh, well, to speak bluntly, it's obvious that mankind is meant to go on. Something, someone, is actively protecting the Habitation, at least for the moment. So you ask, 'why didn't He protect the earth before?' and I haven't an idea. But when God steps in, when something *does* happen, something that makes divine guidance so plain and vivid and obvious – then you'd be mad to close your eyes to it. Perhaps miracles really happen oftener than we think; perhaps we should keep our eyes open for them. Besides, there are two things to consider. The fact is that there are some people, logical people like Malcom, who would have been capable of rejecting the idea of divine guidance, of ignoring what they saw or dismissing it as an accident. And the second, that it all depended on Settle. In other words, it was nothing like a strict proof, nor was it inevitable. If Settle had behaved wrongly in the last hour he would have frustrated it. So, an event like this is not in itself sufficient for converting people. There must, as Settle would have said, be a favourable predisposition.

'God exists, Heaven exists. God is good. The Priests and the common people are right, though many of them fell into the opposite error to Malcom's and Heron's. But they are right to believe and trust in Him. It is faith, which Malcom lacked, that makes the difference between hope and despair, that gives meaning to our existence; faith in God, not a faith in the future of humanity. God must come first. We must live and work only for Him. This is what gives our lives purpose. But if we need occupation, we have it: in working for the good of our descendents; working and trying to our utmost; but never letting this, the business of our daily lives, become an end in itself, a distraction, a God in the wrong place. For us the importance of the future is only as an occupation for the present, an occupation most of us will need, now that the unthinking placidity for our former life has been shattered. It may be that the struggle is hopeless and foredoomed. We will meet huge obstacles. Our efforts may turn out to have been misdirected; our hopes may be mocked, our expectancies dashed. But our success or failure, and that of future generations, in the realm of earthly achievement, is not crucial. There is bound to be some failure; its size and extent are not fundamentally significant, for the end of our effort is not significant. It is the effort itself, entrusting the outcome to the dispensation of Heaven, that matters. All we need is faith, in ourselves, in one another, and in God.'

THE END